Where the Four

By Arlene Pearson

Copyright © 2020 Arlene Pearson
All Rights Reserved

For my family

Contents

Chapter One

Chapter Two

Chapter Three - Callum

Chapter Four

Chapter Five

Chapter Six

Chapter Seven

Chapter Eight

Chapter Nine

Chapter Ten

Chapter Eleven

Chapter Twelve

Chapter Thirteen

Chapter Fourteen

Chapter Fifteen

Chapter Sixteen

Chapter Seventeen

Chapter Eighteen

Chapter Nineteen

Chapter Twenty

Chapter Twenty One

Chapter Twenty Two

Chapter Twenty Three

Chapter Twenty Three

Chapter Twenty Four

Chapter Twenty Five

Chapter Twenty Six

Chapter Twenty Seven

- Chapter Twenty Eight
- Chapter Twenty Nine
- Chapter Thirty - Callum
- Chapter Thirty One
- Chapter Thirty Two
- Chapter Thirty Three
- Chapter Thirty Four
- Chapter Thirty Five
- Chapter Thirty Six - Jeremy
- Chapter Thirty Seven
- Chapter Thirty Eight
- Jeremy
- Chapter Thirty Nine - Jeremy
- Chapter Forty
- Chapter Forty One
- Chapter Forty Two
- Chapter Forty Three
- About the Author
- Also by Arlene on Amazon

Chapter One

It was definitely him. Verity's smile froze on her face. No. It simply wasn't possible. It couldn't be.

He had crinkly lines around his cornflower blue eyes and the hair escaping from a messy man bun wasn't quite as bright a blond as she remembered, but on the whole, she supposed his divine looks hadn't diminished that much.

He looked like he'd just rolled out of bed, wearing a faded checked shirt half tucked in, hinting at a slightly rounded stomach above ripped jeans. His eyes lit up when he saw her and he nearly tripped over the fraying laces trailing from his scruffy trainers.

Bobby Brown, Head of Human Resources who was also Verity's Uncle Bobby, dark and stooped, grinned and said, 'Here we are. Jeremy, this is Verity, our Acting Business Manager. Verity – meet Jeremy - your new Personal Assistant.'

She took a deep breath, feeling the blood rush to her cheeks. She walked round the desk into the middle of the room and looked him in the eye, feeling her smile drooping at the corners. Her new Personal Assistant? What – him? No way! How could fate be this cruel?

His broad frame seemed to fill the entrance. She felt her gut tighten as the memory came shoving its way into the office. And with it heartache and humiliation. The usual slices of late afternoon sunlight thrown from the long windows were today nothing more than grey diagonals on the floor, drab like her frame of mind. Jeremy moved from the doorway to greet her in the centre of the room, hand outstretched.

Uncle Bobby continued, 'Now, this chap has been beavering away as a temp in my department and he's been a real asset. He'll do just as good a job for you.'

For a long moment Verity didn't move. Then, under Uncle Bobby's eager scrutiny she felt obliged to proffer Jeremy her hand to shake. His hand felt warm and she could feel the strength as he pumped hers with such enthusiasm that she felt like her feet nearly left the floor. She attempted to smile back but couldn't quite manage it.

'You?' she said, feeling her cheeks flush deeper red.

'Yes, it's me. And it's really you. Isn't it wonderful?' His whole being seemed to glow with exuberance and his southern accent, loud and rural, was immediately noticeable.

'Please, tell me this is some kind of a joke?' she asked, only slightly aware of Uncle Bobby standing nearby uneasily, looking from one of them to the other.

'Have you two met before?' he asked, one dark eyebrow raised.

'No.' she said.

'Yes.' he said. They both spoke together. There was a sharp silence.

She took another long breath. 'Okay, yes, we've met. A long time ago.'

'Yes. Summer 1997 to be exact. At a writing retreat in Hampshire.' Jeremy said.

Uncle Bobby was watching Verity and she knew he was hoping to please. She couldn't let him down, he'd helped her so much in the past and Callum, the Business Manager was no longer around. There was no-one else to help her to deal with all this work until a replacement was found.

'That's good to hear.' Uncle Bobby said. 'Off to a good start then.'

She straightened up and this time managed to plaster what she hoped was a dazzling smile on her face. She had to be professional. 'Right. Well, let's line up our domestic ducks in a row.'

She noticed a smile of relief begin to appear on Uncle Bobby's face and his eyebrow returned to normal. 'That's exactly what Greyson would say. Greyson's the Chief Executive,' he explained to Jeremy.

'Jeremy,' she said. 'Welcome to the team. We're running a high profile conference in a few days' time. I do hope you're up to it?'

Jeremy winked. 'Oh yes, of course. I'm definitely up for it. In at the deep end. Can't wait to get started.'

'Good man, good man.' Bobby let out a breath of relief and beamed at both of them. 'Great stuff. I'll be off then. Important meeting to get to. With the magic bean counters.'

'Magic bean counters?' Jeremy asked.

'The accountants.' Uncle Bobby grinned as he hurried off.

As soon as he had gone, Jeremy flung his arms around her in a hug so tight her ribs hurt. 'Verity! How awesome this is. I can't believe my luck.'

She felt the warmth of his cheek as it brushed against her face and the power in his arms. 'What on earth do you think you are doing?' she said, extricating herself as quickly as she could.

He let go and she stepped back and glared at him, smoothing down her crisp navy skirt with damp palms. 'That was very unprofessional.'

His face creased. 'Sorry, only it was so, so good to see you again. I can't believe my luck. After all this time.'

She carried on glowering, annoyed with her confusion.

'So what's with the death stare?'

'What do you think?' She folded her arms and continued to stare.

'I think it's wonderful that fate has thrown us together again.' He flung out his arms again and she stepped back.

Her stomach was tied up in knots. 'So you keep saying. Well I don't. How dare you think that after what you did?'

She shook her head. How dare he rock up like this after all this time and smile as if nothing had happened? As if he was totally oblivious to the past? As she looked at his smiling face, she felt the anger rising in her chest. Didn't he know, he'd destroyed her whole life when she was just seventeen?

She felt slightly ill as she thought back to that day, many years ago when he had turned her world upside down. She'd never been the same after that summer. She thought she'd managed to forget what had happened but now the memories were flooding back. How on earth was she supposed to work with him now? She felt like she wanted to scream and shout at him. How dare he be here? What cruel twist of fate was this?

'I haven't done anything. I don't know what you mean?' He shook his head and his forehead corkscrew curls bobbed. 'I am absolutely delighted to see you again.' He took a step towards her. 'If you only knew how many times I've thought about you and longed to see you again. I can't believe you're getting so aeriated.'

'Right.' she raised a hand to stop him, speaking quietly just in case someone was passing in the corridor. 'This ends right here.' She took a deep breath. 'I don't want to hear another word about the past. If you really want this job you've got to prove your worth at the Urban City event. If you don't, you're out.'

'Please, I do really want this job,' Jeremy promised. 'I won't let you down, I promise.'

She ignored him and began logging on to her laptop.

'I need to check my appointments for the day,' she said. 'Sit down for a moment and I'll find you your first task.' Anything to get him out of the way.

He sat down in Callum's ergonomic chair. The one he kept in Verity's Conference Office for the times when he worked alongside her. 'Nice chair.' Jeremy patted the leather back. 'I bet you're wondering what I'm really doing here aren't you?'

She was looking at her electronic diary on her laptop. 'No, not at all.'

'Well, the answer is I don't really know.' Jeremy moved a pile of papers to one side. 'I'm a Screenwriter.'

'I thought you were going to be a Scriptwriter?' she said, looking up. Then she was annoyed with herself for letting him know that she'd remembered that back then, he was just about to go off to study Drama at University.

'Ah', he said. His eyes lightened with a hint of amusement. 'Yes, I'm one of those as well.'

'Really?' she said. 'How fascinating.'

'Thanks,' he said, leaning back in his chair. 'Wow, this is comfy. It is fascinating. Writing is a bit like acting. But I'm in between jobs at the moment. That's why I really need this one. What can I do first?'

She pointed to a tray full of dishes on the adjacent desk. 'There you go. The kitchen's down the corridor on the left.'

'You want me to wash up?' Jeremy looked momentarily surprised.

'That's the general idea.' She sat back in her chair and surveyed him.

'No problem, washing up is a speciality.' He winked at her again as he jumped up.

'Hadn't you better put your shoes back on first?' she asked, glancing at his odd socks.

'Sorry, I'm not appropriately dressed for work today,' he replied, shoving his feet back into his trainers, 'I was out with the dog when Bobby rang and asked me to come straight in. I promise I will be smarter next time.'

'I'm glad to hear it.' She straightened some piles of papers on the third desk.

'Someone's been eating a lot of cereal.' Jeremy picked up the laden tray and eyed the congealed milk and cornflake remains on the cereal bowls.

'When you've done that, could you start putting these Conference Packs together, all the sheets are set out ready to go into the folders. Do you think you can manage that?'

'Of course, I'll do anything I can to help.'

When Jeremy came back with an armful of sparkling crockery, he was humming along under his breath. She could almost see the sparkling soap suds following him along the corridor, like the devoted birds with fluttering eyelashes in Snow White.

'Are you always so cheerful?' she said, not looking away from her emails.

'Oh yes, mostly.' Jeremy smiled broadly and waved at someone out in the corridor. He'd left the door half open. Strange but there seemed to be a steady stream of females walking past the office already to have a peek at the dazzling newcomer. Word travelled fast around the watercoolers and this part of the building had never seen anything quite like Jeremy. She heard snippets of conversations including –

'Is that a Southern accent? Whereabouts do you think he's from?'

She glowered at the latest offender who quickened her pace as she walked past.

'Right, I'm off to a meeting,' she picked up her laptop. 'You won't be here when I get back. I suggest you get yourself sorted ready for Monday because that is when the work is really going to start.' And by goodness, was she going to make sure he worked hard.

'Of course I will.' Jeremy blew at a stray blonde curl which threatened to cover one eye and jumped up in front of the door. He paused for one moment, blocking her way. 'But there is one thing. I really need you to promise me something. It's very important.'

'Hurry up then,' she said, rolling her eyes. 'Well, what is it?'

'After the event, we have a proper talk?' his eyes were soft. 'I can't go on not knowing?'

'If we have time.' Did he really think she was going to waste time on him? She certainly wasn't promising him anything. 'If you don't give me any hassle until then.'

'As if I would.' He looked affronted. 'I'm only here to help you. What do you take me for?'

'Ha! You really don't want me to tell you,' she flung the words over her shoulder as she departed, shutting the door on him.

Chapter Two

Verity was pleased to be back home that evening. Her home was such a haven. When she told people she lived near the banks of the River Tyne and had a magnificent view of the Staiths, a scheduled ancient monument—said to be the largest timber structure in Europe—they told her she was very lucky. As soon as she could afford to buy her own place after her brief marriage had ended, she'd opted for a home on this estate with its community feel, partly because it was near where Uncle Bobby lived and partly because she felt the need to live somewhere vibrant and be part of something. It was small but it was hers and hers alone.

She loved everything about the area where she lived, from the street names which included Autumn Courtyard, to the collective green spaces and the chalet like houses with their cedar wood cladding, warm coloured pink and brown bricks and little balconies. And the Staiths Café was just around the corner, if she couldn't be bothered to cook, with its European feel, providing a welcome relaxing hub for the residents, as well as being a unique stopping point for the many cyclists, joggers and tourists passing by.

She often met up there with Uncle Bobby and his dog, little golden haired Jenny, on warm evenings, as he could also walk there from his home in nearby Gateshead. Sometimes they sat upstairs, on the comfy seats, with a stunning view over the protected mud flats and bird habitat, enjoying a delicious flat white or an expresso. Or on warmer evenings they sat outside looking out over the riverside with a cool lager, listening to the water lapping at the mud flats like the tide coming in at the beach. Not on Callum's evenings though.

After tea, she kicked off her heels, made herself a cup of tea and curled up in the middle of the sofa in the conservatory where she could see out over the back garden, the vividness of yellow daffodils against emerald grass reviving her tired eyes and her spirits. She loved this time of year in her garden where the red tulips she'd nurtured, mingled with fragrant hyacinths and creamy narcissi nodded in the breeze. Uncle Bobby had helped her to plant and create her borders.

A gentle meow signalled the arrival of her beautiful, white Persian cat who quickly joined her on the sofa. Oh, how soft his little head felt.

'How lovely to see you Tom. I'm so glad, I really am, that you simply wandered into my garden and my life one evening and never really left it again,' she thought.

At times she had really needed his unconditional devotion. She rested her head back against the cushions, listening to his contented purring. *Ah, Tom, it must be the legacy of my childhood when I never knew where I was going to be from one week to the next. Funny, though, how you only make an appearance when Callum isn't around...*

She certainly felt lucky to be here in this house today and looking back, she knew that it wasn't for Uncle Bobby, things might have been very different.

For, until her Uncle Bobby rescued her when she was fifteen and introduced her to wonderful Grandma Anna, she'd never known any stability because her mother had died when she was just a baby. Her dad wasn't much interested in her and so from birth she'd been passed around various aunties, anyone who would take her, sharing bedrooms and beds with other siblings and fighting for space. Then he'd turn up every so often to see if she was all right, usually with a new woman in tow. She never went without food or anything like that but felt like she was never shown any love. She was constantly jostling with other kids to make her voice heard, and in the end she gave up and stayed quiet. She knew what it felt like to be lonely in the midst of chaos.

Uncle Bobby was her mother's brother and she'd never met him either until then, due to family politics. It was also Uncle Bobby, in later life, who had helped her to get a job and was always there for her.

She'd moved in with Grandma Anna and adored living there, actually having her own bedroom overlooking the fells of Fell Ridge, instead of being crammed in with other siblings. She only wished that she'd met them both sooner and that Grandma Anna wasn't in a nursing home now but she had to live in the present. She'd only moved out of Grandma's to get married and look how that had turned out. Not good. In fact it had been a huge mistake and didn't last long. Anyway, that was in the past and yes, she felt very content at the moment. And it was all because of Callum. She smiled as her thoughts turned back to him.

He was her boss and head of the Events Team where she worked and she found out they had so much in common. She remembered how she soon established a routine of taking him a cup of strong coffee into his office, first thing in the morning and of the chat that followed.

'Good Morning Verity,' he would say, in his slow, modulated drawl, sitting at his desk in his immaculate suit, crisp white shirt with pastel coloured brocade pocket square and matching tie.

'Good Morning. Isn't it a beautiful day?' she'd reply.

'It is now I've seen you,' as he cleared a space on his desk for his coffee mug. Unlike him, his desk was always untidy. 'You light up the whole room when you walk in. You bring the sunshine in with you.'

'Here's your coffee,' she would smile.

'Most excellent.' He would reply, often rummaging in his briefcase to find a book he'd brought in for her. That was how thoughtful he was.

She grew to look forward to seeing him each morning and would wonder if he would comment on what she was wearing. He did so most days. 'Oh, you really suit that colour, it brings out the golden flecks in your eyes'. Some days he just said, 'You really know how to dress, you've got style.'

After that she began to make more of an effort with the vivid colours she wore and made sure her dark hair always gleamed clean and shiny, even when she styled it in a bun, up and off her face. She always tried to look professional for work anyhow and wore either a suit or a smart dress and jacket. She had her standards and hated how a lot of the younger staff tended to dress down especially in the summer.

After almost a year of flirting he came home with her because she had offered to prepare him a meal. She had felt so sorry for him always having to eat on the run because he was so busy at work, or had to do all the cooking himself at home because his wife was always out working herself. He ate an awful lot of cereal in the office to keep him going.

'Thank you for this and for all you do. You are a remarkable support in my life. I brought you these.' He'd produced an enormous bouquet of flowers from behind his back. She was delighted, because she loved blooms about the place and bringing the garden inside.

He was always courteous and polite and soon they were seeing each other two or three times a week, bringing her flowers most times because he knew how much she loved them. It was only then that he told her he was married and his wife was a real high flyer and wedded to her job. She was shocked at herself but by then she was entranced and couldn't stop seeing him. Uncle Bobby said she had a blind spot when it came to him.

Callum was an attractive man, tall and smart with hair just starting to go grey at the temples. The girls on the switchboard said he had a lovely speaking voice, calm and deep, and used to argue about whose turn it was to ring him. He was always very pleasant to everyone at work and most people treated him with respect.

She was surprised to learn about all behind the scenes work he did for the local Diocese, doing accounts for them free of charge. She admired him for this and sometimes she gave him a hand. After all, the quicker it was done, the more time they had to spend together.

'What makes you give up so much of your time for this?' she asked once. It was late in the evening and he was still looking at the spreadsheets and figures on his laptop whilst yawning profusely.

'Well, I feel I'm very lucky, I've been really blessed in life and I wanted to give something back.' he explained. Verity had never met anyone who did work for charity before. He donated regularly to them as well.

He never stayed the whole night however, always leaving before midnight, even though he had to drive all the way back home. She looked forward to seeing him the next day at work, clasping her secret to herself that she was the one he chose to be with. When other females flirted with him she just smiled sweetly because she knew it was her that he was seeing and not them. She did feel guilty but she couldn't give him up.

Not that Callum was too demanding. He was very courteous and understood when she was exhausted after a hard day at work and sometimes fell asleep on the sofa. He never pressured her in any way, saying he was tired as well, as he worked such long hours and was quite happy to sit and watch TV after she'd cooked him a nice meal. Then they'd spend the rest of the evening relaxing, listening to some of his favourite classical music.

In fact, he often fell asleep on the sofa as well and she felt sorry for him having to drive all that way to the Scottish Borders when he woke up. She knew how hard he worked, as head of their little team he also acted as Project Manager and had to attend a lot of meetings, often staying late to perfect the company's accounts. In fact they both worked hard. They understood each other.

It had been nice tonight though, to have some time to herself, for well, reflection. Why then, was she starting to feel so drained and restless? Probably because of Jeremy turning up like that. She vowed not to let the events of today rattle her and well, she certainly wasn't about to let his re-appearance change anything.

Tom jumped up to leave her side and she grabbed the cushion behind her head and pummelled it before replacing it. She had this place and she had Callum. And she had tomorrow night to look forward to. After a day at work with her new assistant of course. So what? She wasn't even going to give him a second thought until she had to.

Chapter Three - Callum

Callum liked to think he saw a distinguished chap when he looked into the bathroom mirror, one that still appealed to the opposite sex. Even though he was rather grey around the temples nowadays, he hoped it added to his enigmatic look. His wife kept telling him about his bald spot but then he couldn't see the back of his head so he didn't bother about that. He loosened his tie and stood back, pulling in his stomach and turning to the side. The younger guys at work seemed to favour the more casual look but he still believed in the power of the sharp suit.

Back home, Callum and his wife both had spacious his and hers bathrooms and his bathroom cabinet was bursting full of expensive toiletries including lemon water, moisturiser and countless after shave balms. Here, in the 'Penthouse', he had to make do with a mirror over the sink in the tiny en-suite shower room. Not that he cared. It all added to the thrill of the scenario. He splashed some cold water onto his face.

Wandering out into the large outer room, Callum unlocked a pedestal drawer with a little key he had hidden in his inner jacket pocket. Now, for Mrs D, code name only of course, he needed to set the scene. He pulled open the drawer and dug out some items from what he called his serial seduction kit. Not that he needed it, she was always as eager as he was. But it was good to make an effort.

It always amazed him how much stuff he had managed to stash in the drawer. Armed with two scented candles, a tape machine complete with romantic CD, and a box of beautifully wrapped chocolates, he pushed through the second door at the back of the room. This led into a tiny bedroom which was furnished sparsely with a single bed settee, bedside table and wardrobe. He set the candles down on the table top, lit them, dimmed the light and after taking off his jacket and hanging it on the lone hanger in the wardrobe, sat down on the edge of the bed to wait.

He kept looking at the time on his mobile phone, his anticipation heightened by the fact that she was slightly late. Then it buzzed, making him jump.

'I'm in the lift.' The voice was no more than a whisper, like a soft purr, full of promise.

He smiled to himself. 'You know the way.' She loved all this subterfuge and sneaking about. Said it kept things exciting.

Knowing the lift would arrive in a few seconds, he went through to the kitchen and lifted a chilled bottle of wine out of the fridge, picked up two wine glasses off the bench and carried them through to the bedroom. He heard the mechanical noise of the lift as it docked and caught a snatch of the murmured voice of the lift as it said, 'Doors Opening'. Then there came a soft knock at the exterior door. He opened it.

'Darling,' he stood back slightly to appraise her. 'Welcome once again, to the Penthouse. You look absolutely splendid.'

She burst into the room in a flurry of perfume, blonde hair perfectly coiffed in what he would call an up do, pale silk scarf floating out behind her. She always wore neutral colours, today she sported a long biscuit coloured coat which looked as if it had cost the earth, cream stilettos and matching designer handbag worn cross body style. She ran to him and wrapped her arms around him, nearly knocking him over in her enthusiasm. The scent of her filled his senses. She exuded glamour.

She stepped back and pointed to the lapel of her coat with a beautifully manicured fingernail. 'Would you like to know what I'm wearing under this coat?' there was mischief in her eyes. His heart leapt.

'Nothing I hope.' he said, reaching for her. She dodged his grasp, then grabbed him by his tie and pulled him into the little bedroom, chuckling in her excitement, kicking off her stiletto heels on the way.

Much later, he groaned, 'You'll be the death of me,' as he rolled over next to her on the narrow bed to catch his breath. There was hardly room for the two of them to lay side by side, so she balanced on her right side and looked up at him.

'No-one will ever do it for you like I do,' she said. 'Isn't that right, darling?'

He took a deep breath. 'Phew. You aren't wrong darling. You were….spectacular tonight.' He could smell the heat of her body and her strong perfume which was just ever so slightly, cloying.

She leaned on one elbow even further towards him. 'You do know we're destined to be together? She grazed his chest with an immaculately manicured fingernail. 'So, how about same time, same place tomorrow night?'

'I can't tomorrow night, you know that,' he said, sighing, beginning to feel a cloud descend upon him.

'Oh dear, I almost forgot.' She got up and sat on the edge of the bed away from him, her back very straight. Her eyes raked the room for her discarded silk stockings which she snatched up from the floor and began to pull on. 'Tuesdays and Thursdays are her nights aren't it? Verity. Your little Miss Perfect. I suppose she'll be cooking a delectable meal for you once again?'

'Now come on darling,' he chided. 'She's never done you any harm.'

'Oh, but she has,' she accused. 'She commands far too much of your time.' Now she looked around the room for her shoes which she pounced upon. 'Ah, there they are.' She shoved her foot into the right one and swung round. 'Time that could be far better spent with me.'

For some reason, tonight her barbed comments irked him slightly. Maybe it was because he was over tired lately and had started taking tablets for his slightly raised blood pressure, but he was starting to feel uneasy about deceiving Verity. He was very fond of her, that was true but just recently, Mrs D. had come back into his life and he was unable to resist the exhilaration of meeting up with her again. She was so different in every way but he could never relax with her the way he could with Verity. Verity was very easy to be around. Sometimes he didn't know what he wanted the most. Maybe he wanted the best of both worlds?

'Then there's all your charity work. I can't ever see you on Monday nights either because you're doing accountancy work for the Diocese.' She spat out the words. 'I can't think why on earth you would want to spend your evenings doing that.'

He sat up and smoothed back his hair. 'You know why. I've told you before. I want to give something back. I've been so blessed in my life in general.'

'Oh, please,' she snorted.

He smiled to himself. The very idea of wanting to help the community was alien to her but he really did want to give something back. That was why he'd joined the Freemasons as well all those years ago and kept it up. To make a contribution to family and society and even make some donations to charities. As he'd progressed through the ranks, he'd gained more and more seniority through promotions and with those of course, came more responsibility. He'd met a lot of people and they helped each other in the business world. And he'd had fun.

Sometimes all the words he had to learn were rather daunting but he felt it was worth it. He entrusted Verity with helping him learn his lines for one-act plays and rituals sometimes because he knew she was discreet and wouldn't ask questions.

'Anyway, that only leaves Wednesdays for me,' she pouted. 'And Fridays if you're not going home to your wife for the weekend.'

'Come on darling, let's not waste precious time arguing. Help me drink this champagne. You haven't touched it and it is most excellent. And you do know I'd be with you more if only I could.' He handed her a glass.

'Hmmm,' she lay back down next to him, stilettos and all, making the bed bounce. She took a swig from her glass. 'I thought you said you'd chilled this?'

'Actually, darling,' he said, 'there is something I need to share with you.'

She slammed the glass down so hard some of the wine slopped over onto the table.

'It had better not be what I think it is,' she snapped, 'because it's not happening. Not when I've just found you again.'

'No, it's not that at all. You're the best thing in my life, you know that. It's good news actually. You see, I have been thinking along the lines of moving back to the Borders to work.'

'About time too.' She mopped up the wine with her scarf. 'I knew you'd see sense.'

He took her hand. 'I know the perfect little hotel which is halfway for both of us.'

'Not too little I hope.' She looked slightly mollified.

He laughed and stroked her bronzed arm.

'So, this could be our very last time here in the Penthouse?' she asked. 'I'll miss it, I've become rather fond of this place.'

'Me too,' he agreed.

'Although it does have its limitations, for example, no room service or even a double bed, it's rather cosy don't you think?'

'Definitely,' he said, looking around the small room, which looked even smaller with his clothing still strewn across the floor.

'So, does this mean you're going to do the decent thing and call it a day with your precious Verity?'

He ran a hand over his hair. 'There's no need for you to worry about any of that.'

'I disagree. I think it's about time you moved on and…'

'Shhh. Let's just plan the next time we can be together.'

Much later when she'd gone, the scent of her still lingering in the room, he lay on the bed, exhausted but unable to sleep. The air felt stale so in the end he got up, pulled on the silk dressing gown he always kept for these occasions and wandered out onto the adjoining balcony. He looked out upon the winking city lights and the dark mass of the river spread out below him. He went back into the kitchen and came out again with a bowl of cereal and the bottle of champagne.

He sat down at the little table, munched on the cereal and finished off the rest of the champagne, enjoying the coolness of the breeze, looking out at the myriad of stars in the black sky. It was very high up out here and he wasn't keen on heights, but as long as he didn't look over the balcony edge, he'd be okay. He felt the sweat cooling on his forehead in the breeze.

Mrs D was such a bitch and so different from Verity. He felt rather bad that often he was far too tired to do anything when he was with Verity other than sit and relax on her sofa. Verity didn't seem to notice, as long as he was happy, she was content for him just to be there. She was such a sweet thing. She seemed to be devoted to making his life as comfortable as she possibly could both at work and out of it without asking for very much in return. The same certainly couldn't be said for Mrs D. She was like a whirlwind, volatile and tempestuous.

What to do about Verity? Should he do the right thing and let her down gently? He knew
she deserved better than this. Than him. She was a lot younger than him, she'd soon meet someone else. Damm, he felt a pang of jealousy at the thought, goodness he must be fonder of her than he'd thought. *Did he really want to give her up?* Theirs was such an ideal relationship.

It was bad timing that Mrs D had come back into his life at this particular time. But they had history. Too much in fact. And she knew too much about him. He'd always liked living dangerously where women were concerned but she was something else. And she kept coming back for more. He'd always been weak where women were concerned, particularly in the case of Mrs D.

In earlier days, he'd always worked on the premise that if he tried it on with say, six women, one of them was bound to say yes. Any more was a bonus. Nowadays he felt that three was too many.

Something had to give. He was run ragged keeping them all happy, in very different ways. Heaven knows, he wasn't getting any younger although he hated to admit it. And the day job was busier than ever. He'd implemented one or two of his own ideas but deep down he knew Verity was very bright and capable of taking over where he would leave off. She was doing most of it already and he knew she'd make a success of the business. Maybe it was time to call it a day and do what his wife wanted, which was to start up a little business together back in the Borders. At least he wouldn't have all the travelling to contend with and there was always consultancy work if he was bored… He knew Mrs D was willing to follow him wherever he went.

He sighed. Most upsetting but it was time to do the right thing in one direction at least.

Chapter Four

Verity hummed along to the radio as she moved about the kitchen, stirring pans and tasting her pasta sauce. Perfect. Exactly how he liked it. A welcome breeze streamed in from the open window, grazing her flushed cheeks.

She heard his key in the lock and the front door open. 'Hi, I'm in here,' she sang out, the usual thrill of anticipation at seeing him filling her being and bubbling over into a smile. She so looked forward to their evenings together.

'Most excellent,' she heard his low voice.

'Dinner's about ready,' she continued. She hurried into the hallway up to him to kiss him but he moved his head slightly so that she kissed his cheek.

'Ah, Verity, darling,' his voice sounded guarded. 'You're looking most wonderful by the way, as ever.'

She felt a sense of unease as he took a step back. 'Is something wrong?'

'No, no, everything's fine,' then, 'actually that's not quite true.' He hovered from foot to foot. 'Err, I'm afraid I can't stay for dinner this evening. There's something I must say to you.'

'Callum what is it, what's wrong?' she said, taking his arm. 'Are you ill? Come and sit down.'

'No, no, nothing like that,' he pulled back and cleared his throat. 'You've always been a straight talker. I admire that and…and I admire you greatly as you know. Now it's my turn to be straight with you.'

'What do you mean?' The sense of disquiet grew stronger.

'Verity.' He took a step towards her. 'I'm leaving the company. I've handed in my notice.'

'You've done what? But why?' she asked, puzzled, not taking it in. She looked up into his cloudy gray eyes.

'I'm so tremendously sorry, but there's no easy way to say this.' He tried to take her hand but she refused to let him and his arm dropped back by his side. She kept her back straight.

'It's just that I've realised…I want to try and make a go of it with Cindy, my wife. I'm so sorry, I really am.'

'What?' she gasped, feeling the colour drain from her face, 'but, I thought you were happy with me, with us?' No, no, no, this couldn't be happening. She felt her stomach lurch.

'Oh but I am, or I mean I was. I've been happier than I've ever been.' His hands were in his suit jacket pockets now, as if he didn't know what to do with them.

'Then why now?' she demanded. 'After two whole years? What about me?'

'Verity, please don't be angry,' he looked at her with soft pleading eyes. 'Let me explain.'

'Go right ahead,' she stared back at him.

He sighed. 'The thing is, Cindy's had a bit of a health scare, poor old thing. She's come through it but it's really made me think. She needs me.'

Verity was having difficulty in forming the right words. Anger was starting to turn into something else. But I need you as well. What about me? *But I need you as well.*

'And I don't want to waste any more of your life,' he went on.

'Don't you dare turn this round onto me,' she found her voice and flung the words at him.

'Be honest,' he sighed again, 'I sometimes get the impression you're only going through the motions with me.'

'That's simply not true,' she spluttered. 'I'm devoted to you. You must know that.'

'You'll meet someone else who will appreciate you far more than I ever have. Someone more your age maybe.'

'What if I don't want to meet someone else?' Her throat felt choked. 'What if I'm happy with you, with the way things are?'

'I've always been a bit of a blackguard you know,' his eyes were roving around the room, looking at anything but at her. 'The black sheep of my family. I was never very good at settling anywhere.'

'And that's supposed to make me feel better?'

'And you won't have to wash up so much crockery after me at work.'

How dare he be so flippant at a time like this? She was determined not to cry in front of him but she could feel hot tears pricking behind her eyeballs. And she certainly wasn't going to beg and plead with him to change his mind. Did he look a bit relieved that she wasn't going to make a scene? Because no way was she. She'd always been good at hiding her feelings in times of stress. And she was used to people leaving her.

'I'm not getting any younger,' his voice continued, 'I'm tired of travelling backwards and forwards every day.'

'You've always said you love driving,' she stated, thinking of his sleek black Mercedes.

'I do, but it's just too much. Do you mind if I get my things?' he asked. She had the feeling he couldn't wait to be gone.

'Be my guest,' the anger returning, she waved him past into the kitchen whilst she stood there straight and unmoving in the hall, knowing he was gathering up the few possessions he kept here, his spare laptop, a suit jacket, a winter coat, a couple of books. She felt cold and a bit shivery and folded her arms against her body. She couldn't believe this was happening.

'But what will you do?' she asked as he sheepishly entered the hall again. 'Now that you've handed in your notice?'

'I've bought a little business which Cindy and I are going to run together. A village shop. In our village.'

Ha. Best of luck with that one. She couldn't see him behind a counter. In fact it was ludicrous to imagine him organising anything but then, his wife would be there wouldn't she, to help.

'What about her job?' she said. He'd always told her his wife was dedicated to her job and worked all hours.

'She's worn out with it all as well,' he paced up and down the hallway, heavy coat on his arm. 'Particularly after her illness. I, we - just want to make a new start.'

'So it's all arranged?' she had the feeling he couldn't wait to be gone. 'You're going just like that?'

He nodded.

'What about all the plans for our Events Team, all the conferences we were going to organise?'

'Come on, we both know I'm surplus to requirements. Manager in name only. You're the one that runs the team. You're a strong woman you know, much stronger than you think.'

She shook her head.

'I'm so terribly sorry,' he took a step towards her, reaching out for her hand.

'Don't.' She stepped back. 'You've made up your mind. Just go.'

'If I've left anything behind, please just get rid of it,' he said, looking around the room.

She marched up to the front door and flung it open. 'Don't worry. I will.'

He hesitated on the doorstep. 'I am truly sorry. I can honestly say I have enjoyed every single moment we've spent together. You're a wonderful person, Verity.'

'Goodbye,' she said, turning her head this time as he moved to kiss her on the cheek.

'Goodbye then, and take care.' He turned around and gave her a heartfelt, wistful look, shifting his laptop bag slightly on his shoulder. 'I'm truly sorry, I really am.'

'Oh just go Callum,' she snapped and slammed the door behind him. Why was he lingering? Maybe he was disappointed she hadn't tried just a little bit harder to get him to stay.

For a while she just felt numb and it took a while for her to remember he hadn't given her the front door key back.

She couldn't face eating the meal she'd so carefully prepared, so just left it all as it was and sank down on the sofa. She could only think of how empty the place seemed and how alone she felt. Such an empty feeling. Her imagination was running riot and she couldn't work out what's what. She felt too mixed up and too tired to know how she felt.

Indignant? Angry? Sad? She only knew she felt devastated—too numb to cry. Without him she felt so alone.

Well, not *quite* alone. Tom crept up on her and jumped on her lap, bright blue eyes wide. He looked up at her with his bright blue eyes and meowed.

'Sorry, Tom,' she spoke out loud. *'I didn't know you were there. Never know what your meow means, only know you love me. Funny how you always appear when Callum isn't here. Are you telling me something, Tom? . . . Don't know what I'd do without you, little friend. You understand that, Tom, or are you just stroking me with the side of your face before you make your escape? Such soft, white fur . . . You don't need to go you know, he's not coming back...'*

Alone again, a little more positive after Tom's company, she passed her mobile. Tomorrow she would delete his number. She wanted to pick it up and ring him and hear him say it was all a mistake and feel relief flooding back over her. Instead the cold reality hit even further as she realized she would never phone nor text him again. Nor he her. Ever. Oh, stop being so melodramatic, Verity she scolded herself. No man is worth it. Certainly not him.

She walked into the bathroom where it was warm and comforting, and turned on the taps, preparing to bathe in perfumed water. She opened small, luxury bottles of lemongrass and pink grapefruit, then remembered that these were the toiletries they'd brought back from an illicit week-end. She binned the bottles and reached for the Radox. Could it really be two years since they started seeing each other?

Now dressed, she went into the kitchen, one of her favourite spaces in the house, probably because they'd spent such a lot of time in here eating together and cooking, or rather she cooked whilst he sat and read the paper. She caught sight of the poster they'd bought together:

'Life is better when you're laughing.'

They'd certainly done plenty of that in this room. Everything looked so very tidy. Uncle Bobby said she was a bit of a control freak but she just couldn't stand mess and disorder in her own space.

She realised she was absolutely ravenous despite her emotional state and banging headache. It seemed such a long time ago since they'd last eaten together.

As this memory elbowed its way into the room, the tears flowed. She wasn't one to cry, she'd soon learnt at an early age that when she'd been sent off to live with yet another auntie that crying didn't help. She'd had to learn to adjust. And quickly. She often wondered why she wasn't tougher than she was with the upbringing she'd had. Maybe it all depended on the type of person you were deep down, in spite of your past life.

She'd had no inkling at all that anything was wrong and he'd been as attentive as ever the last few weeks. He'd told her he wasn't happy at home, hadn't been for years, her with her high powered job and him with his and they hardly saw each other. Said they only stayed together because of the kids. So it took a health crisis for him to suddenly realise what he was doing to his family. He wanted to spend more time with them. Really? And run a village shop? Hah.

Cold reality took over. Indignation replaced worry and heartache. And let's face it, he was married. It was bound to happen one day. Who needed him anyway? Maybe it was time she thought about herself. She'd been good at hiding her real feelings for years and getting on with things. Uncle Bobby always said she was only with Callum because she wanted a father figure, because she'd lived the way she had. She did so appreciate her own home now because, at last she had something of her very own. She knew how lucky she'd been to be reunited with Uncle Bobby and Grandma Anna and she never ever took her good fortune for granted.

Resolutely, she flung two tea bags into the teapot and then berated herself because there was only herself here to drink it. Then she told herself she could use them both later to soothe her sore eyes and reduce the swelling that was bound to be there in the morning on her eyelids. Be practical, she told herself. She had to pull herself together as tomorrow she had to deal with her new assistant, whose unwelcome presence might rake up all kinds of memories she thought she'd forgotten about long ago.

And she had a meeting with the Chief Executive first thing in the morning.

Chapter Five

Verity never failed to enjoy the walk through country parkland to the office each day but today she was trying hard to pretend to herself that the bottom hadn't dropped out of her world. She was confronted with a huge, hazy orange ball of a sun peeping out from behind the rooftops of the old rustic building nestling in the scoop of the hillside. How unusual. Surely it wasn't usually that big? Maybe it meant the mist was going to burn off and it would turn out to be a beautiful April day. A blackbird was perched on top of the Reception signpost, singing its heart out, the sweet melodic notes sounding so poignant.

She shook herself inwardly and marched straight along to Greyson Parkin's office. What could he want to see her about so early in the morning? It was probably to talk about starting the recruitment process for Callum's replacement. More work to do. Well, she was

 determined she was going to ask him about the possibility of another member of staff, as the Conference Team was way beneath its quota, even with Jeremy on board.

Sophie, the younger of Greyson's two Personal Assistants, was in the outer office, logging on to her computer with one hand and holding a mobile phone in the other, whilst stifling a yawn. When she saw who it was she brightened up, mobile phone in hand.

'Good Morning Verity.' she beamed.

'Morning. Should I go straight in?' Verity asked, walking over to his door.

'He said to tell you, he'll see you in two minutes.' Sophie indicated the chair outside Greyson's office. 'Have a seat. Would you like a coffee?'

She sat. 'No thanks, I'm fine.'

'Actually – while you're waiting, could I have a word?' Sophie fiddled with her mobile.

Verity looked at her watch. Goodness, she had a busy day ahead. She wished Greyson would hurry up so she could get on with it. 'Go ahead.' She was trying to concentrate on the here and now even though her head was all over the place.

'I need to ask you something,' Sophie walked around the desk. 'My dad always tells me I should keep my mouth shut but I find it proper hard to keep quiet.'

Verity liked Sophie. She couldn't help but admire her honesty. 'Me too,' she said, prompting a giggle. 'Go on then, if you're quick.' Behind her the office clock ticked like a steady heartbeat.

'Please can I come and work for you?' she pleaded.

Verity raised an eyebrow. 'Don't you like working for Greyson?'

'Oh, Greyson's okay.' Sophie sat on the front of the desk. 'Sometimes. You'll never guess what I said to him this morning?'

'I have no idea.'

Sophie continued, 'Well, he said to me, 'Did you enjoy my speech at the launch yesterday?' and then I said, 'to be perfectly honest I was bored proper stiff.'

He looked gutted and said 'Why?' and I said, "Because you tell stupid jokes and then you laugh at them. Duh!"

Verity stifled a chuckle.

'Can you imagine, laughing at your own jokes?' Sophie wrinkled her nose. 'He's just like my dad and he's irritating as well.'

'What did he say to that?' Verity asked.

'He laughed like mad.' Sophie leaned forward and her eyes grew rounder. 'Then he told me another one.'

'You know, its hard work in the conferencing world,' Verity told her. 'There are mountains of envelopes to stuff, gear to load in and out of cars as well as lifting banners and lugging heavy equipment in and out of venues.'

'Please. It'll be better than working in here. There's not much to do and I get bored doing nothing.'

'Oh, I'll see what I can do.' Verity looked at her watch again. 'Right, that's it. I've had enough of this waiting. It's been more than two minutes. I'm going in.' She rapped on the door and marched in, buoyed up by the shocked yet approving look on Sophie's face.

Well, he wasn't busy at all. Greyson Parkin, Chief Executive Officer of the entire organisation was short, portly and balding with a strong Geordie accent. He was standing in front of his train set, watching one of the tiny trains chugging around the track with his beady eyes. How annoying was he, keeping her waiting whilst he played trains?

Greyson loved his train sets and apparently had a huge one in his loft at home. He said the one at work helped him de-stress and was always a good icebreaker with important clients.

'Ah, Verity.' Greyson said. He had his jacket on which was a sign he was ready for a meeting. 'Sit down,' his voice boomed out but then he never spoke quietly. 'Have you been talking to Sophie? Can't get the staff.'

'No-one escapes the jesting around here.' He laughed to himself.

One of the mobiles on his desk buzzed and he sat down and picked it up.

For all his joking, Greyson was a family man and several photographs of his attractive wife and children adorned his desk. Although he was often in trouble over the years for his outspokenness, he hadn't got to where he was today without a lot of hard work and effort. He replaced the phone as Verity shot him a look.

'Sorry. Twitter. Football scores.' He pushed the phone away. They eyeballed each other across the desk.

'Now. It's time to do some blue sky thinking.' Greyson reached for his mug which looked like it contained some kind of herbal tea and took a gulp. 'Didn't she offer you a cup of tea? Can't get the staff nowadays.'

'I'm fine thanks,' she shifted forward on her seat.

'You know, not every egg becomes a bird in our tent,' he said, leaning forward across the desk and she noticed the little red flecks in the corners of his eyes. Everyone said he drank at home and didn't sleep much, sending emails at all hours.

'Could you please translate that?' she asked. Sophie was right, he could be irritating.

He continued talking. 'I don't know many women who could rise above the marzipan layer. But I believe you could be one of them.'

'The marzipan what?' What was he trying to say? She felt a prickle of excitement beginning to build in her stomach.

'The layer of execs just below the top level of icing.' Greyson leaned forward a little further so that the buttons on his shirt strained and one in particular threatened to ping off.

'I like you. I think you've got staying power and leadership qualities. That's why I'm giving you the gig.'

'Me?' she gripped the sides of the chair. 'What gig?'

'Yes. You're running the show now. I'm promoting you to Business Manager.'

'Wow,' she said. 'That wasn't what I was expecting to hear.' She couldn't quite take it in but her heart was beating very fast.

'Why not? Surely you can't be that surprised. Come on, everyone knows you run the place anyway. There'll be an upgrade in salary of course.'

'How much upgrade?' she couldn't help asking. Now full blown butterflies were twirling away inside at the thought of being in charge of the Events Team, but at the same time she felt a smile beginning to form and widen. This was beyond her expectations, for a girl with her background to be offered a position like this was truly astounding…

Greyson grinned back. 'Now that's the Verity I know and love.'

He quoted a figure which made her gasp. It was beyond anything she'd expected.

Greyson sat back and thankfully the button stayed put. 'I know you won't let me down and I don't want anyone else for the job. The gig is yours.'

'But...' her face felt as if it was burning.

'No buts. From Soup to Nuts, Verity, from Soup to Nuts.'

'Pardon?' she said, not waiting for the answer. 'I'll need more help. If I accept the job, I want Sophie on my team.'

Greyson nodded. 'Agreed. I knew you'd need more troops. Anything else you need, just ask.' He snapped his laptop lid shut which signalled the end of the conversation.

'I'm off to a meeting. See yourself out.' And off he went, leaving the door open and the little train slowly chugging to a standstill.

Her head was buzzing. Business Manager. She felt sad yet elated at the same time. All at once she'd lost Callum and gained a promotion. And at a salary she'd always dreamed of but never expected to actually achieve. Not for someone like her. But at what a price. She would so much rather have had things the way they were. How could she feel so conflicted, when a job like this was what she'd always yearned for?

Back in the Conference Office, Jeremy and Sophie watched with growing interest as a bloke in overalls arrived with a bag of tools and began prising off the existing name plate on Callum's door and replacing it with one that read:

VERITY RAFFIN – BUSINESS MANAGER

She didn't say anything but couldn't keep a huge grin from spreading all over her face.

'Congratulations boss,' Jeremy beamed, rushing over to pat her on the back.

'Amazeballs!' Sophie said. 'You so deserve this Verity.'

As she stared at her name on the door, inwardly, she remembered Grandma Anna's words. 'Be careful what you wish for,' she always used to say. Because it might just come true.

Chapter Six

Verity couldn't sleep that night as everything was whirling round and round in her head. The air from the open window felt warm. She kept thinking about Grandma Anna, now in a nursing home, and how pleased she would be to hear the news. She couldn't wait to go and see her. Then her thoughts strayed to her Uncle Bobby and how delighted he'd been when she'd told him. She remembered the very first time in her life that she'd met Uncle Bobby. Of course she didn't know at the time who he was…

The years peeled away and she was a young kid again, walking down the local high street with her dad on one of the very rare occasions he took her out. She was hopeful of him buying some her Pic'N'Mix sweets in Woolies. She paused in the shop doorway but he tugged at her hand, saying that they were going up the street to the ice-cream parlour to meet someone. He loved the frothy coffee they sold in there, served in a glass. Today he seemed in even more of a rush than usual.

Verity hung back, glimpsing the bitter lemon sweets she loved through the glass frontage and remembered an oldish lady with thick dark hair and a long face like a gentle horse, charging over the zebra crossing towards them. She carried two shopping bags on each arm and a young man with very short dark hair trailed behind trying to keep up, carrying yet more bulging carrier bags.

'Hello Micky.' The lady stopped right in front of them. She smiled at Verity and Verity felt herself smiling back, thinking how pretty the lady was. She had kind eyes. 'And this must be Verity.' Behind her the young man hastily put down the bags, sighing and rubbing at his wrists.

'We're in a hurry,' her dad said abruptly. 'No time to stop today.'

'Micky, can we talk?' the lady moved closer to Verity, still smiling and held out her hand. Verity smiled back but her dad pulled her away. 'Not now Anna, it's not a good time.'

Verity saw that the lady looked hurt and upset because her dad didn't want to talk to her.

He jerked at Verity's hand. 'Come on, we need to get to D'Nambros. I'll buy you an ice-cream float if you hurry up,' and hurried her off up the street, leaving them both staring after them. Verity craned her neck for as long as she could before the crowds swarmed in front of her and she could see her no more.

'Daddy, who was that nice lady?' she asked her dad as he sat her down in a booth in the ice cream shop.

'No-one,' he said grumpily.

'But she looked lovely,' Verity persisted. 'Who was she?'

'I told you. No-one you need to know about. Now here's a nice lady, and the person I want you to meet, be good now.'

Her dad stood up abruptly to welcome a young woman into the booth. Verity's heart sank. Oh no, not another auntie. .

Due to a long running family feud about which she'd managed to piece together scant snippets gleaned from her various aunties, the second time she saw Uncle Bobby must have been ten years later. He sought her out, together with her dad, in the museum café where she was working as a waitress, one Friday night after school.

It was when they all sat down at the end of her shift and her dad placed a glass of golden Lucozade in front of her, that her dad introduced the man as her uncle. She got a bit of a shock at first but was drawn to him straightaway, because he looked just like her and she thought she was a good judge of character, having come across quite a few of them in her short life.

Uncle Bobby was Verity's mother's younger brother by four years. He told her he had been very close to her mother and was devastated when she died at the age of 21, leaving Verity as a baby. She felt at home with him immediately and wondered if he would tell her some stuff about her mother? Her dad just wouldn't talk about her all. She felt her heart lurch. She knew so little.

Her uncle looked quite old with wiry dark hair starting to go grey, sloping eyebrows and a bristly shadow of whiskers on his chin. He'd come straight from work at the Town Hall and was wearing a smart suit and tie.

She never knew what made her dad change his mind after all those years, but when Uncle Bobby asked if she wanted to come and meet her Grandma Anna and her dad didn't look at all annoyed at the prospect, she'd jumped at the chance. Her dad had always been prone to sharp outbursts of temper whenever Grandma Anna was mentioned and she had soon learnt to keep quiet and not ask about her, or her mother. But she always wondered.

She was still in her waitress's uniform but her dad said they were in a hurry as usual, so she just removed her white apron, grabbed her bag with her change of clothes and the three of them climbed into Uncle Bobby's car. They dropped her dad off first and then began the short drive to Grandma Anna's house, which Uncle Bobby told her was in a tiny moor side village called Fell Ridge. The village was only a couple of miles from the little riverside town where Verity was living with her Auntie Doris, one of her dad's sisters.

The windows of Auntie Doris's house all had grubby net curtains and the rooms always smelt of chip fat but at least she had her own bed, although it was only a tiny box room overlooking the square. It was called Lilac Square, for what reason Verity had never fathomed as she'd never seen a scrap of lilac yet. Not a lilac tree or bush or bloom, just a large square of scrubby grass onto which the sprawling, rundown houses faced.

There were a few random swings and a roundabout which was falling to bits and stray dogs roamed day and night over the grass. She'd even seen the odd horse wandering about the area, looking lost probably due to the fact that beyond the square lay lots of fields and derelict factory buildings, one of which had a goat tethered to the railings.

That first time she saw Grandma Anna's house she thought she'd gone back in time. Uncle Bobby told her he'd lived in this house from the age of six and had had a wonderful childhood, tripping out the back door and off out onto the fells all day, making dens and fires and camping out with his school friends.

She saw an old, neat looking, terraced house right in the middle of a front row of houses with a very tidy front garden full of fragrant, blowsy roses. There were several identical rows of houses sheltering behind this one but from the road it looked as though this front row was the only one. She thought how much prettier this street looked than the one she was living in at the moment, apart from the pit heap of course, which loomed behind the houses.

They parked at the front of the house on the road and she looked to the right where the green and golden gorse of the fells of Fell Ridge rose steeply against the bright blue sky. For a moment she felt panicked and her heart was beginning to thud uncomfortably in her chest. What would Grandma Anna think of her? She didn't think she would be able to speak, she was so nervous. What if Grandma Anna didn't like her? The kids at school didn't. She was just so skinny and gawky and told them what she thought.

They walked round to the back street, where cars were parked nose to tail and there was a little red post box just across the way. She followed Uncle Bobby tentatively through a black gate with the Number 5 painted on it, to a yard which looked like it had just been swept clean, and to the open back door. They entered into a long narrow kitchen, warm with the smell of baking and steamy, with a kettle whistling cheerfully on the hob. Her eyes widened and mouth watered at the sight of two halves of an enormous chocolate cake on the bench and rows of vanilla slices resting on a cooling tray. The heat enveloped her.

Then they were in an immaculately clean dining room where washing was drying, strung across the ceiling on a pulley. A few tins of bread, covered with blue and white checked tea towels, lay resting on the hearth in front of the blazing coal fire. All available windowsills, including the one up the stairs, were covered with ornaments and plant pots bursting full of pink fuchsias.

'Is that you, our Bobby? Turn that kettle off on your way past,' a voice hollered and Grandma Anna marched out of the sitting room and into Verity's life.

'Mam, this is Verity,' Uncle Bobby said and she noticed his eyes were glistening behind his heavy rimmed glasses. She still felt very nervous and hung back but he pushed her forward. Her heart thudded so hard it hurt.

'Hello pet,' Grandma Anna drew herself up to her full height, which in her sheepskin slippers was just a bit taller than Verity, wiped her hands on her flowery pinafore and put her hands down by her sides. She looked right into Verity's face with deep set brown eyes. She was the image of Uncle Bobby, same generous nose and wiry hair. She was smiling. Verity vaguely heard Uncle Bobby saying he was going out for a walk and heard the back door shut.

She stood there, feeling tongue tied, head down looking at the immaculate patterned carpet, her eyes prickling hot with tears that threatened to spill. Her heart was thumping so hard in her chest it hurt. She felt like she didn't dare move in case the spell was broken and Grandma Anna disappeared. Then, looking up under her lashes, she saw Grandma's face crumple. She couldn't stop the tears falling then. Very slowly, she opened up her arms and Verity went into them, feeling Grandma Anna's soft jumper against her hot cheeks. All she could hear was the gentle ticking of a clock somewhere in the room and the crackling of the fire behind her. There was a faint smell of scent, like crushed rose petals.

She couldn't remember ever having a hug like that her entire life. For one brief moment she felt safe.

What seemed like ages afterward, Grandma Anna produced a smooth white hanky with an embroidered 'A' in the corner from the folds in her apron. 'Here hinny, wipe your eyes. Oh dear. Look at you! You are so like my Adele. You've got the same shaped face – a perfect oval.'

'Thank you,' Verity felt her voice croak as she wiped her face, wet with burning tears and blew her nose. No-one had ever paid her a compliment about her appearance.

'Sorry, I'm still in my uniform, I didn't have time to get changed.'

Grandma Anna blew her own nose vigorously. 'You look very smart pet. Look, I've got something to show you. Come on into the sitting room.' She ushered her into the next room and picked up a photo from the mantelpiece of a young woman with very short dark hair, long gangly arms and legs in a short summer dress, grinning widely and playing a guitar.

'That's your mam.' she said proudly. 'Your mam and my Adele. Isn't she lovely? See, look you've got the same beautiful porcelain complexion. She'd be about seventeen then.'

'Two years older than I am now,' Verity's voice still sounded croaky. She'd hardly ever seen any photos of her mam and couldn't drag her eyes away. Oh Mam, why did you have to die and leave me behind? I would have given anything to have known you. .

'I'll make us a nice cup of tea,' Grandma Anna replaced the photograph gently onto the mantelpiece. 'Ooh, the kettle's boiling. You sit down pet and look at the view.'   Grandma bustled out of the room, still speaking over her shoulder. She had a strong voice which carried. 'I'll make a nice bacon sandwich for our suppers' later on.'

Verity dabbed at her eyes again and wandered over to the big picture window with its crisp white curtains pulled back so that a view of the layered fells, topped off by bright blue sky could be clearly seen.

'I like to watch the sun setting over the fells of a night time,' Grandma Anna's voice sang from the kitchen, then, 'Help yourself to a sweet,' her voice rang out again, it was the type of voice which carried. Verity sank down on the nearest edge of the comfy sofa and noticed there was a tin of Roses chocolates on the floor. In fact there was a little line-up of chocolates, just starting to melt, on the lace antimacassar on my left, this must be Grandma's seat.

She hastily bunched along to the far end of the settee, nearer the window. The house looked straight out onto the west and on the way here Uncle Bobby had told her he'd seen some of the best sunsets in his life from that window. Also, from the room that used to be his bedroom which was directly above. She looked out through the lace curtain, marvelling at the sun's dying rays stretching burning fingers of gold across the dusky sky above the carpet of lush green fields and catching the swell of golden gorse which scattered the fells of Fell Ridge, rising gently to the left. She felt hope rising from the pit of her stomach and her mouth felt dry.

Uncle Bobby, so thoughtful and kind, had done just the right thing by leaving them alone to talk. Grandma and Verity talked and cried and talked and cried a bit more. By the time he came back, a few wonderful heart wrenching hours later, Verity knew she wanted to live with Grandma Anna more than she'd wanted anything in her whole life. But how was she to make it come about?

In a short space of time she'd found out lots about Grandma Anna's life, how her second husband, a miner at the drift mine had died several years ago and they said she wasn't due any money after the Miners' Strike because it was a tiny drift mine he'd worked at, not a big mine. She'd had to fight to make ends meet, even had to work as a cleaner and caretaker at the local primary school when Uncle Bobby and his brother Peter were there.

She watched in awe as the fiery golden orb dipped behind the hillsides and the sky became a blazing inferno of brilliant reds and oranges, streaking behind swathes of cloud and emerging among silhouettes of darkened trees and fleeing birds. What a beautiful sight. She'd never seen such a thing, no wonder Grandma Anna loved it.

She felt her heart swell with emotion and she knew in that instant she wanted nothing more than to be able to sit and watch that sky with her Grandma Anna every night. She was the closest link Verity would ever find to the mother she'd never known. She felt all choked up inside. Uncle Bobby came back in then, his eyes light as he looked at the pair of them sitting so close together on the settee.

Shaking inside, her eyes burning with unshed tears, Verity plucked up the courage and asked the question.

'Please, please can I come to live with you Grandma?' she begged. 'I won't be any trouble I promise.' There was silence in the room for what seemed like forever. Uncle Bobby sat down quietly on the edge of the armchair opposite.

'Oh, I don't know pet,' she said at first. 'I've still got our Peter living at home you know. And our Johnny coming over all the time. How would I get all my jobs done?'

'I'm used to looking after myself,' Verity said, the words rushing out as she couldn't bear to see her newfound hopes and dreams crumble at the first hurdle. 'I can cook as well. I'm looking for a job now I've left school and when I get one I'll be able to give you some board money. I think I've done all right in my GCSEs. Please Grandma.'

'I can tell that Verity's a hard worker.' Uncle Bobby said. 'Maybe I could help her out with a job at the Town Hall in a few months when she's sixteen. I'll make some enquiries.'

Her heart leapt with excitement. 'Oh yes please. See Grandma, I'll be able to pay my way.' She found that her nails were digging into her palms as she clenched her fists in anticipation. 'Oh please, don't say no. I just couldn't bear it.'

'Oh well, all right then,' Grandma Anna said after a long pause.

'Oh thank you!' Verity threw her arms around her and they hugged again. 'Thank you so much, I promise you won't regret it.' Uncle Bobby was grinning at both of them.

Grandma Anna went to put the kettle on again for Uncle Bobby and Verity felt so glad she'd worked hard at her studies. She was an avid reader. She'd worked hard at school, spent ages doing her homework and borrowed books from the local library. She supposed she was a very serious and dull child but she had found that once immersed in a book, she could forget what was going on around her. She read anything she could get my hands on, any books lying around she'd pounce on them, even romantic magazines and comics.

It looked as if Grandma liked reading as well. There was a book with a bookmark sticking out with the title *One Door Closes*, on the settee and Verity noticed a shelf bursting full of books above the china cabinet against the back wall. Catherine Cookson was among the titles. She imagined the two of them sitting side by side in the evenings, drinking tea and reading our books with the telly blaring away companionably in the corner.

Soon plans were made for Uncle Bobby to speak to Verity's dad and hopefully she could move in the next weekend. Now her hard work might even pay off. It looked like the feud was forgotten and she thought her dad would probably be pleased as it meant that she would be off his hands. She couldn't see him disagreeing with her wishes as he wouldn't have to worry about which Auntie to send her to live with next anymore. Verity couldn't believe how lucky she was that this was happening, in fact she felt as if her heart might burst with happiness.

'I thought you might be interested in this,' Uncle Bobby said as he dropped her off at Lilac Square later that night. He passed her a piece of paper. 'It's a family tree. I've been doing some research into the family.'

She was fascinated to see her name on it. Verity Raffin, born 23 November 1974.

'You see,' Uncle Bobby explained, 'our circumstances are very similar. My dad died when I was 6 weeks old, so I never got to know who he was or where I came from. I did have a step dad from the age of 5 but it didn't quite work out the way I hoped.'

Poor Uncle Bobby, Verity thought but was too happy to dwell on unhappy thoughts. The words all seemed to blur on the page before her. 'Can I keep this?' she asked.

'Yes, you keep it and have a good look,' he said. 'I'll be back to pick you up on Saturday morning after Grandma's been to the market for her groceries.

Verity produced her key from her pocket, noticing how grey and dingy the net curtains looked at the front windows. She saw the identically grubby curtains at the window next door twitch.

'Won't your Auntie Doris be up to let you in?' Uncle Bobby asked.

'Oh, no she'll be out at the bingo,' Verity told him, getting out of the car.

So, the very next weekend, after an endless week of worrying that it was all a dream and never actually going to happen, Verity eagerly gathered up her belongings and said goodbye to Auntie Doris who told her to come back any time she wanted to visit. It wasn't Auntie Doris' fault, Verity thought as he hugged her, she was nice enough and she'd given her a roof over her head as a favour to her dad, it was just that she had her own life to lead and didn't really need a teenager hanging about the place.

She felt a strange pang in the pit of her stomach as she realised that this part of her life was over, a conflicting feeling as at the same time she hoped fervently she was never coming back. She hoped that she could find out more about her mother, what she was really like. It was too late for her mother to take her to school and pick her up again, wave her off on school trips and come to see her teachers on parents evenings and all of that but maybe, if she could just talk about her now and again with Grandma Anna, it would help to fill the empty void inside.

'Have you got everything?' Uncle Bobby smiled as she fastened her seat beat. She nodded and waved to Auntie Doris who was looking out of the kitchen window. The grubby net curtain flapped and closed as Auntie Doris moved away, probably relieved. Verity didn't look back at Lilac Square as they drove off, curtains twitching all the way along the row of houses.

Then she moved into the sunny little bedroom above the sitting room at Grandma Anna's house, which used to be Uncle

Bobby's and had such a fab view of the fells. Her life had truly begun at last.

Chapter Seven

Jeremy stewed all day Saturday, feeling restless and not at all like himself. As if he'd had all of the breath knocked out of him. It was very rare for him to feel this raw and churned up inside. His step dad, George often said Jeremy had a sunny disposition and was one of those people in life who were annoyingly happy most of the time. He simply bounced along most of the time, enjoying whatever came his way.

Today, though, he couldn't concentrate on his writing, finding himself sitting in front of his laptop up in his study, doodling instead with some force, whilst staring out of the window. He was distracted further by the ace view of a Grecian temple on a green hill set against a hazy blue backdrop of sky with mist swirling into the gaps between the pillars and obscuring the cornices.

He loved the North Eastern village and cottage he and his step dad George had moved into, to be nearer family, after the recent death of his beloved step mum, Cassie in Hampshire, but then Jeremy was used to moving around and was good at adjusting to new places. He was glad of some stability at the moment however, and had come back to live with George for a while to support him, and also because his latest writer in residence job had come to a natural end. He needed a temporary job to tide him over until his next project took off. He hadn't for one moment been prepared for meeting Verity again.

If only he and Verity had got together when we were seventeen at the Writers Retreat, he mused. He knew they'd still be together now. It would have saved him so much hassle. And time. He wouldn't have met and married Yasmin, the girl from the Café Yummy…

It was like a physical pain inside. How could he be feeling like this? He was a grown man for goodness sake. He was annoyed at the fact that so much time had been lost because of someone else's lie. Time spent apart from her. So much precious time wasted.

He had been drawn to Verity on first sight. She was a natural beauty at seventeen although she seemed to think she was too tall and solemn next to her gobby little mate. He'd admired her flawless porcelain complexion, and the way the sun had sharpened her cheekbones with a flushing of red caused by sunbathing in the manor house gardens. She said she'd never really been away on holiday before, just day trips and she wasn't used to sunbathing or using sunscreen.

Okay, so maybe it was just infatuation or lust? No, he just knew that she was his first love and no-one else had ever matched up to her. Not that he hadn't tried to forget her. He'd always been popular with the opposite sex and Cassie had often joked that women liked the scruffy blond surfer look and wanted to mother him which he didn't need. He was an excellent cook and could look after himself. Heaven knows he'd lived on his own and travelled a bit.

He dropped his pencil which stotted off the wooden floor and caused Pedro, his beloved little shaggy Bichon Frise (and other mixes of which he wasn't quite sure) and faithful companion, to jump up from where he'd been snoozing on the floor and move nearer. He put his head on one side and silently stared up at Jeremy with his big, velvet eyes, his tail wagging tentatively.

'If you could talk mate,' Jeremy said bending down to stroke his silky head, 'you'd be saying – I suppose a walk is out of the question?'

On Sunday he decided he would go for a proper, long walk as he knew the fresh air would improve his mood. Or maybe a half pint of real ale in the inn at Low Newton-by-the-Sea, together with some of their home made kipper pate and toast would help hit the spot? Thinking of his stomach again. Not much got in the way of his scran. Not even love. For he was sure that was what it was. Okay, okay, so he was a hopeless romantic. And a day dreamer.

He asked his dad if he wanted to come along but George wanted to get on with some decorating. 'You walk too far for me nowadays.' he said. 'Pedro will enjoy it though.'

So he drove to Northumberland, a place he'd discovered soon after moving to the North East and after all those crowded southern beaches, had been instantly entranced by the deserted, endless sands and big skies.

As soon as he stepped out of the car, the fresh green smell of the countryside with a faint tang of the sea wrapped itself around him.

He laced up his walking boots, strapped on his backpack, snapped on Pedro's leader and hurried on. The view of the sheltered bay with its smooth white sands, rocky outcrops with glistening rock pools and beach huts cosying into the undulating sand dunes, was revealed as he reached the top of the hill, spreading out below him. He felt his heart lift a little. The place had a holiday air about it.

He'd now reached one of his favourite discoveries so far, being the green open ended square facing the sea, edged with cream washed cottages and housing the rustic inn.

The pub wasn't open yet. Lots of people were hanging around outside the entrance, forming a straggling queue, draping backpacks on the outdoor tables and settling dogs on the grass to wait. There was going to be one mad dash to get in and form a long queue for food when it opened so instead he decided to set off along the cliff path to the next village.

He turned his back reluctantly on the beautiful sweeping bay and the jagged fingers of the ruined castle on the headland. He hadn't been this way before but surely there'd be somewhere in Beadnell he could stop for some scran?

The wooden signpost said 2.5 miles. He'd always liked walking and was used to trekking along country roads back home in Hampshire. He felt a sharp pang which soon dissipated. Oops he nearly forgot. The North East was his home now. Oh, if only he could make his peace with Verity. He hated to think that she thought so badly of him. And just what was it that he was supposed to have done that was so bad? He honestly had no idea.

He stomped along for a while, feeling heart sore, with Pedro trotting valiantly beside him. He dipped down onto the beach, flanked on one side by tall white dunes interspersed with sharp, wild grasses ruffled by the warm breeze and the sea on the other. He noticed the smooth golden sand beneath his feet, darker where the gentle tide kept rolling in and out again, creating gentle pools of white froth which soon evaporated. A couple of lobster pots had been washed up onto the beach at the foot of the dunes. What a cracking place this was and what a setting it would make for his next novel.

He soon felt really warm. He loosened his jacket and tied it around his waist, re-arranging his backpack and pausing to take a photo on his mobile. He saw his shadow on the pic and for one blissful moment he felt like he was the only person in the world and almost forgot about everything else.

Standing isolated on a spit of sand in the midst of the ocean, surrounded by layers of gold and blue, he thought how he'd love to walk with Verity on this beach someday…

Back to Verity again. Crap. She knew he'd be able to keep up with his striding pace, enjoying the fresh air and scenery together. His imagination was running wild again. Seeing Verity again after all these years, it had made him want her all over again. It was like a physical pain, twisting at his gut. He might be a bit of a joker but deep down he was a hopeless romantic. The beauty of a place like this tugged at his heartstrings and he felt very alone. Come on Jeremy, crack on, he told himself.

Back on the sands, Pedro trotted along beside him, occasionally getting his paws wet as the surf rolled in. He wasn't a dog that liked to chase a ball into the sea. He didn't like getting wet that much. He was a great little walker for his size, which was a good thing, Jeremy thought, because the signpost was wrong and this walk must have been around four miles long, which meant another four miles back. Still Jeremy clumped along at a rapid pace. He kept feeling his spirits rise slightly, in spite of himself, but nowhere near his normal happy level.

In no time, they arrived at the horseshoe shaped beach at low tide, the red rooftops, rocky harbour and green clifftops of Beadnell becoming nearer. He couldn't see anywhere to eat by the harbour so he walked around further until he found the little village centre complete with pub and café.

He positioned himself at the busy bar, taking off his baseball cap and smoothing down his sweating hair, looking forward to a half pint of real ale. It had his name on it. Not that he was a heavy drinker, but he did enjoy a thirst quenching beer now and again and he felt he deserved this half pint.

Then, Jeremy began to wonder if he was invisible? He'd been standing here for ages, sweating in his walking gear with Pedro panting alongside his feet, watching people being shown to their tables for Sunday lunch. He waited and watched for another five minutes as the young, yellow haired barmaid served someone whom Jeremy was sure had been behind him and had somehow jumped in. Enough. He became more and more annoyed and walked out in disgust. It was obviously one of those days.

Luckily, there was a café across from the pub and they didn't mind dogs. 'I'm starting to feel a bit lear', he said to the chatty waitress as she took his order. When she looked blank, he translated, 'Sorry, where I come from, lear means sick with hunger.'

'Ah,' she smiled. 'We can't have that, then can we? I can recommend our crab sandwiches – freshly caught this morning.' Jeremy was struck by the strong Northumbrian accents all around him.

Walking back against the wind which had sprung up out of nowhere, back on the beach, he spied the castle ruins in the distance on the hill. It seemed a long way off.

He leapt over another stile whilst Pedro ducked underneath and then he stood still for a moment, hearing the silence grew louder. Then he realised it wasn't silent here at all. Apart from the roar of the surf, there was a steady background hum, like a throb of electricity. Feeling the sweat cool on his face, he looked back at a field which was almost entirely covered with gossiping geese, all chattering at once and making a right old racket. Then he saw the curlews, black marks against the bright blue sky, flying in long sequences. One straggler kept falling out of line and struggling to keep up. 'I know how you feel mate,' he muttered.

Eventually he arrived at the track which led up by the little chapel and there was his car parked on the roadside, one of many which lined the road up the hill to Newton.

Jeremy knew they must have walked about 8 miles in total. He'd hardly noticed how far because his head was bursting full of conversations not yet spoken. He walked back to the green courtyard of the pub, full circle, again thinking he'd earned a quick cheeky half of lager before setting off for home. But then he saw it was shut again. Of course it was Sunday. Definitely not his day today. Sighing, he turned around again and made his way back to the car.

Much later, back home, it was dark and Jeremy could see the monument on the hill, all lit up against the star speckled sky. He found a full packet of cigarettes and an old green lighter which he'd shoved to the back of the kitchen drawer when he'd given up smoking. Although he didn't smoke any more, he grabbed one out of the box and marched down to the seat at the bottom of the long garden.

He puffed furiously away, sitting forward on the edge of the garden bench, catching snatches of scented night air. Pedro skittered out of the back door and joined him. He'd nipped straight upstairs to his basket bed when they got back and would probably sleep there for most of the next day.

Trouble was, Jeremy thought, smoking the fag wasn't making him feel any better. If anything, it made him feel worse as guilt added to his woes. What had happened to feeling uplifted by the glorious scenery and salty air he asked himself?

Thoughts crowded back into his head as he remembered the conference tomorrow. Jeremy had never considered himself as being an ill-tempered person, in fact he was slow to anger, but this business of Verity thinking badly of him was weighing heavily on his mind. Why did it matter so much he thought, all these years later? How had he managed before yesterday when he saw her again and his whole world had turned on its head? What if he hadn't ever seen her again?

He took another puff. He was baffled by whatever it was she thought he'd done. Still, he thought, it is what it is. What mattered was, he had been lucky enough to find her again. The question was, what was he going to do about it? How could he get her to like him again?

'Are you all right?' George called from where he was standing at the back door and Jeremy knew he must have seen the light of the cigarette. 'I thought you'd given them up when we moved here.'

'I have Dad. I have.' He looked at the fag in his hand in disgust, took one final puff and threw the cigarette butt over the fence. It sailed over George's hanging baskets into the neighbouring garden. The movement of which prompted a growl from next door's dog who must have been prowling about in the garden, probably having his last pee before bedtime.

An answering snarl from Pedro resounded, he was mooching about in the flower beds on the opposite side.

'Jeremy, what are you doing?' George said. He was padding down the path in his slippers and dressing gown. 'Why are you getting yourself so aeriated?'

'No reason Dad, I'm OK,' Jeremy sighed.

'Is there anything you want to talk about?' George tried to talk quietly. 'You've not been yourself this weekend. In fact, you've got a right old cob on.'

'I'm fine Dad,' he answered. 'Or I will be. You go in. It's late.'

George ignored him and sat down next to him on the bench.

'Whatever it is son,' George said, 'in all the time I've known you – which is a long time considering I've known you since you were a nipper of a few days old – I've never known you to give up easily on anything. Inside that angelic exterior lies an obstinate soul.'

'Ha,' said Jeremy, watching Pedro lift his leg idly on the sweet peas.

'Don't lose heart that's all I'm saying,' George continued. 'As your mother would have said, everything works out for the best in the end.'

Jeremy grinned to himself and thought that this was probably the first time today he'd actually smiled like he meant it.

He was old enough and he'd travelled extensively enough for absence to make the heart grow fonder, and to realise that family was very important. It didn't matter at all to him that George and Cassie weren't his blood relations. He might refer to George as his old man but his step parents were all he'd ever known. Nowadays, he greatly appreciated all that George had done for him and he did actually listen when he talked. He'd never understood this when he was younger and he'd found them annoying.

There comes a point in life, with the passing of the years, when children and parents kind of meet in the middle and feel a connection. They even enjoy each other's company. Jeremy felt he had reached that understanding.

Now he knew there was no point in showing his true feelings at work. He had to smile, grit his teeth and smile some more and get on with the job until he had the chance to find out what it was troubling her about him. Then he could put things right. Yes. That's it. She had promised him she would talk to him after the event. He had to make her trust him. Pedro came and sat on his feet.

'You're right dad. Maybe all is not lost,' he spoke quietly and reached down to pat the little dog's head. He felt like a weight was beginning to lift from his shoulders. This really mattered to him, to win her respect.

He just needed to calm down and keep smiling even though he wanted to grit his teeth. Do a cracking job and show her he was a hard worker and could be of some worth to her. Not just a useless good looking nowt, as her bitch of a friend had labelled him. He was a scriptwriter now. A proper author. Well, in effect, he was a jobbing writer. Okay, so he was only on a temporary contact at the moment, but he was waiting to hear back from his agent about a new project. He had a lot to offer a woman like Verity. Or he would have soon. By some amazing stroke of luck she was single, the gossip around the watercoolers saying that she'd just been dumped by an older man. What an absolute idiot *he* must have been.

No, he vowed he wasn't going to give up that easily. Brave words. But he felt he'd wallowed enough. He'd been given another chance, fate had dealt him another hand and he had to try. No way was he going to let this chance go by. Starting tomorrow. He'd get there really early and make a proper effort. After all, how hard could running a conference be? He'd had worse jobs. And he always enjoyed a challenge.

'Sorry Dad,' he said. He squared his shoulders, shifted Pedro's weight off his feet and jumped up. 'You're right as usual. Come on, let's go in.'

Chapter Eight

Conference Day dawned, a warm Spring morning, and Verity set off early for the city venue which was an unusual choice. Urban City was a contemporary, glass-fronted building, purpose built to host business conferences and events, alongside dance and acting performances for professional and amateurs alike. Delegates were advised to wear trainers on the studio floors.

She drove past meadows of bright green, followed by intermittent, stinging yellow rape fields, so bright they hurt her eyes. The sky was a brilliant blue already and even with all the hurt and trauma of the past few days, she felt her spirits lifting. She was determined to put it all in a box and concentrate on today. Such a lot depended on this, her first conference being totally in charge and she was looking forward to the challenge.

Waiting in a queue of traffic, however, she felt the edginess she always experienced before an event in equal measures of excitement and trepidation. What if she was late? She always set off far too early. What if the main speaker didn't turn up? What if the delegates thought it was rubbish and wanted their money back? She felt like this every time, even more so now that the entire success - or failure of the event rested on her shoulders. Her hands were gripping the steering wheel and her back felt stiff. What if Jeremy didn't step up to the mark?

Unfortunately Sophie wasn't able to attend as Greyson had asked her to fill in for Maureen had gone down with the flu. So, there was no other way round it. Jeremy would have to cope.

'Don't worry there'll be plenty more events,' Verity had told her yesterday. Then she'd given Jeremy a list of verbal instructions:-

- You must look reasonably smart; (even though trainers were allowed)
- No disappearing and getting lost (this was because of an incident on his second day when she'd sent him to escort some attendees to a training room on the third floor and he rang up from his mobile to say he had lost twenty delegates. It turned out it wasn't the delegates who were lost, it was him, for after a detour to the tea trolley, he had ended up on the wrong floor. All the levels had the same layout and beige décor and he'd misjudged the stairs). He was mortified but

soon saw the joke and felt a bit better when Sophie said it happened to her still and she'd worked here for two years;

- No odd socks (because he would have to take his shoes off on the studio floors);
- No helping himself from the buffet until the delegates had all been sorted. ('Do you think I've got no manners?' he'd said, pretending to be miffed. 'No, but I can tell how much you like your scran,' she'd told him);
- No talking to newspaper reporters – that was her job and she had a pitch already prepared.

Everyone he'd come into contact with so far liked him a lot, probably due to his outwardly sunny disposition, eagerness to perform any tasks he'd been asked to do and way of smiling at everyone as he did them. The fact that he wasn't that bad to look at either accounted for some of it, Verity was sure. All the water cooler whispers on her floor were now about him and how hot he was. She knew because they all stopped talking whenever she went past and looked sheepish. She'd heard one girl say yesterday by the main water cooler, 'Stand by your beds. She's coming.'

Why on earth would they think she was bothered? She never joined in with the gossip.

Jeremy pulled up next to her in the car park and jumped out. She need not have worried about his appearance. He was wearing smart navy trainers with blue laces, a navy suit, crisp white shirt, sky blue tie and co-ordinating pocket square which mirrored the blue of his eyes. A few golden curls still bounced on his forehead although his hair was spiked up high with gel.

She could tell from his expression that her deep blue skirt suit and silky blouse flecked with yellow, red and matching blue did her proud. She knew that primary colours suited her dark hair and pale complexion and that the deeper shade of red lipstick she'd chosen made her feel more confident.

He greeted her with a sunny smile and she immediately felt her blood begin to boil. 'Verity, you look fabulous,' his eyes appraised her as she emerged from her car, grabbing a box of leaflets. 'You really suit those colours.'

So much for being heartbroken. How could he smile at her like that as if nothing had happened? She'd expected him to be subdued at the very least. Showed how much cared. How can he be happy after yesterday? She knew she had to quash these negative feelings and act like the consummate conference professional she professed herself to be.

'One day I'll be able to afford a better car,' he said, eyeing all the equipment and boxes in the boot of his car. 'It's always the producers that own the big flash cars, not the writers.'

Glad to see he had his priorities right. Verity gave herself an inward shake. Get a grip Verity, she told herself. This was her day, she'd put an awful lot of work into this and no-one, least of all him, was going to spoil it.

'Glad to see you're early too,' she said, pasting a bright smile on her face. 'Right, let's get on. Pass me a box, we'll unload your car first.'

He gestured to his feet. 'It's the first conference I've been to where I've worn a suit and trainers. 'Do I scrub up well, boss?'

She had to admit he certainly did. 'Your hair looks tidier.' He began stacking up a high pile of boxes in front of his face to carry in.

'I do wash it occasionally you know.' He moved his load to one side so she could see his hair. 'I used my special Chunky Funky hair gel.'

'Very professional.'

Verity grabbed a conference banner, repositioned her leaflets under her arm and hurried on ahead, inwardly gritting her teeth. The area they entered named called the Collective Space, was actually used as a foyer/reception as well. The building was flanked on either side by tall trees, which gave the impression of bringing the outdoor into the heart of the city.

They entered by a side door, as the main doors weren't open yet. It was very quiet, dark purple walls decorated with colourful posters and she could feel the chill of the large room, although she was warm already with carrying equipment around. There was an expectant feel in the air, a tang of energy.

Jeremy pointed to our poster excitedly. 'Look that's us.'

Urban City hosts:

Conferenceque – **A conference for Modern Foreign Language Professionals**

Passing the unattended reception desk, Verity headed for the long tables pushed together at the far end of the square, behind which rows of bare, unpainted steps, wide enough to sit on, led upwards. There was a backdrop of exposed brickwork.

'Right. This must be us for registration,' she said, arranging her bag under the longest table and depositing boxes. Where was everyone?

After a bit of a tussle assembling the banners and under Verity's direction, they began to set out the name badges in alphabetical order. Jeremy started from the left and Verity from the right until they met in the middle. It felt strange to be the one giving the instructions. She'd always had Callum to rely on before, he was the one in charge. Now it was all down to her. Best not to think about it and get on with the job in hand.

Some Urban City staff appeared, drinking coffee from paper cups and looking at clipboards, bustling about in red t-shirts with 'Urban' emblazoned on the front and 'City' on the back. Tea cups clattered from the Urban Café and a tantalising aroma of roasting fresh coffee filtered through. The place was beginning to wake up and one of the red team put on some rousing delegate arrival music.

'Verity? I'm Lynn, we've been speaking on the phone,' a young lady in a smart suit with red heels appeared. 'Would you like to have a quick tour of the rooms you've booked?'

'Good to meet you Lynn.' We shook hands. 'I thought Alisha was looking after us today?'

Lynn fiddled with her clipboard. 'Well, to be honest, we're a bit sparse on the ground today.' She looked around and lowered her voice, 'You see, she's ill. In fact, quite a lot of the staff have called in sick.'

'Oh dear,' Verity said. 'Dare I ask what's wrong?'

'Oh just a flu outbreak. But not to worry. It won't cause a problem at all today.'

Verity hoped not.

'We need to know the layout of the building, so we can direct delegates to their workshops,' Verity intercepted Jeremy who was chatting with two of the red team who had gravitated over to the Badges Desk and started up a conversation.

'So, we're expecting approximately 160 delegates today?' Lynn asked, her heels clipping on the floor, showing us first of all, the UC Café. Was Verity imagining it or did the staff behind the counter look heavy eyed? One of them sneezed loudly, face buried in a large handkerchief.

Verity nodded. 'Yes, it's a very popular event. High profile speakers as well.'

'Remember, no shoes in the Studios.' Lynn reached down and removed her shoes, her varnished toe nails blood red against the honey coloured wood. There were a number of studios spread out over four floors, wide, airy spaces with gleaming full length mirrors and windows looking out onto the busy street.

There was a theatre which had raked seating to hold 250 people. They stood for a moment in the space in front of the stage. 'We'll start off in the theatre and finish off here to wrap up the conference.' Verity checked the programme she held in her hand.

'Wow, this is an amazing venue,' Jeremy said.

It certainly was. Back in the main foyer, she checked her watch. 'The primary school children are coming at twelve o'clock.

I've booked a room just for them to eat their packed lunches in before they perform.'

A passing member of staff with a clipboard said, 'that'll be the Back Room. Right, I need to find the key.'

'The children will sit on those steps to sing their introductory song to all the delegates after lunch,' Verity explained. 'Then they'll go straight to the theatre to wait for the finale to perform their little play.'

Delegates soon started to arrive. The silence in the foyer was filled with chatter and laughter as they were kept busy signing everyone in, handing them their badges, ticking them off on the Delegate List, handing them a Conference Pack, at the same time pointing them in the direction of the introductory teas/coffees and the bathrooms. Most of the teachers were wearing bright, casual gear and looked happy to be here which was a good sign, although some of them had completely ignored the instructions regarding not wearing heels.

'Hi, here's your Conference Pack and badge. Coffee is being served to the right and loos to the left.' Jeremy bounced from one end of the table to the other, picking up packs and presenting them with a flourish and a bright, cheeky smile. Verity noticed the effect he was having on the young teachers, even the older ones looked entranced. She had to grudgingly admit he was a natural with people and creating a good impression so far.

Soon the space was full of people, milling about, networking, helping themselves to drinks and commenting on the croissants. Different perfumes wafted and mingled with deodorant and fresh coffee. The air grew warm.

'This is harder than I thought,' Jeremy said in a lull. 'I'll have a sore throat before long, going through this spiel over and over again. If I'd known I would have recorded a tape.'

'Things settle down when they're in their first workshop.' She told him. 'We should be able to grab ourselves a coffee then.'

'Not that I'm moaning though boss,' Jeremy said quickly. 'I'm really enjoying myself so far.'

'Glad to hear it because you're doing fine,' Verity had to admit.

One of the speakers came and stood looking at the badges. She was absolutely stunning to look at, so petite with glossy hair falling just so around her elfin face, that Verity felt tall and gawky standing next to her. She looked as though she should have a French accent but as she spoke, it was with a loud Southern twang. Soon she and Jeremy were having a conversation about living down South.

'You can call me Kat,' she said as he handed her the Delegate List for her workshop. 'Why don't you come and join in later– I'm doing a parachute game?' she flashed a white smile over her shoulder.

'I'd be delighted,' he said, staring after her as she glided off gracefully.

Verity felt a pang of annoyance but squashed it down straightaway. She hadn't time for any kind of negative feelings today.

'I'm really looking forward to a drink,' Jeremy said, gazing longingly at the table where fresh fruit and croissants were laid out for the delegates during registration.

'Later.' Verity looked around at the emptying room. 'I'm off to sit at the back of the auditorium and listen to the intros. You stay put for a while and sign in any late-comers, then point them in the direction of the theatre.'

'Yes, no problem boss.' he said.

The morning passed in a whirl. In the lunch break, people were milling about with plates of food, looking for somewhere to sit. There wasn't really anywhere, as the UC Café wasn't big enough, so they congregated in groups or sat on the steps.

Verity began to relax just a little bit and thought maybe today might not be as bad as she had expected. In fact she was beginning to enjoy herself when Lynn mouthed from across the floor space. 'It's going well.'

Famous last words.

Chapter Nine

Jeremy disappeared and the children arrived, excited and wide eyed, resplendent in their blue and yellow uniforms, all carrying their little lunch boxes. They paraded past Verity and the conference desk as their teacher shepherded them onto the steps behind. Carly was still looking for the key for the Back Room where they were to eat their packed lunches.

'Now, can we all sit down nicely on the steps,' the teacher said. Then she repeated the sentence again in French, gesturing with her hands. They all sat.

Carly appeared at Verity's elbow with the key, sneaking a peek past her to see where Jeremy was.

'Some of the children are on an exchange visit from France,' she said as, oohs and aahs abounded from the staff and delegates standing around watching, as the children sat docilely.

'Verity. We have a problem.' A booming voice echoed and one of the workshop presenters began nudging her elbow.

'How can I help?' she said, thinking that things had been going too well.

'Our mid-morning teas and coffees haven't turned up.'

'No problem, don't worry,' Verity smiled. 'I'll sort it out.' She turned around to find someone from the UC Café but instead found Kat gliding towards her.

'Verity.' She gestured with her slender hands. 'Our workshop room – it's far too hot.'

'Ours is too cold.' Another workshop leader crowded around her. 'Can you get someone to turn the heating up?'

'And turn ours down?' Kat asked, then added, 'if you please.'

What, at all once? Honestly, sometimes people could be so annoying. Refusing to let herself feel flustered, Verity looked around for Jeremy who seemed to have chosen the very worst moment to wander off.

'I asked you first to sort out the teas and coffees?' came the first voice. Was she expected to deal with everything on her own?

Before she had a chance to do anything at all, a loud, shrill shriek ensued, cutting through the warm, cosy room like a knife. The young teacher accompanying the children had tripped up on one of the steps and was half sitting, half lying on the floor, clutching her ankle. The children looked on, their eyes growing wider.

'Miss, are you all right, miss?' one of them said.

The trio of complaining workshop leaders dissipated on both sides of Verity and she spied a very red faced Jeremy moving towards her at a fast pace. 'Verity, Verity,' he said and pulled her to one side. 'I need to speak to you.' His tie was slightly crooked. 'It's important.' Then he saw what had happened and waded in to help.

'Good of you to bother to put in an appearance,' she muttered and immediately felt mean, trying to hurry along the workshop leaders and dial the number Lynn had given her to summon the porter at the same time.

She spotted Carly with a handkerchief pressed to her nose, holding the lost key, opening the room and sneezing loudly.

'Bless you miss,' said one of the children. Then another couple of the kids muttered 'Bless you' in unison. A couple of them giggled.

'Can you please go and turn down the central heating dial in Studio No 1?' Verity spoke into the phone. Next, she instructed Carly to usher the kids into the Back Room and keep them quiet for a little while. Off they went, all craning their necks to see what was happening to 'Miss.'

She seemed to be in a lot of pain but kept saying she didn't want any fuss. People crowded around her until Lynn took her off to Accident & Emergency. Which meant there was no-one to supervise the kids in the Back Room apart from Carly.

'What's going on in there?' Verity saw what looked like a sandwich go flying past the window amid shrieks. She could see cheeky little faces pressed up to the glass pane of the door. Carly was no-where to be seen. A banana was next to be seen sailing through the air.

'It's descending into chaos,' Carly said, squeezing out of the door and sneezing again. A hubbub of chattering voices abounded which was silenced as she shut the door quickly. 'One of those kids has ADHD and he's going berserk in there. I'm surprised he hasn't reached the ceiling himself.' She leant her head back against the wall. 'I don't know if he's had his medication today.'

'Are you okay Carly?' Verity put an arm around her.

'OMG, I think I'm going to faint.' She slid down the wall into a sitting on her hunkers, her handkerchief fluttering to the floor.

Verity helped her put her head between her knees. 'I think I've got that flu.'

'What about the kids?' someone said. Jeremy took a deep breath and opened the door. Noise bounded out, followed by a cheese and tomato sandwich. She ducked. Jeremy shut the door again and the roar was instantly subdued.

'They say you should never work with children or animals.' Jeremy leant against the door for a second.

'What are we going to do?' Verity thought to herself. 'The whole day is ruined. Everything I've worked for is in tatters. I'll be a laughing stock.'

Jeremy bounced forward. 'I've got an idea. Is there anywhere else I can take them – somewhere with a bit more space?' he asked. 'It's so airless in there. They need to spread out a bit.'

'What about the space in front of the stage?' she suggested. 'Then they can practice their song.'

'Great idea boss,' said Jeremy. 'I'll take them there straightaway.'

Carly looked up, weakly from between her legs to nod her approval. 'Atishoo.'

Jeremy braced himself and opened the door again. 'Come on kids,' Jeremy shouted, above the din, gesturing to the children. 'Follow me!'

'Sir, sir, what about these?' a young voice asked as they began jostling and vying with each other to get out of the door first, clutching their lunch boxes.

'Oh, just leave them on the steps,' said the Pied Piper. Lots of kerfuffle followed as they all began depositing their lunch boxes as requested but then, to her surprise, they all dutifully started to form a tidy line behind him, each manoeuvring the child behind them into place. Even the child throwing the sandwiches seemed intrigued. Jeremy had him at the front. 'Where are we going sir?' he asked loudly.

'To the stage,' Jeremy said, with a grin, flourishing an arm into the air. 'What's your name again?'

'He's called Ethan,' came several young voices, drowning out Ethan's reply.

'Right, Ethan. I have a special job for you. You can be the leader of all the children. I'll go first and then you next. Okay? Can you do that for me?'

Ethan nodded. Then he straightened up and shrugged but he moved into place, hopping from foot to foot. His red face became buoyant with pride as he looked back over his shoulder at the line of little faces behind him.

'Now, everyone please follow Ethan. Then, when we get down to the stage could you all please take your shoes off and leave them nice and neat at the side of the room,' Jeremy called, from the front of the line. 'Pass it back to everyone – whisper.' The children began whispering loudly all the way back down the line.

'Will Miss be going in an ambulance?' said another youngster followed by a few more mutters, then they all happily traipsed after Jeremy, some of them reaching down to start loosening the buckles on their shoes.

'He seems to know what he's doing.' Carly said sitting up. 'I feel a lot better now.'

Verity hoped so. After fetching Carly a glass of water, she crept along into the theatre to have a look and was stunned by what she saw. Oh, my word. All the children were sat cross legged on the floor in front of Jeremy. And they were smiling, even Ethan looked rapt. Jeremy had rolled up his shirt sleeves, revealing tanned forearms, and discarded the tie and he was leaping around the floor space doing lots of actions and interacting with his entranced audience. He was telling them a story. Part of it was in fluent French. He was speaking quickly in what sounded like a perfectly authentic French accent. She couldn't believe her ears. Or eyes. The kids were loving every second. Was this the same person?

Much later, when the lunchbreak was over and the delegates were in their final workshops of the day, she was standing by the registration desk trying to shovel in a cold chicken leg before anything else happened when Jeremy caught up with her, looking a bit breathless. The immaculately gelled hair of this morning had flopped into unruly, damp curls onto his forehead.

'You didn't tell me you could speak French.' She said, picking up a glistening scotch egg from my plate.

'You never asked.' He grinned, looking at her plate.

'True,' she shrugged.

'I used to be a tour guide and I've worked in a few different countries.' He looked longingly at her plate. 'Are you going to eat that pickled onion?'

'Yes, I am actually.' She watched his face fall. 'Here, I saved you a plateful,' she produced it from behind her. 'Great storytelling.'

'Thank you so much.' His eyes lit up as he grabbed the plate, sat down and bit into a piece of spinach quiche. 'I used to be part of a group that went around schools acting and telling stories to kids. I've done a bit of acting as well.'

'That I can believe.'

'And kids like me for some reason.' Jeremy blew a spiral of hair back off his forehead and picked up a sandwich.

'Probably because you act like a big kid yourself.'

The curl bounced back over his right eye. 'Are you impressed?'

'No, well maybe just a bit.'

Jeremy looked up from his food to grin at her. Then there was silence as they demolished what was left on their plates.

'What was it you were going to tell me? Before it all kicked off?' she said.

'Oh that, he said, looking around. 'It was nothing really.'

'Oh, I thought you said it was important?'

Jeremy gathered up the last crisp from his plate. 'In the big scheme of things probably not so important. I think I might have, sort of got the wrong end of the stick.'

Oh, not again. She began tidying up the desk as she waited for him to continue.

'The Chair, the Scottish speaker lady said she had a task for me.' He brushed crumbs off his once pristine shirt. 'She said…we need four flapjacks.'

'Flapjacks? Only four? That's a strange amount.'

'I know. So I asked her to repeat it…and guess what she said? He put on a posh accent. 'Four flapjacks, darling. Can you arrange this for me straightaway?'

'So what did you say?' she picked up a banana from what was left of the fresh fruit platter.

'I said yes, of course, and off I went to the UC Café. Only they didn't have any, so I trotted across the street to the Patisserie.'

'Well, as I told you, we're here to help.' she pushed the fruit plate over to him. 'We always try to accommodate our speakers' requests as far as we possibly can.'

'Yes, well they put them on a nice plate and everything because I said it was for an event at Urban City and I was so happy I'd managed to get exactly what she'd asked for.' Jeremy bit into an apple. 'I ran up the stairs to the Studio at the top, she was in the one that overlooks the street.'

He paused to finish his mouthful. 'I knocked on the door and went in. She came over and looked at me with my hand outstretched with a plate with four flapjacks on it. You'll never guess what she said?'

'No,' I can't guess, what did she say?' She felt like she was waiting for the punchline to some really bad joke.

'First of all she laughed. Then, she said, 'thank you very much, they look wonderful.'

'And?'

'Then,' he paused and his eyes twinkled, 'then, she said, 'but I actually asked you for four flipcharts!''

She was speechless for a moment. 'Oh no,' she said, suppressing a giggle.

'I said I was sorry straightaway. I was mortified.'

'What happened next?'

'Well, when she'd stopped laughing, which took a while because everyone in the whole room was absolutely hooting with mirth as well, she said she knew how strong her accent was and it wasn't my fault.'

'Oh my goodness.'

'She said I'd made her day and she was keeping a little black notebook of sayings just like this. It wasn't just me. In the notebook I mean.'

Verity shook her head but then saw the funny side and began to chortle.

'Watch it boss, you're laughing.' Jeremy said.

Hysteria more like. 'What did she say next?' she composed herself quickly.

'She said she would have a word with me at the end.'

Verity felt her heart sinking. What if she wanted to complain? That was all Greyson needed to hear, a complaint from the Chair.

'And then they abandoned the original workshop idea which needed flipcharts and they ate the flapjacks instead.'

'Honestly Jeremy, chaos just seems to follow you about.' She shook her head. What if he'd ruined all her hard work? Then she felt immediately guilty because he'd been so wonderful with the kids.

'I know, you're right, it does,' he frowned and changed the subject by asking, 'Where are the children now?'

'They're backstage, getting ready to perform.' She smoothed down her skirt. 'The day is nearly over, thank goodness.' The children were going to sing in French and as a special finale, were going to perform the song they sang when they won a song contest which was held as part of the International Festival of Culture at the University a few weeks earlier. 'I think we should get down there for the wrap up of the event.'

There was nothing more to be done until the big tidy up at the end now, so they were free to sit at the back in the auditorium and enjoy watching the wind up of the event. If that was possible after everything that had happened today. She relaxed slightly until the end when the Chair was thanking everyone. Morag was in control of the final proceedings up there.

'I'd also like to thank the organisers for their expertise in running such a professional and informative event,' she said. 'I'm certain everyone will join me in saying they've had a very enjoyable day.'

'She must be crazy,' Verity whispered incredulously to Jeremy as murmurs of assent and clapping rang out. It had been the event from hell from their point of view.

'As for the sheer entertainment value,' the Chair continued, looking towards Jeremy who was on the edge of his seat, 'I'd like to thank Jeremy for the best laugh I've had in years.'

Verity thought of the lost 20 teachers. This was déjà vu. How was it he managed to mess things up but always came out smiling?

A ripple of laughter flowed around the theatre. Jeremy had the grace to look slightly sheepish but then, to Verity's horror, he stood up and mock bowed very low to the audience, his hair flopping over his eyes. Everyone roared with laughter then. She smiled even though she wasn't sure if she was amused or not. Then, at the end, when she was saying goodbye to the delegates and making sure that they didn't leave without handing in their feedback forms, she noticed that yet again Jeremy was no-where to be seen. What mischief could he be getting up to now?

He re-appeared with another man, complete with camera equipment, whom he showed to the door.

Verity was standing at the entrance, in a prime position to say goodbye and collect in the feedback sheets and badges. Everyone seemed to have enjoyed it, as she heard snatches of conversation:-

'Great event, really beneficial.' 'Great to be able to do a bit of networking.' 'Nice looking chap.'

'Who was that man by the way?' she asked Jeremy as they tidied up.

'Which man?' he unwrapped a glassy green sweet and popped it in his mouth. 'Oh, you mean Ken, the reporter from the local paper.'

'What? Why was he with you?' Verity began putting the plastic badge covers in a box to be reused.

I was just showing him out.' Jeremy looked away and raked his fingers through his flopping fringe.

'Out from where exactly?' she pushed a pile of badges towards him. 'Here, help me with these.'

'Backstage. He took a photograph of the children just after they'd performed.'

'You should have come and found me straightaway.' Verity ripped up some cardboard name tags and threw them in the bin.

'I did try but I couldn't see you,' Jeremy said. 'Sorry, but he said he had to conduct a very short interview there and then.'

'Interview?' she said, her head snapping round to face him. 'I'm the Business Manager and it should have been me dealing with the press.'

'Yes, don't worry, it was all fine.' Jeremy helped himself to another sweet. 'Chill out, boss.' He smiled broadly at another delegate as she unwrapped her badge from around her neck and handed it to him. 'I didn't say anything I shouldn't.'

'Let's hope so.'

'You're such a hard woman to please V,' he said, straightening the evaluation sheets.

Someone had put the music back on to play the delegates out and a few of them did a few dance moves along to the music as they departed.

'See, they're all leaving in a happy mood.' Jeremy said.

Verity felt a sudden burst of exhilaration. Everything had gone well and she had to admit, however grudgingly, that Jeremy had really proved his worth. Soon everything was packed up, ready to go back in the cars, but she didn't feel like going home just yet.

'Sit down, I'll buy you a coffee before we go,' Jeremy offered, soon returning with two mugs. 'This feels like I've been acting in a play. It's always hard to go home and sleep afterwards. It's the adrenalin kicking in.'

'Well done,' Verity went to take the mug from him, 'you've done a great job today.' Her feet were throbbing in her conference day heels.

'Don't sound so surprised.' There was a wistful look in his eyes. 'Now it's just us. Are you ready to talk?'

Chapter Ten

The foyer was quieter now everyone had gone and the music had stopped. The remaining staff members were upstairs tidying up the studios. The place was beginning to cool down so Verity reached for her jacket and pulled it on. She had hoped he'd be too tired to talk.

He put his coffee mug down on the floor and sat down in the first row of the steps, gesturing to her to join him. 'Come and sit here – please.'

She shivered slightly, but sat down next to him, arms folded about her knees.

Looking out of the corner of her eye she saw that his white collar was ruffled now, his sleeves creased and his hair back to normal but he still exuded vitality.

'I don't know about you but I've been talking all day,' she said.

'Not about this,' he moved closer so that their knees were nearly touching. 'I waited until after the event as you asked me to. I'm sorry but I can't wait any longer.'

She reached forward and took hold of her coffee mug with both hands, taking a gulp she hardly tasted. She turned to face him and shook her head, thinking of the best way to begin.

'Look,' his bright blue eyes met hers. 'You've accused me of doing something and I need to know what it is. I can't bear the fact that you think badly of me for something I can't even begin to remember. You did promise me we could talk.'

'Okay,' she sighed heavily and replaced her mug on the floor. 'I know I did. It's just that I find it rather incredulous that you can't remember how you ruined someone's whole life.'

'Someone? Who are you talking about?' Jeremy's knee pressed against hers.

'Ellen of course.' She reached for her coffee mug again for something to do with her hands and to move away from the disturbing pressure of his knee.

'Who's Ellen?' he blinked as if in disbelief.

'Oh come on, don't try to pretend you don't know.'

'Well I don't. And I'm sick of being blamed for something you won't even talk to me about. Please tell me, who's Ellen?'

She rolled her eyes. 'My friend Ellen of course.' He still looked blank, so she added, 'from Little Wallop House Writing Retreat.'

Verity remembered every moment. Ellen, who lived next door to Grandma Anna, had wanted to be a journalist and had won a competition in the local paper to attend a weekend writing retreat in Hampshire. They were both seventeen. She was allowed to take a friend and it was so exciting, as Verity had never been away anywhere before except on camping trips to the Durham Dales.

She could still picture in her head the quintessentially English village situated in the heart of a National Park, chocolate box style complete with sixteenth century thatched cottages and a manor house. There was also a cricket pitch, set amidst fields with grazing sheep and shire horses looking on. She could almost taste the delicious cream tea they'd eaten in the sunshine, the warm scones, covered with thick clotted cream and lavender jam, accompanied by cooling elderflower cordial. She could smell the scent of summer flowers wafting everywhere and could almost feel the burning pain of her sunburned arms.

She hadn't been bothered about being a writer, but loved floating about the gardens in the sunshine in a new summer frock and scribbling a couple of words down now and then in a new flowery notebook bought specially for the occasion. She'd been surprised to discover she was actually expected to produce some words and attend tutorials and classes. They were given a tour of the big house and their tour guide was none other than Jeremy, young and glorious in period costume, Mr Darcy style with rippling white shirt, long well cut coat and Regency styled blonde curls tumbling onto his forehead. Ellen had fallen instantly in love. Verity was also entranced. She remembered the bittersweet pain of first love, how her heart thudded and her body seemed to turn to liquid when he smiled at her. And how it had all turned sour.

'Ellen?' he repeated, bringing her back to the present.

'The very same.' Had realization dawned at last? She felt slightly ill at the thought of him not even remembering her name. How could he not?

'Ah. Ellen. Sorry, I remember her now.' He nodded his head thoughtfully. 'What about her? What's she got to do with anything?'

'Are you being deliberately obtuse?' Verity felt as if her blood was boiling.

'Please tell me, this is driving me insane,' he got up and paced around the conference table. 'I really like you, Verity and I hate it that you think badly of me.' He came to a stop and looked down at her. She stood up and took a deep breath.

'How can you blame me? You were the one that abandoned her.' She took a step towards him. 'You abandoned her – after you got her pregnant.'

She watched his face crumple and turn ashen white.

The silence in the room was growing edges and elbows.

Slowly, Jeremy sat back down on the steps. It seemed like an age before he eventually spoke.

'What did you say?' Jeremy grasped the mug of coffee and she noticed his hand shook slightly as he took a long gulp.

'You heard.' She walked round to stand in front of him.

'That is absolutely ridiculous. As well as being impossible,' he said. 'It's, it's ludicrous.'

'Is it?'

'Yes, because I never touched her.' Jeremy put his head down. 'I swear.'

'Don't lie.' She leant her arms on the table and looked straight into his clouded blue eyes. 'You kept in touch with her for a while then, when she discovered you'd made her pregnant, you didn't want to know. How could you take advantage of a poor defenceless girl with a broken ankle who was so besotted with you?'

Jeremy was running both hands through his hair so it stood on end and he looked like a wild man and all semblance of tidiness had gone. 'I never even heard from her again. I can't believe what she told you. It's all lies.' He stood up in front of her with his arms down by his sides, rigid. 'I would never, ever do such a thing.'

They faced each other over the table in a stand-off. He grabbed her hand and stared into her eyes, the deep blue growing darker.

'Now you listen to me Verity and I'll tell you exactly what did happen that night.' His forehead was creased in a deep furrow.

'Come on then, tell me your version of events.' He was still holding her hand firmly as they both sat back down.

'Well, as far as I can remember we, I mean you and I, had a fabulous time dancing at the evening barbeque. Then, I escorted Ellen to her room as she'd sprained her ankle dancing to Strip the Willow.'

'Go on.' She remembered how Ellen had clung to him, placing his arm tightly around her waist.

'I helped her onto the bed and put a cold compress on her ankle. Then,' Jeremy raked his fingers through his hair again, 'she put her arms around my neck, really tightly and tried to kiss me and I pushed her away. I was so keen to get back to you at the barbeque. But she started crying and making a fuss and said if I didn't stay with her for a bit she'd scream and tell everyone I'd attacked her.'

'Ellen would never have done that.' Verity felt absolutely furious, it was too ridiculous to be true.

'You obviously had no idea what she was capable of. She was bitterly jealous of you.'

'Jealous? Of me?' She sat back, unable to believe what she was hearing. 'Don't be ridiculous. How could anyone ever be jealous of me?'

'Quite easily I would imagine. And, she was.'

'But…she was the popular and the pretty one.' Verity got up and began pacing around the table. She was in turmoil.

'I didn't think so.' Jeremy raised an eyebrow. 'Not for one moment.'

'And she was my best friend.' Verity remembered how close they were, doing everything together. How she'd missed her when she moved away.

'Believe me she was no friend of yours. Are you still in touch with her?'

'No, no, she married someone else from our village pretty soon after and they moved away. He was besotted with her and happy to take on someone else's child.'

Jeremy shook his head, his words coming out faster than usual. 'I'm absolutely gutted to think that you've thought so badly of me all of these years. She very well may have been pregnant but I swear to you that *someone else* wasn't me.'

Jeremy grabbed both of her hands now and she felt the strength in his forearms and the warmth of his hands. She could see the hurt in his eyes as they bored into hers, they were heavy with unshed liquid. 'Verity. I swear on my life. You have got to believe me.'

She wanted so very much to believe him. What if he was telling the truth? Grandma Anna always said that Ellen was very envious of her, but she just used to laugh at the thought of it. In fact, one of Grandma Anna's most popular sayings at the time was, 'If Ellen jumped off a bridge, would you follow her?' Along with 'If you lie down with dogs, you'll get up with fleas.' Verity was never sure what that one meant at the time but knew it wasn't complimentary.

Jeremy sighed. 'Sounds to me like your Grandma Anna knew what she was talking about.' Verity flinched, she hadn't realised she'd spoken aloud.

Just maybe he wasn't lying? She had to admit to herself that she hoped so. He was so close now that she could feel his breath on her cheek. The beseeching look in his eyes made her think he could not be anything but innocent. His forearm was resting on her knees.

'I would never do such a thing to anyone. How could you even think it? But then we never really had the chance to get to know each other, did we?' Their heads were very close together now. His nearness was making her a bit giddy on top of her growing headache, but she so wanted to believe him. 'I did think about you a lot,' he added.

She felt a sudden rush of air behind her and a voice said, 'Excuse me, are you about ready to go now? It's just that we need to lock up.'

'Yes of course,' she regained her composure and jumped up to her feet. In silence they began a final check of the venue, avoiding each other's eyes.

Just as she was about to get into the car, Jeremy caught her eye. He didn't smile and she was struck by how tired he now looked.

'Verity,' he said, pausing with a hand on the car door, 'I am telling the truth you know.'

'Look, we're both shattered,' she said. 'It's late. Let's talk again tomorrow.'

'I'll hold you to that.' He nodded, paused as if to say something else, then got into his car and drove off into the sultry summer night.

Chapter Eleven

Verity couldn't sleep that night. Her head was buzzing and as she tossed and turned, trying to find a cool spot on her pillow, she kept thinking about Jeremy and wondering if he was telling the truth. She so wanted to believe him but how did you undo a belief you'd held for twenty odd years?

Her stomach was churning with unease at the very thought of his revelations and so instead, she tried to focus on the success of the Urban City event. She kept thinking of the little boy who threw the sandwich. The one with ADHD, Ethan he was called. As so often happened at emotional times, her thoughts began to stray back to the past. Ethan reminded her so much of someone….

Grandma's house 1989

Verity was doing her ironing in the dining room of Grandma Anna's house, feeling a sharp pang of happiness as she looked through to the sitting room window at the changing skies. She could see bands of sky ranging from china blue through to subtle hues of purple and pink, hinting that the sun was about to set. She always looked forward to this time of day. It was a nightly ritual of Grandma Anna's, and hers too now, to put down the books they were reading and look out at the sun setting over the fells.

Delicious smells of garlic and frying onions wafted in from the kitchen. They were having homemade pizza tonight because Our Johnny was here and it was his favourite.

Our Johnny was Auntie Bertha, Grandma Anna's sister's kid, the youngest of three brothers who lived across the road. He was aged nine and was often in trouble at school for being unable to concentrate. He frequently came over to Grandma's for his tea when Auntie Bertha got fed up of his antics. He was prone to tantrums and used to do daft things.

Like collecting empty tobacco tin boxes and throwing them all out of his bedroom window at six o'clock in the morning. They fell with such a loud clatter on the street pavement below that the din woke up all the neighbours, and all the dogs in the street. The miners who were on shift work at the drift mine over the fells weren't happy at all and Auntie Bertha had quite a confrontations in the back street that day.

Verity didn't think he was a bad kid though, but he could be a handful when he went off on one.

When he'd been in trouble and banished to his room, which was often, he used to jump out of the window on to the coal house roof and run off up the back street to the fells where he'd be out for hours. Then he'd come back hungry to Grandma Anna's, scared to go home and face Auntie Bertha's wrath. Grandma Anna could be scary when she lost her temper, not that Verity had seen that happen very often, but she had a gentle side, unlike Auntie Bertha who was in another league altogether. She used to stand at the top of the stairs brandishing a hair brush at Ethan and his brothers.

Verity was busy ironing her smart black skirts and white blouses for work next week, getting it out of the way before the weekend. Uncle Bobby had got her a job as an Office Junior in the typing pool and she'd never been happier, living here with Grandma and walking down the bank to Fell Ridge every day to the Town Hall. She'd only ever helped out in pubs before, collecting glasses, but she'd learnt how to type at school and had been the fastest in the class. She found the job fairly manageable and the pay was good for her age. She didn't go out much at nights although she'd just got to know Ellen who lived next door and she kept asking her to go out with her and her friends. She was quite happy staying in.

In fact she was more than happy, she adored living here. She had her own bedroom for the first time ever, her own space, and a view over the fells from her window. Keeping her room tidy and doing her own ironing didn't bother her. Grandma taught her how to cook properly and in return, Verity introduced her to Spaghetti Bolognese and pizza.

She giggled to herself because it was her who had persuaded Grandma to try to make pizza with her homemade bread as a base and also her who tricked her into using garlic.

Our Johnny's tummy rumbled. 'I bet you're laughing,' he said, 'because you're thinking about the garlic trick?'

She nodded.

'I don't like garlic,' Johnny mimicked.

'Ssh, she'll hear you.'

A few weeks ago when Verity had made the tea, she'd added some chopped up garlic cloves secretly bought from the local shop. Grandma Anna had thoroughly enjoyed her tea. Then Verity broke the news.

'Eee, our Verity, how could you?' she was astounded. 'But I don't like garlic.'

'Oh yes you do,' Johnny sang back to her. 'You do, you so love it!'

'You two are like partners in crime,' she scolded. But Verity noticed she added garlic to her shopping list from then on.

Tonight, our Johnny was lying stretched out on his front on the carpet in the front room in his school uniform, stockinged feet up in the air, engrossed with a microscope set she'd picked up from a charity shop in town. It had cost her next to nothing, but she knew he'd love it. He was right, he had spent hours after school finding things to look at under the microscope. Some quite gross things actually.

'Verity come and look at my snots under the microscope.' he said. 'Come here now.'

'How about a please?'

She switched off the iron and went through to the sitting room, ignoring the view outside and joining him on the floor. Science was one of his favourite subjects at school and she was amazed because he could talk about cells and evolution for hours.

She couldn't do that, nor could she recite every country in the world off pat like he could. Geography was his next favourite. It was easy to see he was a very bright kid. Clever even and she wished wholeheartedly that his teachers could see him now.

'I picked my own snots,' he said, making her pull a face and then laugh.

But when he had a tantrum, no-one seemed to be able to deal with him. He'd sit on the toilet screaming for ages, just because the toilet roll holder was empty. He'd run up and down the stairs or round and round the football field across the road like a mad man, as if he just couldn't get rid of all his energy.

Auntie Bertha used to leave him with Verity all the time as he'd taken a liking to her for some reason. Probably because she was used to dealing with kids. She found the best way to deal with him was to keep him interested in stuff and give him loads of one to one attention.

'Our Verity's got a lot of patience with him,' Grandma Anna would say to Auntie Bertha.

'I got wrong at school today,' our Johnny told her, resting his chin on his hands. 'Again.'

'What for this time?' Verity asked.

'Throwing pencils on the floor.'

She shook her head. 'Never mind, it's the weekend now. You don't have to think about school until Monday.'

'I hate school,' he said.

'No, you don't, not really. You enjoyed that school trip last week to the Science Museum in town didn't you?'

'Yeah, suppose so,' he shrugged.

Grandma's voice boomed in from the kitchen. 'You don't know how lucky you are Our Johnny,' she tutted. 'Do you know, when our Verity was little, long before she lived here with me, she sometimes wasn't lucky enough to go on a school trip like you did. Isn't that right Verity?'

She cringed inwardly at the memory. 'Yes, that's right.'

Johnny's eyes grew rounder. 'What do you mean?'

'I mean that, our Verity was the only one in her class who couldn't go on the school trip because her dad hadn't got enough money to pay for it.'

Johnny turned round, a look of horror on his round face.

'I was the only one left in the classroom with a teacher,' Verity picked up the tale.

'Can you imagine how that must have felt?' Grandma Anna demanded. 'Watching all the other kids get on the bus and wave goodbye, leaving her behind?'

'Well, it wasn't all that bad really,' Verity lied. 'At least I got to read a book all morning. And I could pick which one I wanted from the school library.'

'If it was me, I would have gone without something rather than let you stay behind,' Grandma Anna said. 'But that was your dad for you. Selfish he was at times.'

A cloud shifted across the sun and the room darkened for a second. Verity remembered how she'd felt back then. Miserable and alone, she'd made a pact with herself that day. The teacher keeping an eye on her had felt sorry for her and let her spend ages in the library choosing a book. She vowed she was going to read every book she could get her hands on, work hard at school and learn as much as possible so she would get a good job, be in charge and never be in a position like this again.

Brave words. Sometimes it was hard as the only reading material was a superman comic or a trashy newspaper. The teachers and librarian in the school library used to point her in the right direction and her obsession with books never waned.

It had worked to a certain extent though, as now she did have an excellent vocabulary and at work in the typing pool, it hadn't taken long for the Assistant Manager to come to her to ask for a suitable word to fit into his report. It never ceased to amaze her how someone so clever with figures could be so rubbish at spelling and not have the sense to use the spellchecker thoroughly.

Our Johnny pulled a face and grabbed at her arm. 'Never mind Verity, don't think about that now, come and look at my snots under the microscope again.'

She had to laugh at that.

'Oh and don't forget, you two. You promised you'd help me with blackberry picking on the fell tomorrow,' Grandma Anna bustled back into the room to remind them. 'I need a glut of them to make pies and blackberry jelly.'

'Picking blackberries? That's boring.' Our Johnny wrinkled his freckled nose.

'You don't have to come then.'

'If Verity's going I'll come,' he said grudgingly. 'If we can we take a picnic?'

'Yes, we can,' Grandma Anna agreed.

On blackberry picking day, Verity laughed as Our Johnny did his usual thing of running like a mad thing round and round the tarmacked football pitch at the bottom of the fells.

'He's dafter than an old wet hen,' Grandma said, leading the way past the allotments and a rain fed pond. 'Come on, up the hill.' Our Johnny ran on ahead as they joined the original stony path, made by years of pounding feet, overgrown with tufty grass and flanked on both sides by tall, elegant silver birch and sturdy oak trees.

Verity reached the top of the hill first, loving the way the wild heathland opened out all around, surrounding them with by purple heather like a blazing carpet alive with the buzz of honey bees diving alongside dancing butterflies and damselflies.

'Can you hear the skylarks?' Grandma Anna indicated as they tweeted overhead, treading their pockets of air, mingling with the plaintive cries of what she said were curlews.

'Not that path,' Grandma Anna said as Our Johnny hurried on. 'We'll take the high path.'

'That path is the one I go along with my friends to make camps and dens,' Our Johnny said, pointing and whirling back to them. 'It's where the railway line is.'

'The lower path is the way to the spot where the four streams meet,' Grandma Anna said. 'My mother used to take me there when I was a kid. It's my favourite. We'll go there next time when we've haven't got blackberries to pick. And the middle leads the way to the drift mine where Charlie used to work.'

She told them this every time they came up onto the fells but Verity didn't have the heart to say she already knew. Oh, how lovely and pure the air was up here and the stillness of the open space.

'Can I play near the pit heaps?' Our Johnny asked, running from side to side. He was more interested in that monstrosity than the beauty of nature.

'You know the pit heaps are out of bounds,' Grandma Anna tutted. ''They could still be smouldering.'

'I know some kids who play on them.'

'It's very dangerous, you're not to go near them,' Grandma Anna went on.

'Can I have something to eat now? I'm starving.'

'You kids of today don't know you're born,' Grandma Anna scolded. 'Do you know when your Uncle Charlie used to work down the Smithy Dene, all he used to have to eat was jam and bread for his bait, washed down with water so he didn't get heartburn?'

'What's heartburn?' Our Johnny danced on ahead, not waiting for a reply. Then he turned back to continue with another question, 'Why is that bracken all flat?'

'You don't half ask a lot of questions, Our Johnny,' Grandma Anna sighed. 'The summer bracken bashers must have been out.'

'What's bracken bashers?' he wanted to know.

'They use horses to crush the bracken because it would spoil the heather.'

'Ha, this ground feels springy.' Our Johnny bounced along, plunging into the heather.

'Keep out of the heather,' instructed Grandma Anna. 'Stick to the path.'

'Why, will there be snakes in it?' Our Johnny asked, leaping back to the pathway.

'Oh yes, there'll be grass snakes, Verity told him, and as Our Johnny's eyes grew wider she added, 'although I've never seen any.'

'I know the best spot to find the biggest blackberries,' Grandma Anna moved briskly along the path surrounded by the glorious heather on both sides. She always walked fast. 'Only pick the ripe ones, mind.'

Of course, Our Johnny was eating more blackberries than he put in the baskets and soon his mouth and hands were stained with the dark purple juice.

'You'll not eat your picnic,' Grandma Anna scolded him.

'I bet I will,' he said.

'I know you will,' Verity laughed.

Soon they were sat on an old stone seat with their plastic bags bursting full of purple blackberries so dark they were almost black, overlooking the panoramic countryside view. She looked across the wide expanse of vibrant green rolling fields, past a clump of trees which Grandma Anna had told her were called *The 30 Trees,* over to where the grey and red rooftops of the neighbouring villages snuggled up to the hazy blue sky.

'I think we've got enough now for me to make my famous blackberry jelly,' she said.

'I love your blackberry jelly coz' there aren't any seeds in it,' our Johnny said. 'It's

nice and smooth.'

'That's because I strain them through gauze,' Grandma Anna began laying out the

picnic and Verity marvelled at the spread of ham bread buns sliced and filled with homemade Pease pudding, hard boiled eggs sprinkled with salt from the tiniest of salt cellars, plump sausage rolls made with flaky pastry and a selection of little cakes on the stone between them. Our Johnny ate standing up, rocking on the balls of his feet, devouring his food and flicking crumbs everywhere. Grandma Anna had even brought a flask of hot water and two cups, to make tea outdoors and a bottle of dandelion burdock.

Verity felt the warmth of the late summer sun upon her face and felt so content. There was a peace in the air up here, something she'd never experienced before. The only thing that niggled at her happiness was that it was very difficult trying to get Grandma Anna to talk about her mother. Her need to know more just grew and grew but the more she tried the worse it became. Since the first meeting when she showed her the photograph on the mantelpiece, conversations about her mother were rare.

Grandma Anna was always so busy, working hard to keep the house sparklingly clean and tidy. She had set days for washing, baking, washing the windows and so on. She reminded Verity of a busy little blackbird, always hurrying here there and everywhere, always on the go.

Or, Our Johnny was there. If he was in the other room and she was helping Grandma Anna in the kitchen and happened to mention her mother, she'd tap on her nose and whisper, 'Sshh, walls have big ears.'

Then, when she sat down to watch television she didn't want to talk, same as when she read her library book. She read for half an hour every morning and usually the same at night, before she went to bed. She never stopped still for long, apart from when she read or watched the sunset. Uncle Bobby said it upset her to talk about it and that was the last thing Verity wanted to do, upset her when she was always so kind. So she totally savoured the bits of information she did manage to find out.

How her life had changed over the past year and oh, so much for the better. She could hardly imagine that not long ago she hadn't even met Grandma Anna or Our Johnny…

Back in the room she plumped up her pillows once more. Wide eyed, she sat up. Today they'd probably diagnose Our Johnny as having ADHD. Back then, they only thought he was naughty or hyperactive. In her whirling brain she remembered reading something on the subject at work just the other day. She thought it was in Callum's filing cabinet which hadn't been opened since he'd left. Now why would Callum have a file on ADHD? She wasn't sure why it was important but it must have piqued her interest because she got out of bed and padded along to her laptop in the spare room and emailed herself at work to remind her to have a look the next day.

Chapter Twelve

Next morning came all too soon, with Verity having had very little sleep. She opened the window in her office, letting in cool fresh Spring air and the sweet, plaintive notes of a little blackbird perched on a branch just outside, singing his heart out. She sighed as he flew off at her intrusion. She didn't blame him. The euphoria of the successful event had worn off, the feedback forms awaited and she felt exhausted and rather raw inside. Post conference day always felt like a let-down.

'Good Morning team,' she called out as Sophie and Jeremy rocked up in the outer office. Must put on a professional front at all times, no matter how tired she felt. 'How are we this morning?'

'I'm good.' Sophie wandered in, mobile phone in hand. 'Which is more than I can say for him.'

Verity waited for some comment about the dark shadows under her own eyes, but Sophie scrutinised her phone instead.

'Well, thanks a lot,' Jeremy replied, shrugging and burying his nose in his coffee mug, then grimacing as he realised it was empty.

She guessed he was feeling as bad as he looked, which was heavy eyed, his hair all tousled, (definitely no sign of the chunky funky today) and as if he had the whole weight of the world on his shoulders.

'Was the event crap then?' Sophie asked.

'On the contrary,' Verity logged on to her computer and opened up her emails. 'It was a massive success. Jeremy was a total star.' Well he was, he'd saved the day.

She saw Jeremy's back straighten up.

'Aren't you joining us out here?' Sophie wanted to know.

'No, I'm working in here today. Lots to get through.' Verity grabbed some change from her desk drawer. 'After I've been along to the restaurant for a proper coffee.'

'I'll come with you,' Jeremy said and before she could dissuade him, they were walking along the corridor in an uneasy silence. She could have done without his company and the awkward gulf between them.

Jeremy broke the silence when he spotted the back staircase. 'Where does that staircase lead?'

'Right the way up to the roof,' she said. 'To the Penthouse to be exact. Strictly out of bounds.'

'That's a shame,' Jeremy said. 'The Penthouse sounds interesting. I'm going up for a look.'

'Wait,' she said, 'staff aren't supposed to go up there and I don't want you getting lost again.'

'Then come with me. I need the exercise,' he called from the first landing. 'Come on, it'll brighten us up.'

She looked around. There was no-one in sight so she sighed and began to follow him.

'All right, wait for me.' She supposed she could do with the exercise as well and didn't feel like going straight back to the office just yet, feeling a bit restless.

So she followed him up ten flights of stairs in silence and joined him to rest on a dusty landing, both of them taking deep breaths. 'Only one more flight to go.'

There was colour in Jeremy's cheeks now and she was sure her face must be purple with all the effort. She felt the pain in her calves. Why hadn't they gone in the lift?

'Is this where the top director guy lives?' He bounced along ahead to arrive first. 'Is there actually a Penthouse Suite?'

'No, there isn't,' she said. 'Although people did try to tell me there was when I first started in this building. No-one actually works up here.'

'Then just what is up here?' he asked.

'Nothing,' she shrugged. 'Just unused offices.'

Then Jeremy ran up the final staircase and disappeared through the door at the top. She heard him snapping on lights. How did he have so much stamina?

'Hey wait,' she said, joining him. 'We've only come for a quick look at the view. Staff aren't supposed to be up here.'

'Please, let's just have a scout about.' he said.

The first thing she noticed was that everything seemed to be light. As opposed to the rest of the building. The walls resembled outdoor bricks painted cream and the walkway was wider than the usual corridors. It was so very quiet.

'So you've never been up here before?' Jeremy asked in lowered tones, looking around.

'Never. Never had any reason to.' Her voice sounded loud.

She could hear ticking pipes, a familiar noise which reminded her of Grandma Anna's ancient central heating system and a faint electrical humming. On their left, sprawling boxes of musty papers bound by string and papers with curling edges rested against the walls and stretched for the ceiling, like tendrils of a giant beanstalk reaching for the sky. To their right the windows were obscured by grubby vertical blinds. Jeremy tentatively opened one to have a look outside, causing a glittering storm of dust particles to do a crazy dance in front of his face.

She gasped as she looked down upon a world of greenery, the tops of the trees ensuring that everything in her line of vision consisted of roof, bright sky and foliage. She could just see the open, glass fronted tower which housed the front stairs and caught a glimpse of people below scurrying up and down it, about their everyday working lives, going off to meetings or to the nearest watercooler.

'Let's just see how far it goes, there must be an even better view from the end window.' Jeremy seemed to have forgotten his woes as he excitedly hurried along.

She shivered as she walked on, thinking she could hear the faint, far off hum of voices. The passageway was so uneven in places at times it felt like walking uphill. Surely it couldn't be safe? The floor creaked and the hard skin on her feet in high heeled shoes was beginning to rub after climbing all those stairs.

She heard another groaning noise and jumped side wards as something hit her in the small of her back. 'Ouch, what was that?' she winced.

She whirled round to see what looked like an enormous electricity meter, reminding her of a one armed bandit, boxed in and painted light grey to blend in with the rest of the walls. It had a large protruding lever which had nudged her back. What a monster. Did she imagine it, or had the lights flickered?

Thinking of all the floors and people that were underneath us, she looked at Jeremy in horror. 'Do you think that meter controls the whole building?'

'Probably, yes.'

'What if you've fused all the lights?' Jeremy sipped at his cooling coffee and pulled a face. 'What if all the computers have gone off? 'And the boilers and kettles?'

Verity stared up at him and they locked eyes. 'Don't be so ridiculous.' She sometimes couldn't tell if he was winding her up or not.

'Disaster. Can you imagine? A day here without caffeine? They'll be a mass walk out. You stay here and I'll go and look.' He handed over his coffee and was off, hurtling back off back along the corridor to the windows.

'All clear boss,' he bounded back along the walkway, his smile huge. 'Productivity won't be lost. Chaos averted.'

Verity couldn't help smiling back. What a big kid he was. Goodness, was she warming towards him?

'Glad I've cheered you up, boss.' He looked pleased with himself.

The boiler groaned again as they continued walking. It felt as if she'd walked for ages along the walkway with walls on both sides, but the overhanging structure that was the top floor didn't go that far along. It stopped in the middle of the building.

'How many people do you reckon work here?' Jeremy asked.

'Oh, a few thousand at least,' she replied.

'Wow! Think of them all below us. We're walking on top of them.'

Jeremy's phone rang and he answered it quickly. 'Hi, Sophie. Okay, right I'm on my way.'

He looked at Verity. 'She needs a hand with a delivery.'

'That's fine. You go on down. I'll just have a little look along here.'

'How do I find Reception?'

'Take the lift directly to the Lower Ground Floor. Here, get rid of these,' she handed him our empty coffee cups to carry back. 'It's impossible to get lost.'

'Ha. Famous last words. I'll come straight back.'

'No, I'll follow you down.' Anything for some breathing space. 'I just want to see how far this walkway goes along.'

'Of course boss. Whatever you say.' He made for the stairs and spoke over his shoulder. 'Will you be all right up here on your own?'

She shot him a scathing look. 'I can look after myself thank you very much.'

'Of that I have no doubt. I'll see you in a few minutes in the office.'

Glad to be on her own, she kept on walking, then stopped and for a long while just looked out of the window and enjoyed the silence. Then she noticed that there was another door at the end of the walkway. She turned the handle half-heartedly not expecting it to give but it jumped open to reveal a secret, enclosed staircase – or rather, a few, steep, narrow steps leading up to another doorway.

She didn't think twice but scrambled up the staircase and stood on the top step and grabbed the handle. What could this locked room possibly hold up in the attics? Probably more boilers.

It was locked. Disappointed, she shrugged and turned away.

She didn't know why but something made her turn back again. Had she heard something? A hint of a noise. Coming from the empty room. What on earth could it be? What could be in there? She strained her ears to try and work out what kind of sound it was. A whirring whishing sound. She felt the sweat prickle on her forehead. Was it a human sound? Or was it machinery?

She bent down and peered shamelessly through the keyhole. Something caught her eye. Something was definitely moving in there. Round and round. In the middle of the room. Her head moved in time as my eyes tried to focus on the movement. She began to feel dizzy.

'What are you doing?' she heard a voice behind her.

Her heart jumped. She fell backwards onto his toes. She'd forgotten all about Jeremy. How could he be back so quickly? He put his arms out to steady her and they both teetered on the stairs, scrabbling at the stairwell walls for balance. She felt anger rising in her chest.

'What the hell are you doing creeping up on people like that?' She almost pushed him backwards down the little staircase. 'You're supposed to be in the office helping Sophie.'

'Hey, steady on,' he righted himself, arms flailing against the wall. 'It's fine. She's sorted. It's lunch time now anyway.'

She stared at him. 'Anyhow, what does it look like I'm doing?'

'Snooping?' He grinned at her. 'Peeping through keyholes.'

'I was not snooping.'

'No?'

'Well maybe just a bit.' She shrugged her shoulders.

Why don't you just open the door?' he said.

'Because it's locked.' She hissed through clamped teeth.

'Why are we whispering?'

'I don't know.' How annoying was he?

'Have you tried turning the handle?'

'Yes, of course I have.' Did he think she was stupid or something? She was beginning to get a headache and felt irritated.

'Let me try.' He bounded up the stairs again, and turned the handle, pushing down and lifting and astonishingly, the door swung open a crack.

'There you are you see. It wasn't locked after all.' he grinned.

She glared at him. Why did he always manage to get one over on her?

'Wait. Do you want me to go in first?' he said, a trace of wariness in his voice.

'No way. I'm going in first.' She ran up the stairs, pushed past him and opened the door fully. She took a few steps into the room and stopped still. It took a few seconds to register what she was seeing.

'Oh my stars and garters!' she uttered one of Grandma Anna's favourite sayings out loud before she could stop herself. She heard Jeremy's intake of breath right behind her and she thought he might have uttered a stronger expletive. 'A secret room!'

They stood in silence for a couple of seconds. This room was certainly the most beautiful, gleaming, streamlined office space she'd ever seen. They must have wandered into another dimension. The contrast with the rest of the building was astounding. Surely no-one had ever actually done any work in a room such as this?

'Wow. It's like the Tardis from Doctor Who.' Jeremy said with delight. 'It's awesome. Incidentally, where did you get that Stars and Garters saying from?'

'My Grandma Anna,' she said. 'She has one for every occasion.'

One wall was partially covered with tall, gleaming, steel grey filing cabinets like a line of silent robots with a wall clock suspended in the space above like a disjointed head. They were all padlocked. There was a large boardroom table at the other end and one solitary shining new desk, compact with a pedestal drawer underneath. Smart grey blinds obscured one wall of windows opposite the filing cabinets. She could smell old fashioned furniture polish and air freshener.

'Oh my days.' Jeremy said, 'it's like a ballroom in here.'

The rest of the room was just, well, space apart from, another table in the middle of the floor space on which was a train set complete with hills and tunnels. The entire model must have been about three times the size of the one in Greyson's office.

Round it went, disappearing through a tunnel in the cliffs with a jaunty turn, muffling the sound and then re-appearing, chugging and clicking at regular intervals as it moved over the tracks. 'That's the sound I heard through the keyhole,' she said.

Someone must have been in here very recently unless the motor's stuck,' Jeremy paused. 'Maybe someone is hiding out on the roof?'

She held her breath as he moved over to the window and tugged the cord at the edge of the blinds which moved them along a few inches. She noticed that there was a small open window which belonged to a patio door. And oh my goodness, it actually opened onto a spacious balcony on the flat roof. Complete with a table and two chairs. Thankfully, there was no-one there.

Jeremy moved beside her and she could see his mouth was hanging open with amazement. They both looked at each other and then beyond the balcony at the panorama below.

It looked as if she could just take one giant step off that grey, green flat roof and be in the midst of the glorious tableaux. Verity felt like the Greek gods must have felt like gazing down on Earth.

There was a whole hillside scene laid out before them. She could see where the main road trawled, where the river meandered, the turrets of the castle on the top of the hill hiding behind sharp black branches. It was like gazing onto a painting. Beyond the vegetation, wind turbines twirled on the horizon against the light blue sky. Jeremy winced and shielded his eyes. Secondary roads glistened like silver snakes winding their way upwards, cars flashed as the sunlight glinted like a blaze of lightning. Her eyes stung from the brightness but she couldn't look away.

At the very bottom of the canvas, she saw the trickle of silver and counted one, two, three, four streams merging into a crossroads and meandering into the larger body of the river itself.

She gasped and turned to Jeremy. 'It's the spot where the four streams meet.'

'Is it? Where is that?' he asked.

'Oh, just a place from my childhood,' she said, unable to look away.

She'd been there so many times in the past and now she was looking right down upon it. This was a magic moment. Oh, those few short golden summer months each year when Grandma Anna had taken her and Our Johnny there for picnics. It held so many happy memories. Her heart lifted. She could almost taste the salt on the hard boiled eggs, and remember how the tart of the home made lemonade made her pull a face, the bubbles prickling her nose. Most of all, she remembered the sense of belonging she had on those outings. It was the only time she could ever remember feeling that way in the whole of her childhood years. She felt tears behind her eyes and her throat tightened. Standing there, she felt an overwhelming pull of deja vue, so strong that it exerted a physical pressure around her chest. The pain of nostalgia was both acute and pleasurable at the same time.

'Wow,' she murmured. 'It's…it's…incredible.' She felt an uncomfortable warmth on her lower legs from the sun behind the glass but she couldn't move.

They stood there transfixed for ages. Then Jeremy broke the spell by trying to take photos on his mobile. He prowled around the room and opened one of three doors at the back.

'OMG,' he said. 'Look at this.'

She tore herself away from the view and looked. It was a tiny en-suite shower room. Behind the second door was a bed settee and a wardrobe. There was nothing in the wardrobe and the action of opening it caused the two lone coat hangers inside to swing and hit the back of the wood. Beside the bed, on the floor was a filmy silk scarf. She went over to pick it up, feeling it's softness between her fingers. She dropped it into onto the bed.

Obviously, this room was used regularly. But by whom? And what if they appeared without warning, found them intruding and shut and locked the door on them, imprisoning them in this glorious office space in the clouds?

'What happens now?' Jeremy turned his back and without thinking, she grabbed the scarf from the bed and shoved it into her suit jacket pocket. It was so sheer it hardly made any impact.

'How on earth should I know?' This was not a situation she'd been in before and she felt unusually out of her comfort zone.

'Well, you always seem to know the right thing to do.'

'I just want to gaze at the view,' she said, moving back to the window.

A sound behind her made her jump and she felt the cool river breeze cut through the warmth of the room.

It sounded like a Puffing Billy train whistle.

'Where did that come from?' she looked at the model then at Jeremy. 'It's coming from you.'

'Is it? Oh. It's me.' Jeremy checked his phone. 'I forgot I changed my text notification last night.'

'Trust you to choose that one,' she breathed a sigh of relief.

'Yep. Sorry. I must have known.'

The train on the track moved slower and slower until it finally stopped altogether, half in, half out of the tunnel, emitting a final click. Silence and then she could hear the ticking of the disjointed robot head wall clock. Then Jeremy's voice distracted her from the daydream she seemed to be in.

'Have you seen the time?' He looked at the robot head clock. 'What a day.'

'We need to go now,' she said.

'Just a minute, we haven't tried the third door.' Jeremy dashed off to have a look and she followed him into a very compact kitchen, complete with sparse units and a bench with a tiny hob and a kettle. Then she saw it. An object behind the kettle on the shiny draining board. It was the last thing she saw as she pushed Jeremy out in front of her and shut the door behind them. She felt as if her heart had turned over.

It was a dirty cereal bowl.

Chapter Thirteen

'Going down,' said the slow mechanical voice of the lift. Everything went dark for a second as Verity shivered and the old lift shuddered and creaked on its descent, making her stomach lunge. She'd felt a bit faint and told Jeremy to walk down if he wanted but he wouldn't hear of it.

She felt as if she'd been hit over her back with a heavy shovel and bent her head, taking deep breaths. She'd been doing so well. So much for managing to convince herself that she was moving forward by throwing herself into the job. It only taken the sight of that bowl, milk congealed with muesli or whatever it was into a lumpy brown mass, to turn her into a quivering wreck. Also, she felt that the scarf was burning a hole in her pocket.

It hadn't been hard to put two and two together and come up with the upsetting image of Callum and another woman up in the Penthouse. Surely not? Although Uncle Bobby had tried to warn her. He'd always said Callum was a philanderer, a serial womaniser with form and nowhere near good enough for her. She'd shrugged off his comments because she didn't want to believe him and was happy to think that he'd changed his ways.

'What is it? Are you okay?' She felt Jeremy put his arm around her shoulders as she straightened up. She couldn't betray her suspicions to him.

'Nothing. I'm fine.' She wasn't, she still felt like she was going to faint. She closed her eyes and for one moment, relaxed and let herself enjoy the comforting nearness of his body. He took the opportunity to put his other arm around her. She leaned in, resting her head down in the direction of his chest, feeling the softness of his shirt against her forehead. The woody aftershave was stronger now and she could also smell mints and a faint trace of coffee.

Her vision lightened again and the world seemed to regain its equilibrium. Her head cleared as she broke apart from him in the enclosed space and pushed him away. He stepped sideways, his face showing his hurt.

'Sorry about that, I'm fine. It's just lack of sleep. Or Conference Fever.' She was starting to feel angry with Callum now, rather than sorry for herself. How could she have let herself be so duped?

'Look.' He opened his hand and on his palm was the key to the secret room. 'Here.' He took her hand and put the key in it. His hand was warm but dry. He closed his fingers around hers. 'The key was still in the lock on the inside so I grabbed it and locked the door.'

'Quick thinking,' she said. 'I am impressed though quite what I'm supposed to do with it, I don't know. I mean, should we be pinching keys from a room we're not supposed to know is there? What if…oh never mind.'

He was still holding on to her hand and then he began to stroke the inside of her wrist with his long slender thumb and she felt a bolt of electricity surge along her arm. How could this be happening? She wasn't sure about this man's integrity so what on earth was she thinking about?

'What are you doing?' she wrenched her hand away and stepped back against the lift wall, the buttons prodding her back.

'Verity. You must know how I feel about you.' Jeremy took a step towards her which, as they were in such a small space, brought him very close indeed. This was all she needed. There was a mirror in the back of the lift.

She caught a glimpse of their reflections and almost gave herself a fright, looking at her white, shiny face with tendrils of sweating hair escaping from her bun and sticking to her forehead, and his tanned face with messy blond curls standing up on end. 'I look a sight.'

'You look beautiful.'

'Well, I feel awful,' she said, reaching for a tissue in her pocket and blowing her nose loudly. Her eyes and nose were both starting to run. She noticed the floor number on the lift trundling past slowly. Only at Floor Six. Oh why couldn't they be on the ground floor? She heard a smattering of voices as the lift began to slow right down. Quickly, Jeremy pushed the button for the Floor 10 again, confusing the machinery and it jolted, the doors started to open but started to shut again before the people waiting could get in. Verity saw heads turn to each other with confused expressions as Jeremy gave them a little wave and looked sheepish.

'What did you do that for?' she hissed as the doors shut.

'I need to talk to you some more,' he said as they began to ascend, making her stomach pitch again. The lifts in this old building were past their best.

'Because, Verity', he made as to rest his hands on her shoulders, 'I absolutely adore everything about you.'

She raised my hands to ward him off, feeling her nose run again. 'What, after two days? Don't be so daft.'

'It's not as if we've just met.'

She immediately jabbed at the lift buttons. 'That's got nothing to do with it.'

He looked mortified. 'Then why not? I can't help how I feel. You must have felt it too. I really hoped that…'

'I'm sorry,' she said. 'I truly am.'

'Really?' he said, hope sounding in his voice. 'What for exactly?'

'For – for not believing you for so many years.' She blew her nose again.

His eyes lightened. 'So you do believe me?'

'I want to,' she said. She really wanted to.

He ran a hand through his hair. 'That's better than nothing I suppose. To tell the truth, since you told me, it's been weighing very heavily on my shoulders. When I think about what we've lost because of someone else's lie and what we could have had.' His curls sprang back. 'I didn't sleep much last night.'

Tell her about it. 'We were very young you know,' she said. 'Life moves on.'

'No-one else ever quite compared with you. Can we start again? Come out for a drink with me this evening.'

'No, not tonight,' she said.

'You are single aren't you? I tried to find out about your situation, discreetly of course, and I was told that you were.'

'I am now,' she admitted. Had they really fooled the watercooler whisperers? Ha, they were wrong for once. 'I've just split up with someone. Literally a few days ago.'

'Oh, I see.' He raked his fingers through his unruly hair again. 'I'm sorry, well I am and I'm not, if you know what I mean.'

'It's too soon,' she said, feeling her voice wobble to her annoyance. 'And too raw. I…I just can't think about starting anything else up right now. You do understand that, don't you?' It wasn't that she didn't find him disturbingly attractive, yes, she was admitting it to herself, it was just that it was the wrong time.

'Yes, I do,' he looked crestfallen again, then his blue eyes began to sparkle. 'You did say *right now* though. So, I won't give up on us, Verity, you'll see.'

She felt thankful as the lift bumped to a stop. Too many turbulent thoughts were racing around in her head.

'Doors opening,' said the voice of the lift and she escaped out and was off along the corridor with Jeremy in close pursuit.

Looking around at the drab, dirty beige walls and brown doors, stretching on and on as if to infinity, she was struck by the stark contrast of the sleek and gleaming office space she'd just seen on the penthouse floor. She stopped for one moment, opened her sweating palm and glanced down at the key, clutching it even tighter before hurrying on back to the Conference Office.

Chapter Fourteen

Back in the office, the team were waiting for Greyson to come along for a post conference debrief. 'Hey, look outside, it's snowing.' Jeremy said.

'What! Snowing in May?' Verity shot him a look. 'Don't be so silly. It can't be.'

She joined him at the window where sherbert pink petals from the two breathtakingly beautiful cherry blossom trees outside floated idly downwards to dust the grassed area below with a glorious profusion of pink and white confetti. She forgot about her streaming nose for one delightful second as she gazed at the carpet of pink.

'Good Morning guys, wait until you read this.' Greyson bowled in, waving a folded newspaper in the air. His eyebrows were raised which meant that he wasn't displeased but he thought that she might be. She knew him so well. Oh, oh, this must be the article. Filled with apprehension, she hesitated for a second before taking the paper proffered by Greyson and then Jeremy took the other corner and they both sat down at the conference table to read it.

'Ooh! La! La! – Class act by pupils', was the heading.

Underneath was a coloured photograph of some of the children kneeling on the reddish boards of the stage. In the midst of them all posed Jeremy, a cheeky grin on his face with all the little ones turning their heads to gaze up at him with rapt expressions. The strapline underneath read, 'Star Performance – pupils from the Salt of the Sea Primary School perform at The Moving On Up Conference at Urban City, being inspired by Jeremy Soderland, Conference Organiser.' Then there was also a tiny square photo of him in the top right hand corner, grinning at the camera.

Being inspired by Jeremy? A few weeks ago she wouldn't have believed it possible.

'Is that you?' Sophie jabbed at the photograph. 'I'm well pleased I wasn't there, you're so embarrassing. Just like my dad.'

'Gee, thanks a lot,' Jeremy grinned.

She didn't know the half of it. 'Let's see the damage,' Verity thought to herself before reading the text. It opened with a quote from Jeremy -

'The only conference I've ever been to in trainers and a suit.' His favourite line. Then a short description about the event followed. It was fairly well written actually. She breathed a sigh of relief.

'Maybe not such an entire disaster after all then?' Jeremy laughed. 'In my line of work I have come across journalists before.'

Verity felt bad for doubting him but was it her imagination or did he look just a tiny bit pleased with himself?

'You can have that copy, I've got one pinned on my noticeboard.' Greyson stood up. 'Oh by the way guys, I've had a phone call from the Chair.'

Her back felt stiff as she sipped at her plastic cup of water. Surely this wasn't going to be about the flapjacks?

Greyson stared at Jeremy. 'Apparently your help with the kids saved the gig from disaster. In fact, the whole event was a huge success.'

Jeremy positively glowed and she felt his eyes on her, as if begging for approval. She felt her body visibly relax and had to give in. He did deserve it.

'I have to agree,' she said. 'He saved the day.' Jeremy's eyes lit up.

'Good man, good man'. Greyson shook hands with Jeremy vigorously. 'Onwards and upwards.'

'Verity is the one you should be praising,' Jeremy said. 'She keeps it all going and I only did what she told me.'

She knew that wasn't strictly true, in fact his quick thinking and skills had got them out of a tricky situation.

'Greyson patted her arm with vigour, 'I knew I was right to take a punt out on you. Good luck on going forward with the team.'

Luck would have nothing to do with it but she did have an idea crystallising at the back of her mind.

'Right, I don't want to be disturbed for the rest of the morning,' she said, as she walked into her room and made to shut the door.

'What are you going to do?' Jeremy asked, swivelling round in his chair.

'Look at the budget.' Among other things.

She shut the door, shutting out him and Sophie and surveyed her new domain. It looked rather different in here now as she'd thrown away every last trace of Callum and brought in a few plants to create some greenery and a couple of photographs adorned her new desk, one of Grandma Anna, Uncle Bobby and Our Johnny and another of her mother.

Callum was always looking at the budget and he constantly shut himself away to do it. It was his most important task of the week. Used to be his most important task of the week, she corrected her thoughts.

She was struck by how cool it was in there and enjoying the quiet whilst waiting for the computer to load up, she steeled herself to open the first desk drawer. She hadn't cleared anything out of his desk yet just in case…She rifled through all the cardboard coloured files, noting their names, until she found one named *Trainers for Medication Course*. Great, this was the one. She put it in her laptop bag to take home with her, to read at her leisure. Now she was ready to check the budget and needed to focus.

Playing around with figures was one of her favourite work tasks and she had to admit, it felt good to be in charge of the finances and sitting in the Conference Manager's chair with her own name on the door. She could even order herself a brand new docking station and a lighter weight laptop so it would be easier to carry about with her.

She then logged into the Company's Internet Banking Account to have a quick check of the finances.

She clicked onto the most up to date bank statement and looked at the balance. She looked again. There must be some mistake surely...This couldn't possibly be right. They weren't in deficit last time she looked. She cast her eye down the page for outgoings. There were two transactions she didn't recognise, one for £10,000 and the other for £700.00. What was going on here? Now she knew the meaning of the saying when your blood runs cold...She felt as if ice water was running through her veins.

Taking deep breaths, she rang the Bank, sweating and stressing, as she went through the rigmarole of security questions. She eventually got through to the Account Manager, who calmly advised that the transaction for £10,000 was payable to a company called Bulleted and was authorised by Dr Callum Doyle on 28 March.

'There must be some mistake,' she spluttered. 'What on earth was BluLite?' And the transaction pending for £700.00?'

'That was to a company called MMM,' came the steady reply.

'Who was the account holder?' she asked. What was going on here? She'd already been told but needed to hear it again.

Such a calm voice. 'Callum Doyle, Conference Manager.

She put the phone down in bewilderment. Her heart was beating so fast it was hurting my rib cage. She googled BluLite. They were an exclusive web designer company. But he'd told her he had designed the website himself to save money.

She was just about to google 'MMM' when there was a knock at the door and Sophie burst in.

'Sorry to interrupt, but there's a delivery for you in the Conference Office.' Sophie had her mobile to her ear. 'I've signed on your behalf.'

'What delivery?' she said. 'I haven't ordered anything.'

'Dr Callum Doyle ordered it for you,' Sophie said.

Verity was fed up of hearing his name this morning. What had he done now?

Verity gritted her teeth as she followed her into the outer office where a smart young man was directing two porters who were wheeling in a huge box on a trolley.

'If you could just deposit it on that side table,' the young man was saying.

'What's this?' she said, in what she believed to be her firmest Conference Manager's voice. 'What are you depositing on my Conference Table?'

'I'm Steve from Multi Magic Machines. So pleased to meet you,' he said, holding out his hand for her to shake, which felt cold. 'I've heard such a lot about you from Dr Doyle. All good as well.'

His attempt at a joke didn't amuse Verity. Multi Magic Machines. MMM on the bank statement. 'I haven't ordered this,' she repeated, her voice sounding strange to herself. 'What on earth is it?'

'It's your new Stack N Go Multi Magic Mailer Machine.'

'It's my what?'

'Stack N Go Machine. It's all been paid for and specially arranged by Dr Doyle. He wanted it to be a surprise for you.'

Well it certainly was that.

'Can't you take it back?' she folded her arms. 'I don't want it. Can I send it back?'

Steve looked shocked and hurt. 'I'm afraid not, Dr Doyle agreed to our No Returns Policy.'

'Let me have a look at the paperwork.'

He handed her the signed agreement, and as she read it through, realised he was right.

'I need to carry out a demo now with the luck users,' he went on, adding, Dr Doyle said you'd be so pleased.'

A memory jerked into her mind. *'You shouldn't have to stuff all these envelopes at your level. It's such hard work. As soon as the budget allows it, I'll buy you a machine that stuffs them for you...'*

'Right,' she said, speaking quietly and moving into the centre of the office, 'here's what's going to happen.' She hardly recognised her own voice it was so controlled but she knew when she was beaten. She looked round at the three of them in turn. 'Steve, I can see there is no way out of this so you go ahead and do your demo. In the meantime, I...'

'But for protocol, I need three people before I can do the demonstration,' he interrupted weakly.

'Sorry, that's not possible,' Verity continued, narrowing her eyes. 'Jeremy, you and Sophie stay here and watch and learn. Now if you'll all excuse me, I've got some proper work to do. She stared at Steve. 'Do you have a problem with that?'

Steve shook his head and looked at his shoes.

'Good. Thank you.' She did a sharp turn and walked through into the other office with her back rigid, shutting the door as calmly as she could behind her. She wanted to stand and scream at the wall in fury. Could things get any worse? Callum had spent all the company's money on web design and a Stuff N Go Machine. How was she supposed to singlehandedly stop the company going under? And, for the moment, how could she let Jeremy loose on such a thing as a Multi Magic Mailer? That had to be a recipe for disaster.

What should she do? Tell Greyson they were in dire straits with no money and have him disband their little Conference Team in disgrace? She'd only just been made Business Manager. She had to do something and it had to be done quickly.

She clenched her fists by her sides. How dare he do this? He must have known that they didn't have the money for such a contraption. Or a brand new website.

She felt her knees begin to give way. The silence thundered in her ears and pain burst from her heart. Humiliation spread and the hurt that had been smouldering surged, as she saw the red mist in front of her eyes and found her voice. It came out as a low growl of anger which was swallowed up by the grind of machinery from next door. Then Sophie opened the door again.

'Verity, please come and look, you've got to see this.' She indicated behind her where a bewildered Jeremy was being attacked by envelopes which were spitting out at him from the machine at a rate of knots. Steve was nowhere to be seen but the door was wide open.

'He's gone. I think he was a bit scared of you,' she giggled.

Verity suppressed a hysterical chuckle and went back in to her office, closing the door firmly behind her. A few minutes later, Sophie knocked and popped her head in, her eyes wide.

'I'm proper sorry to disturb you again, but we need help out there,' she jerked her head towards the noise. 'I think the machine's stuffed and gone.'

Chapter Fifteen

Next morning Verity marched along the corridor along to her office, hearing a whisper as she passed the most popular water cooler which sounded very much like:

'Here she comes girls, stand by your beds.' What a cheek. She didn't really care though as, today, after lots of reading and research last night, she truly felt like she had a purpose again.

'Tell Sophie I've called an urgent team meeting in ten minutes,' she announced to Jeremy, without even giving him a chance to say Good Morning.'

'Good Morning to you too,' he smiled. She idly noticed that he looked smarter today, although the sleeves of his soft blue shirt were rolled up. The morning sunshine slanted through the blinds, turning his unruly hair to gold.

'Morning. There's something I must do first.' She hurried into her office and shut the door. She picked up the phone and dialled the number from the file she'd found in Callum's drawer. Having arranged a visit, she put down the phone, breathing a sigh of relief. She had to pull this off.

Jeremy and Sophie were assembled around the meeting table in the outer office, looking expectant when she bustled in with a file under her arm. Sophie had quickly brewed some filter coffee for them which smelt delicious, and had even poured out three mugs and arranged them in the centre of the table, together with a plateful of chocolate biscuits. It was good to see she was learning fast.

Shutting the outer door behind her to block out the general hubbub of corridor traffic and the metallic ping of the lifts, Verity then made herself comfortable in her seat at the top of the table. Head of her tiny empire. Goodness, she was enjoying this so much.

'Can I just say,' Jeremy said, dunking a biscuit in his coffee, 'that I think I am mentally scarred from that…that doobrywotsit yesterday.'

Well, he wasn't the only one. Verity opened her file.

'It is actually called a Stack N Go Multi Magic Multi Mailer,' Sophie told him. 'Not a doobrywotsit. You come out with some proper weird words.'

'Well, I don't know what to call it.' Jeremy ran a hand through his hair.

Verity knew what she wanted to call it but was far too polite. 'Right,' she sat up straighter. 'Let's get on with the meeting. I have an idea and I need you both to listen to me very carefully.'

They sat and listened intently as she outlined her plan. When she'd finished speaking she laid her elbows on the table and looked from one to the other. There was silence for a moment. Sophie's phone in her hand flashed but her eyes didn't move from Verity's face.

'So what do you think team?' She watched their earnest, animated faces.

'Wow,' Jeremy said, exhaling slowly, his eyes widening. 'I could never, ever have thought of that.'

'I think its proper awesome.' Sophie said. 'Greyson told me that you totally think out of the box. Now I know what he meant.'

She shrugged. 'It just seems logical to me. Now do you both understand why Greyson can't know about the finances – or rather the lack of them?' She straightened up the papers in front of her. 'Not now, not ever?'

They both nodded. 'We're with you, boss,' Jeremy said.

'It will be our secret,' she looked around the table. 'The three of us, I really think we can do this but it's not going to be easy.' She felt so excited at the challenge. 'However, I'm sure there's a gap in the market and it's up to us to grab the opportunity.'

'More coffee?' Jeremy asked, reaching for her mug.

'No thanks, not for me. I've got to get on but there's one more thing. Call it Any Other Business if you like. This is a task for you guys.' Guys? She was sounding like Greyson already.

Both heads jerked up in her direction. 'Sounds intriguing,' Jeremy said. 'What is it?'

Verity smiled at both of them. 'We need a new name for our team. A new brand.'

'Oh, right boss,' Jeremy and Sophie exchanged glances.

Verity stood up and pushed in her chair. 'Yes, I want something smart and snappy we can use on all our merchandise and on our website.' She made for the door, stopped and called over her shoulder.

'Oh, and I want it by this afternoon.'

'No pressure, then boss,' Jeremy muttered under his breath.

'Well, you call yourself a writer,' she smiled, opening the door and nearly bumping into Uncle Bobby who was hovering in the passageway.

'Sorry if I'm interrupting your meeting?' He always gave off a nervous energy even more so now since he'd been ill last year and hadn't put all of the weight he'd lost back on.

'No problem at all, we're finished now,' she said.

'I just wondered if I could borrow your magic machine to do a mailshot?' Uncle Bobby asked.

'With pleasure. Jeremy will show you how it works.'

'Must I?' he said, eyeing the machine warily which sat sentinel in the corner, mocking us. 'I've still got scars from yesterday. Machinery isn't really my forte.'

Sophie snorted with hysteria. 'I'd never have guessed. Can I just thank you for the best laugh ever at work,' she said, getting up to assist him. 'I haven't stopped giggling since yesterday.'

'Thanks a lot,' Jeremy said, but he did have a wry smile on his face. Verity liked the way he seemed to react to most situations with good humour.

Verity left the three of them to it. So now, she had her team and a plan. A feisty teenager, an exuberant Scriptwriter and a newly promoted Conference Manager. She'd certainly set herself a challenge. Just what had she let herself in for? She knew she had to make her idea work. First of all, she needed to go and see Greyson.

She caught him at a good moment. His PA wasn't around and so she knocked straight on his door and barged in. He was sitting in front of his train set, holding one of the little carriages. It helped him to think, apparently.

'Come in, come in why don't you?' he said and launched straight into one of his anecdotes which began 'Did I tell you what happened on the train yesterday?'

At least it wasn't a football story, she thought, waiting for an opening.

She sat down on the other side of the train set and waited for him to draw breath, laughing in the right moments at his tale which involved little bottles of wine and the people sitting around him who told him that he'd livened up their journey. Eventually he stopped talking and so she waded in.

'I would like to ask you a favour,' she began.

Greyson snorted. 'What is it this time? Surely you don't want another temp?'

'Oh, no thank you. I'm very happy with my team. It's about the Secret Room.'

Greyson's face changed and he sat back with a little train carriage still in his hand. 'What Secret Room? I presume you're talking about the Penthouse. How do you know about that?'

'We…I discovered it by chance,' she said, knowing that the Penthouse Floor was supposed to be out of bounds for staff and hoping he wouldn't reprimand her for that. 'What is it used for anyway? Is it for top secret meetings?'

Greyson laughed. 'Nothing so very exciting, I'm afraid. It's being trialled at the moment as a venue to hire for private organisations, just to bring us in some extra income. It's been specially designed as a brand new blueprint of an inspirational meeting room of the future.'

'I've had a really good idea and it's all for a good cause,' and before he could say anything else, she launched into her plans for the Big Event, ending with, 'So can we have your permission please to use the Secret Room?' Please, please, don't say no or my plan won't work...

Greyson replaced the carriage thoughtfully on the track. 'Well, I suppose it's for a good cause. Yes, I'll arrange it with the powers that be.'

'Great, thanks so much. You won't regret it.' Magic. She knew he made up the majority of the powers that be, so it was a done deal.

'I'm sure I won't. What would you have done if I'd said no?'

Verity rose slowly to her feet and uncurled her palm to show him the tiny key which lay there.

'Not sure, but seeing as I have the key already in my possession...'

'I presume that's the key to the Penthouse?' How did you come by that?' Greyson shook his head. 'Never mind, don't answer that. Verity Raffin. Sometimes you remind me...'he lent right back, swung all the way round on his chair, lacing his fingers behind his head. He came to an abrupt stop.

'Of me.'

On that note, Verity made her exit before he could say anything else, striding along the corridor and curling her fingers around the key once again, elated that another part of her plan had fallen into place.

****

The team reconvened later on that afternoon around the Conference Table. Sunlight poured into the room through the long office windows, casting the usual slanting patterns across the floor.

'Well?' asked Verity. 'I can't wait to hear what you've come up with.'

Jeremy's eyes twinkled. 'You're going to love this, boss.'

'I certainly hope so.'

'We made up a shortlist,' Jeremy produced a notebook open at a page where many shorthand outlines jostled for space. 'I kept mine secret for a while.'

'Do you do shorthand?' Verity queried. 'I didn't think anyone used that anymore.'

'I did a course once. Well that's a better reaction than hers,' Jeremy pointed at Sophie who was rolling her eyes. She said – 'Shorthand - what the…'

'Okay, I get the picture,' Verity clasped her hands together on top of the table.

'He could be swearing at us and we wouldn't know,' Sophie giggled.

'Right, come on then I'm waiting.' This had better be good. The way forward depended upon it.

'Well it took a while to come to an agreement,' Jeremy continued. 'We both had some ideas and we kept them secret until the last moment.'

'It was well exciting. Let me tell you what the final shortlist was,' Sophie broke in. She opened the book with a flourish.

'Drum roll.' Jeremy begin tapping his fingers on the desk.

No. 1 – The Conference Gang – Jeremy's idea

Verity's first thought was Oh no, Yuk, it made them sound like a bunch of reprobates.

No. 2 – Conferenceomatic

(Sounded like a washing machine).

No. 3 – Conference Consultants

No 4 – Conferenceable

(Hmm, not bad but imagine answering the phone 'Good Morning, Conferencable?' No maybe not)

'And the Piece de Resistance,' Jeremy took over. We both agreed on this one.'

No 5 – he paused for effect, looking at each of them in turn. Da da! -

'Conferenceque!'

'Really?' Verity said. What, was this the best they could come up with?

'Yeah, we like it,' Sophie said. 'It's awesome.'

'Short and snappy like you said, boss.' Jeremy's eyes twinkled. 'And you can say it with a flourish in your voice. Like this, Conferenceque!' he demonstrated.

'Well you might.' Sophie giggled.

'No, it will be a good talking point. Smart piece of marketing Soph. I can see it now on all our merch.'

There was a long silence and Verity kept her face straight as she looked around the table. Jeremy's smile faded a bit and Sophie was beginning to look mutinous. Jeremy looked down at his hands. She could hear the faint chirping of the birds from the open window.

She took a deep breath and smiled. 'I get it. Yes, it could work. It's different. Yes, that's it. I like it. You've done it. Well done team.' Their faces cleared and broke into smiles of relief.

They all shook hands in agreement. Jeremy raised his mug half full of cold coffee. 'To us. Conferenceque.' They all raised their mugs and clinked together.

Onwards and upwards thought Verity with hope in her heart.

Chapter Sixteen

Early the next morning the pavements were dark with rain, as she walked through the streets of the town, thinking about her idea. It had come about when she'd read an article in a file left behind in Callum's drawer, written by someone called Martyn Kingston. A professional consultant, he had just begun to provide courses to manage medication in educational settings.

In the article he was passionate about how school staff needed to be properly trained in administering medication to the growing number of hyperactive children in schools with ADHD. He promised a new training course, in accordance with current guidelines which would provide delegates with a qualification at the end of the course. If only she could persuade him to work for their team, maybe they could roll out the courses over the North East, spread awareness and also put their team on the map. And claw back some money at the same time.

If only Our Johnny had had more help at school. His teachers at the little primary school had no idea how to deal with him when he ran riot, scribbling on the other kids' drawings, making them cry and throwing stuff about the room. Back then Grandma and Auntie Bertha had no idea that Johnny could be suffering from such a condition as ADHD. They just thought he was being naughty and that he was lazy and silly which was far from the truth.

She still missed Our Johnny and she really had a vested interest in this course. If only she could help other kids in the same situation in some small way so that they didn't have to go through this alone, she would feel that she'd achieved something of real value. She felt the excitement rise in her stomach at the thought.

The next part of her idea was to organise a Big Event, a high profile conference to showcase the courses, with Martyn as the lead speaker. It would be the event of the year for school staff. And to be able to hold it in the Secret Room was an amazing coup. No overheads, no venue costs and a beautiful view. An inspirational speaker whose passion for his work would shine through. All she had to do was get Martyn on board. He had a reputation for being rather abrasive. She was to meet with him in twenty minutes time.

She soon found the street where Martyn Kingston's offices were situated. Dark heather clouds directly overhead promised further cloudbursts, although a watery sun was striving to peep through.

She caught sight of herself in a glass fronted coffee shop as she walked and thought she looked different. She was moving forward and felt tall and confident. She wore a new smart, dark trouser suit she'd bought at Callum's request after their last event, teamed with some spiky navy heels. Come on Verity, you can do this, this is your forte, she thought to herself.

She liked this part of town. She'd done her research and felt quite excited when she realised he was based in an old building where, many years ago she'd worked as an agency temp for a few weeks. She used to work on the fourth floor and the office was but a few minutes' walk from the town centre. She was an office junior and it had been her very first position, before Uncle Bobby found her a job at the Town Hall.

She remembered the bitch of a supervisor telling her that in the past this area had its roots in a much darker history, that of public execution and hanging of witches. She'd tried to unnerve her but Verity didn't scare easily. In fact she only succeeded in making the surroundings more intriguing.

Funny, looking across the street today, she noticed stuff about the building she'd never even thought about when she worked there. From the other side of the road, it was like looking at it from a totally different perspective. The old, earth coloured building dominated much of the street and she craned her neck to look upwards at the six storey building with its art deco style terracotta panels featuring stylised human figures, symbolic of power.

Her team had agreed that she was the only one who could negotiate with the best trainer in the area. Her plan was coming together. She looked at her watch. It was nearly time.

When she entered the foyer, she didn't recognise it. It was very modern with a glass fronted reception desk and there was even an escalator where the rickety lift had been.

She smiled at the immaculate receptionist who had long dark hair held back from her smooth forehead by a tight white hairband. It made her look younger than she was, Verity figured. What a good idea, the hairband did the job of a mini facelift by stretching and ironing everything out. She made a mental note to try it herself.

'Good Morning,' she said with a welcoming smile which didn't crinkle the smoothness of her cheeks. 'Can I help you?'

'Good Morning, I'm here to see Mr. Kingston.'

'What was the name?' she asked.

'Verity Raffin. On behalf of Dr Callum Doyle.'

'Aha. Found you on the system,' she said. 'Shouldn't there be two of you?

'Just me today. Amazing foyer.' She looked around.

'Do you like it?' she said, checking her screen.

'I used to work here a long time ago and it looks so very different now.'

'Did you really?' she said. 'It's a very old building which has been revamped.'

She remembered the archaic switchboard she used to manipulate, flicking the cream switches back and forth and the relentless callers. 'I remember going up to the top storey.'

'I've never been past this floor,' she said. 'How did that come about?' She looked genuinely interested.

'Well, one day, someone took me on a tour of the building and showed me the room where the telephone mechanisms were. It was a hot, dark room at the very top of this building. It was like seeing it from the inside out. There were lots of switches and mechanisms up near the roof making lots of clicking noises. When the red light flashes that meant there was an incoming call,' he'd said. I was nervous then, thinking I might get into trouble from the matriarch lady who was in charge because the calls weren't being answered.'

'Was she that bad?' she asked.

'Oh yes. I only lasted there a few weeks because she used to make me spend most of my time secreted away in a dark cupboard filing. When I wasn't filing I was plonked in front of the switchboard.'

'So what happened?'

'I told her to stick her job if I remember rightly.' Verity never did like people telling her what to do.

'Good for you,' Claire said. 'I really admire you for that.' Then her demeanour changed as an electronic bell notification sounded.

'Mr Kingston will see you now.' She jumped up. 'He'll meet you at the top of the escalator.' She briskly walked Verity to the elevator and shook her hand. 'It's been really nice talking to you.'

Verity noticed a tall, frowning man, looking down through the glass and plants. He seemed to be looking way past her. She turned to Claire but she was already scurrying back to her desk.

Martyn Kingston was waiting at the top of the stairs with an air of impatience.

Unsmiling, he barely touched her hand as he shook it, then he ushered her into an airy office with glass panelled walls on two sides.

'Sit down err, sorry what's your name again?' he glanced behind me. Up close he was tall with a fleshy round face, long haughty nose and red veins on his cheeks. He was wearing a sleek dark blue suit with a sheen to it. 'Verity isn't it? So where's Callum?'

She was a bit unprepared for the hostility in his voice. The file she'd read on him had stated that he was the most experienced person in the region, perhaps the whole country, with an exalted history. Ex-Army, Drugs Squad, Consultant, Lead Trainer.

'He's not coming,' she answered, 'I'm here in his place.'

He was still towering over the desk. He finally sat down and looked her straight in the eyes. She felt like squirming as the silence stretched on. 'Then, you've got yourself this appointment on false pretences.' He leaned back in his chair. 'I only do business with Callum not his minions.'

'I am not a minion.' She said, bristling angrily inwards. How rude was he?

'So, who *are* you exactly?'

'I'm the new Conference Manager,' she tilted her chin. 'Callum has left the company.'

'I see.' He nodded to himself. 'You've taken his job. I bet you couldn't wait to jump into his shoes. You look just the type.'

'I beg your pardon?' Why was he being so rude? Didn't he want the work?

He steepled his fingers and rested his long, bulbous nose on the top of them. The silence in the room was growing edges and elbows. She could hear the thrumming of the rain on the roof.

'Do you realise just how very important this course is?' He leaned forward in his chair to illustrate his point.

'Yes, of course I do. That's why I'm here. The way I'm thinking there's going to be a huge demand for this type of training and we need to reach out to the market now. This is a really exciting opportunity for us to be involved with.'

His eyes flashed. 'At some schools, the kids line up outside the school office waiting for an admin person to give them their ADHD medication.'

She thought of the kid at the conference throwing the sandwiches. And Our Johnny.

'An admin person?' she asked.

'From the school office. Usually an untrained administrative person. There's no-one else to do it. It's a huge responsibility. It's a necessity, otherwise the whole class would be disrupted in the afternoons.' His gun metal eyes bored into hers.

'What about the parents? Can't they come in to administer their child's medication? Or give them their tablets before school?'

'Not feasible sometimes. The parents are quite happy to leave it to the school.'

There was a bloated silence.

'So, as you can see, it's a disaster waiting to happen.' He brought the heel of his hand firmly down on the desk, shifting some papers. 'Every school needs someone to be trained.' He banged his fist on the desk as he uttered the last few words to prove his point. 'Before some child is given the wrong tablets or the wrong dosage and then it's too late.'

'So how would you feel about doing some training for Conferenceque again?' she asked. 'We were thinking about starting off with the One Day Courses?'

'Absolute waste of time,' he picked up the pile of papers and arranged them strategically again. 'It has to be the Multi Days Course which has a portfolio at the end. I absolutely wouldn't consider anything else.'

'Do you have a note of your fees?' she asked.

He slid a business card over the desk. Thank goodness, she seemed to be making headway now.

'How much?' She must have sounded incredulous. 'That's extortionate.'

He shrugged his shoulders. 'I don't come cheap. Callum didn't have a problem with my prices.'

She felt her stomach churn. Well, no, he wouldn't would he?

'Would you be willing to negotiate?'

'There's always room for a bit of negotiation,' he said. 'Except about my fees.'

She slid the business card back across the desk. 'I was going to ask if you would come along to our next conference, to be our Lead Speaker and talk about Medication in Schools. It's going to be a very high profile event with around 200 delegates. It would have been a perfect opportunity for you to showcase your courses.'

She saw his eyes flicker with interest. 'Verity,' he picked it up and stood up. He walked around his desk and moved into her personal space. It was all she could do not to shrink backwards but instead she stood up and faced him. He sighed and moved closer, and thrust the card back into her hand. 'I don't think you realise just how important this is. Look, give me a call tomorrow when you've had a chance to think about my fees. I won't negotiate any further, however.'

'In that case, I'm afraid we won't be able to do business with you.' She stood her ground. What an utter creep he was.

'Well in that case.' He whispered close to her ear. 'Goodbye. Enjoy the rest of your day.'

He strode across the floor and flung open the door, standing to one side and making shooing gestures as if he couldn't wait to be rid of her. She leapt up and strode through it, staring at him the whole time. As she passed him she went right over on her left foot in her killer orange heels. Insult was added to injury as she saw him smirk. She drew herself up and hobbled to the escalator, trying to ignore the pain.

Well that went well. She winced inwardly as she heard the door slam behind her. What an absolutely awful, atrocious man. Oh, what had she done? She'd completely failed the first simple task she'd set herself. Now she had to go back and tell the others how she'd failed to get the trainer on board. The best trainer in the region who had the monopoly and without whom her plan was doomed. She couldn't even do a simple thing like that.

Cheeks burning, she tramped through the foyer, knowing that Claire's eyes were on her. She tried to smile and gave her a quick wave.

Back at work, she caught sight of herself in the full length mirror in the Ladies Room and got a bit of a start. She looked awful. The suit was far too dark for her colouring and the jacket was too long and made her look totally washed out. How could she ever have thought she looked like she was power dressing? She had two high red spots on her cheeks which clashed with the dull orange.

There was no-one in the office thankfully, so she went straight into her room, shut the door and slumped down in the chair. She pressed her fingertips onto her burning eyelids and the world exploded blue, pulsating. How could she have fallen flat at the very first hurdle? He'd made her feel exactly like the silly little girl of her childhood, blushing and stumbling for words.

After a while she made herself a coffee and took a series of deep breaths before opening the drawer and raking through the trainer files once more. Aha. Here it was. She knew she'd heard that name before. She cleared her throat and picked up the phone, hoping it wasn't too late in the day. She was nothing but resilient. Time for Plan B. Did she have one?

Chapter Seventeen

Grandma's House December 1991

It was a few weeks before Christmas and Verity was walking home from work, hugging her coat around her and enjoying the crispness of the frozen puddles as they cracked under her new work shoes. There was snow on the tops of the fells and below them the wind was gusting across the fields where sheep were flattening themselves against the fences. A few random snowflakes floated down in the frosty air.

She couldn't wait to get home out of the cold. She knew there'd be a roaring fire in the grate and the delicious smell of baking. Verity loved Christmas time at Grandma Anna's house, especially the Christmas decorations. She'd never known anyone put up so many. As well as the strips of coloured paper streamers which she'd helped drape from all four corners of the ceiling, twisting them in the middle so they hung gracefully, Grandma Anna had suspended a mixture of brightly coloured concertina style lanterns, snowmen and bells overhead. The ceiling was almost covered which proved a problem when Grandma Anna wanted to dry her washing by stringing it up on the pulley.

She was halfway up the back lane when she heard the noise. What on earth was it? It sounded like the howls of a banshee, interspersed with loud yells. And it seemed to be coming from Grandma Anna's house.

As she grew nearer, Verity thought she could make out some words which sounded suspiciously like,

'GRANDMA, GRANDMA, COME HERE NOW!'

Oh no. She had an idea what might be going on. The wails grew louder as she approached the house and she began to hurry, sliding on the snow dusted path in her haste. She yanked open the sneck of the gate into the back yard, seeing the curtains switch next door at the house where Ellen lived.

The back door was ajar, which wasn't unusual as Grandma Anna often left it open so that her neighbour friends knew they could pop in for a gossip and a cup of tea and a homemade vanilla slice.

Verity rushed into the kitchen, feeling the warmth hit her. The kettle was singing away cheerily on the hob. 'Hi Grandma, I'm back.' The horrendous yelling seemed to have subsided.

'What's going on?' she hurried through the long kitchen into the dining room where she encountered Grandma Anna in her flowery pinny, eyes popping with temper and a pair of scissors held aloft in one hand. A couple of hair grips dangling out of the side of her mouth. Her face was bright red.

In front of Grandma Anna, sitting in a straight backed chair was her friend and neighbour Mrs Hubbard, with half a head full of purple perm rollers, obviously waiting for Grandma Anna to finish the job. An array of twink rollers, pins, combs and brushes were laid out on the dining room table which was covered with a protective foam tablecloth.

Oh my stars and garters. Did you hear that?' Grandma Anna hollered.

A series of wails erupted, then Verity heard, 'GRANDMA, GRANDMA, COME HERE NOW!'

'I heard it right down the street,' Verity said.

'Thank the Lord you're back,' Grandma put down the scissors and brandished a roller in the direction of the bathroom which was next to the dining room.

'Would you just listen to that,' she wiped her forehead. 'I can't get a blasted thing done for him. I don't know how I've managed to get Ethel's fringe cut.'

'Our Johnny?' Verity presumed. 'What on earth is wrong with him?'

'Nothing at all.' Grandma indicated her guest's head of rollers. 'Oh dear, I should be finished doing Ethel's perm by now and getting on with the tea. I'm right behind.'

Grandma Anna hated any disruption to her routine.

'He's gone off on one.' Mrs Ramsay sniffed. 'The kids of today just don't know how to behave.'

'Sorry about this Ethel,' Grandma Anna said. 'You must be getting cold sat there with a wet fringe. Don't worry I'll make us a nice cup of tea when we're done.'

Mrs Ramsay sniffed again. 'Tea? I was hoping for a nice little port and lemon.'

'It's not New Year's Eve yet you know,' Grandma Anna chastised her.

He's stopped now,' Verity said, flinging off her winter coat and unravelling her scarf. 'Don't worry, I'll go and see to him.'

'It's Auntie Bertha that should be dealing with him,' Grandma Anna put down the scissors and wiped her forehead on the edge of the faded towel around Mrs Hubbard's shoulders.

'GRANDMA, GRANDMA, COME HERE NOW!'

Grandma shook her head. 'He's flipping nine years old. My kids are grown up. I'm not going to do that when I've been through it all once. For lawd's sake, I swear I'll swing for him in a minute. I've already shut the middle door on him but it hasn't drowned him out.'

'Something will have to be done,' Mrs Hubbard said, 'because if you don't get these rollers in my hair shortly, I don't know what will happen with the perm solution…'

Grandma picked up another roller. 'Verity, can you run straight over and fetch her? Let her sort him out.'

'Who, me?' said Verity, feeling dismay rising in her chest.

'Well, I can hardly go and get her can I?' Mrs Hubbard said, gesturing to her half-finished head of perm rollers.

Verity's heart sank. Grandma Anna could be scary when she lost her temper but Auntie Bertha was in a whole new league altogether when she started. Poor Johnny would be in for it. She'd be round here with a man's slipper in hand in no time.

More shouts erupted. 'Verity!' VERITY! COME HERE NOW.'

'Oh my stars and garters,' Grandma Anna said, winding a curl of hair around the roller so tightly it made Mrs Hubbard pull a face. 'He's heard your voice Verity.'

'Verity! Is that you, our Verity? You can come and do it.' Our Johnny yelled from the bathroom.

'I told him,' Grandma Anna spat out the words. 'There's no way I'm doing it.'

'Doing what?' Verity asked on her way to the bathroom.

'He's refusing to get off the toilet.' Mrs Hubbard volunteered.

'No need to bother Auntie Bertha.' Verity said quickly over her shoulder as she began to open the bathroom door. Anyway she's probably gone to the bingo if she's left Our Johnny here.

As the door opened, the cacophony of sound spilled out.

'Verity!' yelled Johnny. 'VERITY!'

'Tell him to sort out his own backside,' Grandma Anna bellowed back.

Verity stifled a giggle as she entered the bathroom, shutting the door behind her. Perhaps it was hysteria because she certainly didn't find this situation funny. She detested seeing Grandma Anna getting upset or angry. In fact she'd hardly seen her lose her temper in the two years she'd known her. After years of living in crowded houses with lots of other siblings vying for attention, Grandma Anna's house was a haven. Nobody shouting and arguing. It was bliss to live with someone who put you before themselves. No-one had ever been as kind to her as Grandma Anna was. Sometimes she just felt like her heart would burst with happiness.

Our Johnny was still sitting on the toilet, trousers around his ankles, but having a proper temper tantrum, thrusting his legs up and down and squealing at the same time. His face was bright red and screwed up. He was still wearing his school blazer but his shirt was sticking out and his tie was strewn across the floor.

Johnny stopped shouting mid bawl, the second he saw Verity's face. 'Verity! Where've you been? Oh, thank goodness you're back home.' His face lit up and her heart went out to him, because, for all his naughtiness, she was very fond of Our Johnny. Well, most of the time anyway. Verity sat down on the side of the bath so she was on his level.

'Now, what's all this about?' she said. She always used her extra calm voice in situations like this. She put her arms around him and gave him a hug which usually managed to calm him down.

'You'll do it won't you?' He smiled, lighting up his round face, which was wet and streaked with black tear tracks of frustration. Verity immediately tore off a sheet of toilet paper and wiped his hot face, leaving black marks on the tissue.

'Ow,' he said.

'Come off it, that doesn't hurt at all,' she reprimanded him.

'That toilet paper's scratchy.'

'Rubbish. 'You're so silly getting yourself in this state,' she used the same calm but firm voice. 'Now, are you going to tell me why you are making all this fuss when you know Grandma is very busy?'

His looked mutinous. 'They were being horrible. I just got in from school and they were whispering and ignoring me,' he said. 'I thought I heard my name mentioned so I asked them what they were talking about.'

'And?' Verity asked. She knew full well what it was like to be ignored.

'That old wifey told me to shush and said I had big ears.'

'Don't be rude,' Verity said. 'She's Grandma's neighbour and friend.'

'She's an old bag,' Johnny shifted from side to side. 'Then, she said kids should be seen and not heard. So I went and sat on the toilet. So now will you do it?' he handed her the toilet roll.

'If you promise me this is the last time,' Verity shook her head. 'Why can't you do it yourself anyway?'

'I dunno,' he shook his head. 'I just want you to do it. Please?' he wheedled.

'I want you to realise how lucky you are,' Verity scolded. 'No more screaming?'

'Not today,' said our Johnny solemnly. 'I'm getting a sore throat.'

'Verity had minded young kids all her life so she didn't flinch from the task in hand.

'There all done,' she said in a brisk voice. 'Now come on, wash your hands and splash your face with cold water.' Our Johnny jumped up, pulled up his trousers and did exactly as he was told. 'It stinks in here, doesn't it?' he smiled as Verity opened the top window.

'That's nothing to be proud of. Now, you can go and apologise to poor Grandma Anna.' Verity tidied up the bathroom behind them. 'You should think yourself lucky Grandma didn't go and get your mam.'

Our Johnny ran back into the dining room, all smiles now. Grandma Anna was fastening a hair net over her friend's head of rollers. 'There you are Ethel. All done. Time for a nice cup of tea.'

'I'm sorry Grandma,' he said. 'I didn't mean it. 'Can I have something to eat?'

'You'll be getting the slipper on your backside if your mam finds out about the fuss you've made,' Grandma Anna admonished.

'Please don't tell her.' He jumped up and down on the spot. 'I'm sorry, sorry, sorry!'

Verity bore him off to the kitchen. 'I'll make him something, Grandma. You sit down. Our Johnny, you come with me and we'll have some bread and dripping before tea.'

'What about some fizzy lemonade?' he said, rummaging in the pop cupboard. 'My throat's a bit sore.'

'I'm not surprised,' Verity said. 'After all that commotion.'

'And can I have a chocolate éclair?'

'Not before your tea,' Verity chided him. Honestly, sometimes she felt like his mother.

'Please?' He lifted the bottle of pop onto the kitchen table.

'Well, maybe one of those mini ones,' Verity acquiesced.

Verity wasn't sure, but she often wondered if Our Johnny's behaviour was linked to his sugary drinks and chocolate intake. He always seemed more hyper after eating sweets.

'Have you been pinching chocolates from Grandma's stash behind the settee?' she asked him but he shook his head.

'That's good, you've picked Dandelion and Burdock pop instead.' she said, pouring him a drink.

'Thank you,' he grinned at her. 'After tea, would you like to come and look at my snots under the microscope again?'

Chapter Eighteen

A few days later, Verity came across Jeremy holding court at Watercooler No 2, a pile of Conferenceque literature under his arm. He was surrounded by two girls simpering and smiling at him, and asking him questions.

'I do love your Southern accent,' said one. 'It stands out amongst all us Geordies.'

'How interesting it must have been working for Adem's Amazing Adventures in Turkey,' said the other in a breathy voice. 'Are you still married to the girl from Café Yummy?'

'Oh goodness no,' he sighed, topping up his plastic cup with the coldest water option. 'That was all a very long time ago.' He caught sight of Verity approaching and grinned. 'Well, it's been lovely chatting to you ladies but I must go. Please excuse me.'

'Jeremy have you a moment please – I need you to collect a visitor?' she asked. If he could be bothered to tear himself away of course.

She then turned to speak to the others, 'Haven't you got any work you could be doing?' She watched the little gathering disperse.

'Of course, boss.' Jeremy threw her a dazzling smile and disappeared along the corridor to Reception.

He was back in five minutes, beaming, with Katrina Devine in tow.

'Hello, hello,' Katrina Devine floated in. She was wearing a fresh white, shift dress with a tiny scarf around her elegant white neck. Once again she made Verity feel tall and gangly.

'Good Morning,' Verity greeted her. 'How lovely to see you again.' She wasn't sure if she entirely meant it, but needs must.

'Why, hello Kat,' Jeremy said, his eyes twinkling. 'This is such a pleasure.'

'Lovely to see you Jeremy,' she said. 'Ah, I have something for you from Morag McCallum.'

'The Chair of our *The Only Way is Up* Conference?' Verity asked.

'The very same.' Kat brought out a packet from her designer handbag and made a big show of handing it over to Jeremy.

It was a box containing four flapjacks.

Jeremy laughed out loud. 'How delightful, thank you so much.' He winked at Verity.

'I hope you realise you can't eat them until you've filled in a Gifts Declaration Form, she told him, folding her arms.

'I do have another reason for being here.' Kat told Jeremy. 'Verity and I have been having some discussions and I would like to offer my services as a trainer. You see, I've had first-hand experience of ADHD and I am accredited. I've worked in schools in the South East.'

'I'm sure we can negotiate something.' Verity ushered her into her inner office and shut the door.

A little later on, Jeremy had gone to escort Kat out of the building and Sophie brought up another visitor. It was none other than Martyn Kingston, bringing with him a kind of disturbed energy into the Conference office.

Verity stood up, stunned to see him. 'Well this is a surprise. What brings you here?' she said, definitely prepared to give him a hard time. He was wearing a Visitor's Badge which was a bit crooked.

'I'm very sorry to disturb you.' He stepped closer and offered his hand and she shook it warily, catching a glimpse of a delicate aftershave. 'They let me come straight up. I'm well known here.'

'I see.'

'Yes, well, I'd very much like to discuss your offer further with you Verity.'

There was a sharp silence as Verity raised an eyebrow.

'I'll get you some coffee,' Sophie said, rolling her eyes.

More silence.

'Well, you'd better sit down then.' Verity gestured the seat in front of the spare desk, not bothering to show him into her office. She sat down slowly in the superior black leather chair behind the desk, leaned back and waited. This was going to be interesting.

'I'll get straight to the point,' Martyn said. 'I couldn't help feeling I'd been a little hard on you the other day but I was expecting Callum. Sorry, I know I'm old school. Old fashioned if you like. To be honest, you were so sure of yourself that I wasn't convinced you wanted to run the course for the right reasons. And I'd had a really bad morning but never mind about that. I know that's no excuse. Anyway, I'd thought about it and well, maybe I can help you after all.'

She was stunned. This was unexpected.

'Firstly, I'd like to apologise for my behaviour.' He ran a hand through his hair. 'You see, that's just my way.'

Really? Well it wasn't good enough. Verity wasn't sure she wanted to work with such a person. Still, she supposed, it was good of him to bother to come along and apologise.

She leaned right back in the chair. 'Apology accepted.' This turnaround of events was rather enjoyable.

'Secondly,' he went on, 'I'd like to offer my services as Leading Trainer on the Medication Management Project.' He sounded like he was presenting her with the moon.

'Thank you very much,' she said, leaning forward. 'However, I'm not sure the offer is still open.'

'What?' His smile sagged like his badge.

'You see, the thing is, I've actually engaged someone else.'

'I see, you know you won't find anyone better qualified than I, the original author of the three day course. I didn't think you'd move quite so quickly.'

'I saw no reason to wait around,' she said. 'Might I ask what made you change your mind?'

'My son.' Martyn gave a wry smile. 'You see, I've had first-hand experience. My son Damian, he's eight. He suffers from the condition. And from Autism as well.'

Sophie came back in at this point with his coffee and he stopped speaking. I introduced them and he carried on.

'I give him his medication every morning and evening. The thing is, he's a very bright child.'

Verity nodded. 'I know what you mean, my nephew suffered from the same condition.'

Martyn was in full flow now. 'Then you'll know where I'm coming from. He absolutely loves Science at school. He can talk about cells and evolution for hours. 'That's part of the condition you see. He can focus on one thing and he's really good at it.'

She felt a sharp pang, as I thought about Our Johnny and his Microscope Set from the charity shop.

Martyn waited for his words to take effect. 'However, without his medication he can't concentrate for long and would be climbing the walls by lunchtime. So, surely you can see why I'm so precious about the subject? More people need to be educated about administering the medication. I'm definitely the right person for the job.'

'Hmmm,' she looked back at him and rested her elbows on the desk.

'It causes a lot of disruption at home. A few arguments. That's why I was a bit tetchy with you that morning. And then, after speaking to Callum, I knew that working for you and your team, would be the right decision.'

She stood up, her voice sharp. 'You've spoken to Callum about this?' How dare he?

'Yes,' he nodded. 'He said he wished he'd had the idea himself. So now we can move forward quickly without any more ado?'

She was absolutely livid at the thought of him clarifying everything with Callum, of all people. Couldn't he make a decision on the strength of their first meeting? Callum had nothing to do with this. It was her project.

Before she could voice her thoughts, Jeremy and Kat joined them, Kat nodding her head so her shiny bobbed hair danced around her elfin features. 'I forgot my scarf,' she said. 'Oh, so sorry to interrupt.'

Verity made the introductions.

Martyn turned to them. 'We're just finalising my services for a brand new project. Medication courses in schools.'

Making a huge effort, Verity swallowed down the anger that threatened to bubble over. What did it matter, if the end result was the same? She had a result and certainly didn't want everyone to know that it took a discussion with her ex- lover to seal the deal so she gritted her teeth inwardly and plastered a smile on her face. Sometimes you just had to swallow your pride to get to where you wanted to be.

'Wait one minute.' Kat strolled across the room to stand in front of Martyn. 'I've already offered my services as Lead Trainer on the course and been accepted.'

Martyn shook her hand. 'The thing is, Kat, I've already been in earlier discussions with Verity.'

Soon their voices were raised and a lively debate was taking place. They stood opposite each other.

Jeremy, Verity and Sophie watched and listened. Kat's voice was loud with her rural Southern accent whilst Martyn's was very calm and measured and carried across the room.

Verity and Jeremy looked at each other. 'Well, Verity, what do you think?' Jeremy said.

She thought some negotiation was needed. Rising to her feet, she slipped in between Kat and Martyn and raised her hands upwards to separate them.

'One moment, both of you,' she said, looking from one to the other. 'We have capacity for two trainers.' She was so enthralled in this now she'd gotten over her initial displeasure regarding Callum.

Martyn and Kat continued to eyeball each other, moving away from her so they could do so.

'Why don't you both sit down for a moment?' Verity said, indicating the seats at the meeting table and reluctantly, they sat, warily glancing at each other.

Verity sat opposite them and explained, 'This course needs to be rolled out right over the region so we are definitely going to need more than one trainer. Of course, I'm going to have to look at the budget first. Martyn, if you could see it in your heart to offer us a decent discount, I am fairly sure we can work something out?'

She could see out of the corner of my eye that Jeremy was gazing across the room at her with a growing smile on his face and a look in his eyes which looked like something akin to, well admiration. He had such faith in her, goodness knows why.

Martyn made a grumbling sound then said, 'I wrote the course. I should be the Lead Trainer.'

'You can both be Lead Trainers,' Verity said. 'You can each be back up for each other. It makes sense.'

They were both starting to look mollified.

'Well, maybe this could work out,' Kat said slowly.

'Brilliant.' Martyn Kingston grabbed both of Verity's hands in his to shake them with enthusiasm this time.

'And you'll speak at the conference as well?'

'I'll get my people to talk to your people,' he released her hands at last.

'You mean you'll get Claire to ring me.'

'Ah, yes Claire. Oh, well to be honest I'm in the process of talking her into not leaving. She tried to hand her notice in the other day.'

'Did she really?' Verity said. She couldn't say she was surprised the way he treated his staff.

Then he turned to Kat and they began shaking hands as well.

'Welcome to the *Reach the Stars* Conference,' Jeremy said.

'What an inspiring title,' Kat said, beaming at him.

'Well, I don't know about anyone else but I'm starving,' Jeremy said. 'Chicken Kebabs and Chips in the canteen today if anyone is interested?'

'Thank you for the kind offer,' Martyn said. 'But I need to get back to the office. I said I'd let Claire know how this meeting went. She seems to have taken a bit of a shine to you Verity. And I must admit she's usually right.'

'You'd do best to listen to her then.' Verity showed him to the door.

Martyn raised an eyebrow and smiled. He looked as if he might voice a detrimental comment then seemed to change his mind.

'Oh, before I go, one thing. It may be a good idea for you to visit a school with me so you can see what we're up against.'

'I'll check my diary,' Verity replied.

'I'll be in touch very soon. 'I'll see myself out.' He was smiling to himself as he went through the door, nearly falling over two girls who were standing right outside.

'Well I think that sounds absolutely wonderful. I'd love to see your canteen. You can show me,' Kat swept her arm through Jeremy's and bore him off into the corridor leaving Verity and Sophie in the room.

Verity went to shut the door and noticed the gaggle of girls along at the water cooler looking on enviously as Kat glided past with Jeremy, her laughter tinkling. Then Jeremy looked back and raised an eyebrow as if to say sorry, as Kat bore him off down the corridor. Verity shrugged inwardly, why on earth would he think she was bothered?

'Aren't you just a tiny bit jealous?' Sophie said as Verity pulled out her lunchbox which was full of Slimming World quiche and green salad and placed it squarely on the desk. 'You're both quite old… I mean you're both about the same age and you seemed to be getting on quite well together?'

'Not at all,' she said. 'I'm delighted. This morning I didn't have one trainer for this course. Now I have two.' All she cared about at this moment in time was making a success of Conferenceque. Wasn't she? Well, maybe she was just a little bit envious.

She noticed the unopened packet on Jeremy's desk and pounced on it. They'd forgotten all about the flapjacks. Opening it hastily, she pushed away her salad. They should be celebrating. Two trainers on board and a reduced fee, this was a good day and another part of her plan was falling into place.

'Fancy a flapjack?' she said.

Chapter Nineteen

A few days later, Verity and Martyn Kingston visited a nearby comprehensive school to see how they administered their tablets.

'The Office Manager's a friend of my wife's,' he said. 'There's such a lot to be done. You'll soon see what I mean.'

They rang the bell at the main Reception and were let in and greeted by a harassed looking woman wearing black t-shirt and jogging bottoms.

'Morning Jan,' smiled Martyn. 'Lovely to see you, I hope you're well?'

'Oh, I'm well enough thanks, just rushed off my feet. I'm Jan, the Office Manager,' she turned to Verity.

'I'm Verity, Conference Manager,' Verity shook her hot, dry hand. 'Thank you for agreeing to talk to us.'

'I'm afraid we're in a state of chaos at the moment,' Jan went on. 'Not enough staff.'

Jan showed them into the general office where four other women, all casually dressed, were hard at work, answering phones, getting up and down to deal with queries at the hatch and typing furiously in between time.

One lady was surrounded by money, on her desk was a coin counter, aligned with rows of coins in varying sizes and in front of it, neatly arranged piles of notes.

'Petty cash,' Jan explained. 'Right, it's a bit noisy in here so first of all, I'll show you where we give out the tablets.'

Leaving the hubbub of the general office, they were shown into a dark room off the corridor to the main office which was little more than a cubby hole with a sink, a stack of plastic cups and a battered filing cabinet.

'The children line up outside here in the corridor at lunchtimes,' Jan explained. 'Then we call them in one at a time.'

'Where are the tablets stored?' Martyn asked, looking around.

'Oh, in this top drawer,' Jan indicated, opening it.

Verity saw the look of horror on Martyn's face which he quickly managed to hide. 'So you don't have a…a proper medicine cabinet which locks?'

'No, afraid not,' Jan snapped the drawer shut and indicated a list of names on the wall. 'We tick off this list when we've given the tablets out.'

'How many children do you have with ADHD?' Verity asked.

'Around fifteen at the moment,' she said. 'The numbers are growing with each new term.'

'Fifteen? That's an awful lot,' Verity said.

'And that's without the ones that have epilepsy. And one who has fainting spells. Oh, and the ones with EpiPens.'

'Really? Isn't there a school nurse to help?' Verity asked.

She could hear Martyn snorting behind her.

'No, I'm afraid not,' Jan answered. 'We don't have a school nurse on site. She only comes once in a while to check for head lice or such like.'

Verity was beginning to realise she had a lot more research to do into this field of administering medication in schools project.

'Who actually gives out the tablets?'

'Whoever's available in the office,' Jan gestured. 'We do have a rota but it's difficult. Most of the time we don't have time to have a proper break ourselves.'

Martyn asked. 'Do you do it in twos? One to hand the tablets out to the child and the other to check the records and tick the sheet?'

'Not at the moment. When its tablet time there are so many other things to be done. The reception hatch has to be manned, the phones constantly ring. Then there's library duty and story sack duty and…I could go on and on.'

'I totally understand,' Martyn patted her arm.

Jan led them deeper into the building into an untidy office, indicating they take a seat. 'We can sit down for a moment in here, this is the Bursar's Office.' She shut the door. 'I'm so sorry, I should have asked earlier if you would you like a cup of tea or something?

'Oh no, thank you, I can see how busy you are,' Verity said. 'I've brought some leaflets and flyers describing our Conference. Do you think the Head teacher will let you attend?'

'It may be made compulsory very soon by the Government', Martyn explained, 'that every school has a proper Medication Policy and at least one trained person to administer the drugs.'

'Oh,' Jan said. Her neck was growing redder by the second but she accepted the flyers. 'I'll certainly ask. Something needs to be done. We're not coping very well at the moment and I'm scared in case someone makes a mistake and gives out the wrong tablets. We can't go on like this.'

'I'm not here to judge, you know,' Martyn said kindly. 'This is happening all over the region, perhaps the country.'

'It is a bit of a nightmare at the moment,' Jan admitted.

'Do you mind if I ask how the drugs are disposed of at the end of term?' Martyn asked.

Jan went redder. 'I'm afraid I don't know, I've just taken over this role and the lady who did it has left.'

Verity thought she didn't blame her. Things were worse than she had imagined.

'Don't you worry, it's not your fault. We can help.' Martyn said. 'Some training courses will be available shortly from

Conferenceque especially for school staff, which will explain how to put a policy in place in your school.'

'So will it be up to the school staff to write the policy?' Jan asked, pulling at the skin on her neck.

'Yes, but the training course will help and I'm sure it will be much easier with a set procedure in place,' Martyn said.

Jan didn't look convinced, saying, 'Maybe, but it's all extra work isn't it?'

As they passed the hubbub of the General Office on their way out, Jan popped her head in. The phones were ringing in unison. 'Where's Angie?' she asked.

'She's had to pop out to pay the School Fund money in at the Post Office,' one of the other ladies answered, as she picked up her ringing phone. Placing her hand over the mouthpiece she added, 'Oh, and by the way the fax machine has jammed so we're getting even more phone calls than usual.'

'I'll be back in a moment, I'm just showing my guests out,' Jan ushered them out of the building and they all walked together to the car park. Verity was glad to be out in the sunshine away from the taut atmosphere of that office. She could hear the shouts of the children out on the playing fields behind the school building.

Jan was still clutching their glossy conference fliers in one hand. As Martyn shook her other hand, Verity heard him say, 'So sorry if I've been hard on you with all the questions. You seem like you're having a rough time at the moment.'

'Thanks Martyn, I do appreciate it,' Jan looked around to make sure no-one was listening, 'it's just that things are set to get worse. The Head teacher wants the school to be run as a professional business. The Bursar is being replaced by a Schools Business Manager.

Jan indicated her casual trousers and feet encased in trainers. 'She wants the office staff to wear a uniform, which she is going to pick for us. Namely being a smart suit and heels. No more trainers and track suits. The ladies aren't happy at all about that. They say they've always worn comfy gear and don't want to look pretentious. Imagine running about the building in heels. But that's another story and not what you've come for. I am worried about the medication.'

Martyn looked concerned. 'You know you can ring me anytime, Jan for a chat about the medication, or come and see me and I'll help as much as I can. I must advise that it is in your best interests to try to come to the Conference and then sign up for some training.'

'Thanks, I'll hand these out in the office and request that at least two of us attend. If we can be allowed time off together. You know I used to love working here.' Jan said, shaking Verity's hand in goodbye.

'Maybe you will again one day soon,' Martyn said, now please, remember, I meant what I said about keeping in touch.'

'See what I mean?' Martyn said to Verity as the door closed behind Jan, flyers under her arm and they drove off along the long drive. 'No locked medical cabinet for the drugs, anyone could walk in and help themselves. No back up staff to check the right drugs are being administered to the right child. It's a disaster waiting to happen.'

'It's certainly been an eye opener,' Verity agreed. 'That poor woman, I felt so sorry for her. I hope she's not heading for a breakdown.'

'This could be happening all over the North East,' Martyn said. 'Now do you see, how the proper training could really make a difference?'

Verity nodded. Martyn had impressed her today and she was glad she had him on side. Now, more than ever, she knew just what they were up against and how important this conference was going to be. Her resolve was fired, here was an area in which she, and her team, could really change things. The conference was a starting point, a trigger for bigger things and it was up to her to ensure it was a success. The pressure was mounting.

Chapter Twenty

Greyson had checked with the 'powers that be' and agreed that Verity could use the Secret Room for the Conference, although he did say she was taking a helicopter view. She didn't even bother to ask what that meant. He was delighted to be chairing the event. She knew he loved any sort of opportunity of talking to an audience and would perform his duties in such a way as to keep the whole thing moving along in a lively fashion. As long as he didn't swashbuckle about the place too much, they'd be fine.

'I hope he doesn't tell too many crap jokes,' Sophie said.

Verity was sure the delegates would all sign up for the three day course once they'd heard Martyn Kingston in action. All they had to do was get them there. They decided upon the first week in September, on the inset day which was often used for a morning's training out of school. She was convinced that if one school signed up, then the rest would follow. 'Sophie, could you get to work on designing the marketing literature?'

'Ace,' she said.

Verity had been pleased with Sophie's attitude and how animated she'd been since she joined the team. She had no time to sit and look at tattoo plans on her phone whilst she was working here.

'Jeremy.' She swung around to face him.

'Yes, boss?'

He was sat straddling his chair the wrong way around, arms resting on the back, ready to spring up into action after having received his instructions. And she had to admit he was working out well too. The three of them made a solid team.

'You can start ringing around the schools and persuade them to book onto the Big Event.'

'Right away,' he jumped up.

'Oh, Sophie.' Verity remembered, 'Don't forget you must add in the programme that lunch is included in the price.'

'I get so excited for food.' Sophie looked up. 'Especially if it's a MacDonald's or a Nandos. As long as it's not like the last event I went to. Lunch was a tiny sandwich, a yoghurt, an apple and a small bottle of water.'

'Sounds like a kid's lunchbox.' Jeremy said.

'Yeah, well, it was rubbish,' said Sophie. 'Everyone was moaning about it. Can't we just give them a Domino's pizza?'

'No, we can't,' Verity said firmly. 'I have plans for the catering, don't worry it will be fine.' She looked sideways at Jeremy. She'd tell him later about her idea to combine the use of their culinary skills.

She was thinking about using a mini picnic table for each delegate's conference lunch, laden with savoury sandwiches and quiche followed by miniature chocolate eclairs and vanilla slices which Grandma Anna had taught her to make. Delegates always appreciated a decent lunch. After all, a lot of them didn't get away from the day job very often and she wanted to ensure they enjoyed it when they did. The mini picnic table would be a novel idea.

'We can start advertising on our website soon, as well as Twitter, Facebook, LinkedIn,' she continued. 'Sophie, can you lead on social media seeing as you're always on it?'

'Defo', she said, mobile phone in hand.

There was just so much to do. Verity began to help Jeremy with ringing around the schools and was speaking to one of the teachers who had been on the Mrs Potter training course when the teacher asked, 'Will he be there?'

'Who?' Verity said at first, misunderstanding and thinking that she meant Callum.

'Lovely young chap with a man bun and cheeky smile who got us all an iced bun?' came the ready reply.

Goodness. He was definitely making an impact on the female population in the North East.

'Oh yes, Jeremy will be helping me at the Conference,' she said, rolling her eyes.

''That's settled then. I'd like to book myself a place. Oh, hold on, some more colleagues here would like to go as well. Six places please.'

Unbelievable. A forgone conclusion. It was proving remarkably easy so far to get people to sign up and they would invoice them beforehand, to ensure they turned up on the day.

Later that day the Stuff N Go Machine was being utilised to the maximum and Jeremy had now managed to master the art of putting the envelopes in the right way. The room was warm even though they had the windows open, letting in the soft summer breeze. There was a real crackle of energy in the air as they all tried to get as much done as possible. Five o'clock came and went and they just carried on working. At five thirty she sent Sophie and Jeremy home. It was Friday evening after all.

She was just about to leave herself when Uncle Bobby appeared in the doorway, tie loosened and jacket over his arm.

'Still here? Great stuff, I'm pleased I've caught you. You haven't forgotten you agreed to host the barbeque tomorrow evening?' he said. 'I thought I'd just remind you.'

'What barbeque?' she asked, closing down her computer.

'The barbeque for George's birthday?' He leaned against the door. 'We agreed to hold it at your house as you've got the biggest garden remember?'

She hadn't quite forgotten. Well, not that she'd promised to host the barbeque but that the Saturday in question was tomorrow. Unfortunately, Bobby's wife was away on business, so there would be four of them.

'No, of course I haven't forgotten. It just slipped my mind with all the work stuff that had been going on. Jeremy hasn't mentioned it either.'

'Probably too scared to talk about anything but work.'

'I'm not that bad am I?'

Uncle Bobby laughed. 'Course not. George says Jeremy's been busy preparing stuff in the evenings all this week.'

She felt a touch guilty, as she'd kept him late most nights to promote the Big Event.

'I thought it would be a good idea with them being new to the area.' Uncle Bobby ran a hand through his hair. 'George and I used to get on so well when we worked together years ago. You don't mind do you?'

'I don't have much choice do I?' she said, snapping the window shut, then felt another guilt pang. Uncle Bobby had done so much for her and here she was moaning about one small thing he'd asked her to help with.

'No, sorry, I didn't mean that at all.' She reached under the desk for her handbag. 'I'm just a bit tired. Of course I don't mind. It will be a lovely change.' If only she wasn't so exhausted, she could have done without this barbeque.

Uncle Bobby looked relieved. 'Jeremy's doing all the cooking remember and I'm going to help him. You won't have to do a thing.'

She gave a light sigh. 'Sounds good.' Marvellous. So not only did she have to work with Jeremy all day, now she had to socialise with him at the weekend as well. The strange thing was, it wasn't entirely an unappealing prospect.

Chapter Twenty One

It was Verity's idea to take Grandma Anna out from the home for the day so she could come along to the barbeque as well. They did this from time to time and she always seemed to enjoy herself. The staff always encouraged family outings, saying a change of scene was good for her. Uncle Bobby went to collect her and Verity wondered if it would be one of her good days as they arrived in the kitchen, Grandma Anna clutching an umbrella, a big handbag and a bunch of flowers which she pressed into Verity's arms.

'For me? Oh thank you so much.'

'They're from him,' and she pointed at Uncle Bobby.

Oh, how slight she was nowadays. Uncle Bobby had helped her take off her mac and as Verity hugged her, she noticed at once how sharp her shoulder blades felt beneath the soft wool of her best lilac cardigan which was buttoned up to the neck. Lilac was her favourite shade. She must have just had her silvery hair done because it felt soft to the touch and looked clean and shiny. She was also wearing her favourite necklace.

'Come on through and sit down,' Verity took her hand and led her through to the conservatory where she stood looking out onto the soft summer rain falling onto the garden until Verity sat down and she sat down too. She was quiet but smiling at them all, which was what she did on bad days. Not that they were really bad, it just meant that she didn't speak unless spoken to, whilst on good days she had really lucid moments where she would talk about the past for ages.

In one elegant move, Tom appeared, jumped up and sat next to her, his front paws on her lap, purring as she began stroking his silken head, her eyes lighting up. She loved animals, particularly Tom.

'Typical barbeque weather as predicted,' Uncle Bobby made conversation.

'What would you like to drink Grandma?' Verity asked. 'Orange Juice? Lemonade?'

'With a touch of sherry in it?' Uncle Bobby asked, heading through to the kitchen to where Verity had assembled the drinks on the island bench in the centre of the room.

Her deep set eyes flickered. 'Ooh, yes please,' she said.

'I'll put some music on for you as well,' Verity rifled through her CD rack for the Alfie Bo music Grandma Anna loved.

Then Jeremy and his father George arrived, laden down with bulging carrier bags which they dumped in the kitchen.

'Wow, you look fantastic Verity,' Jeremy appraised, appreciation gleaming in his eyes as he surveyed her, taking both of her hands in his. 'I love that outfit.'

'Thanks.' She glanced down briefly at her floaty indigo blue summer dress and flat, jewelled summer sandals. She'd left her hair hanging straight and loose, still damp from the shower. For once she did feel comfortable with her appearance. He didn't look so bad either, wearing cut off denim frayed knee length shorts and a blue cotton shirt which complimented his cornflower eyes.

'And who is this?' she asked as a bushy grey haired little bundle launched himself excitedly at her ankles. He was a gorgeous looking dog with eyes like melted chocolate and silky grey hair flopping onto his tiny face.

Jeremy released my hands. 'This is Pedro.' There was pride in his voice. 'He likes you already. I hope you don't mind dogs? We didn't want to leave him home alone.'

She wondered what Tom would make of that. 'Fine with me,' she glanced into the conservatory but Tom had made a hasty exit into the garden.

George, Jeremy's father, was tall and pale with sandy hair. 'So pleased to meet you Verity,' he said, extending his hand in greeting. 'I've heard ever so much about you.'

'Good to meet you too,' she shook his hand, thinking he didn't look anything like his son.

He pushed his glasses back onto his nose. 'I hope you don't mind me having a plain chicken breast. I don't eat anything too spicy. Nervous stomach you see.'

'I don't mind at all, she said, 'however, if it's your birthday and Jeremy's cooking all this food, isn't it a shame you won't be eating it?'

'Oh he's doing some special dishes for me.' He leaned forward and lowered his voice. 'I'm just glad to get out of the house to be honest. And Jeremy loves having people to cook for.'

She heard the skittering of paws on the wooden floor and looked to see Pedro sat down right in front of her, tail wagging and staring with those velvety eyes.

'He wants to know if he can go upstairs and lie on your bed,' Jeremy said, and as he spoke, Pedro's tail wagged even more furiously and he let out a little whine.

'Yes, I suppose so,' she agreed. Little Jenny, Uncle Bobby's dog, often did the same.

Pedro jumped up and made off up the stairs. Then at the top he stopped and sat and looked down again, wagging his tail furiously.

'He's waiting for you to go and physically lift him onto the bed,' Jeremy explained. 'He's too small to jump up on beds himself.'

Verity shook her head and dutifully followed Pedro upstairs where she picked him up carefully, and placed him onto the throw on top of her double bed. Oh, what a roly poly tummy he had. She stroked his silken head. After licking her hand gratefully, he curled up straightaway and shut his eyes.

'He's a very silent dog,' Jeremy remarked as she re-joined them downstairs.

'He's adorable,' she said. Goodness knows what Tom would make of him though.

Jeremy and Uncle Bobby cooked outside under a huge umbrella and soon everyone was sitting around the dining table with a view of the rain swept garden. Jeremy insisted on sitting on the end of the table so he'd be nearer the kitchen so Verity sat opposite Uncle Bobby and placed Grandma Anna next to her, facing George.

For starters Jeremy had made puffy bread and mezze like she'd never tasted before. 'It's a mixture of Turkish and Lebanese,' Jeremy said, bringing out olives wrapped in vine leaves.

'This is wonderful,' Verity exclaimed, dipping bread in hummus with lemon juice.

'Now this one's for Dad,' Jeremy said, bringing out a huge dish which looked a bit like quiche. 'Now this is a speciality I discovered at my mate's place, in Turkey and replicated a version for myself. It's called Georgian Pie and it takes hours and hours to make.'

'It looks very good as usual,' George said. 'This is an excellent birthday treat.'

'I had to get up at five a.m. to cook this so it would be fresh for this evening,' Jeremy's lips twitched.

'Yeah, right,' Verity moved dishes about the laden table to make room for the latest offering.

'Well, that's what they do in the Sunset View Restaurant.'

Wow. And these were just for starters. It was certainly very impressive. She'd drunk a few glasses of wine by the time they reached the main course, which had helped just to take the edge off everything. She wasn't used to entertaining, preferring to stay in her safe haven on her own and was feeling a bit apprehensive at having people in her house.

She was also a bit awe of Jeremy's culinary talents. Uncle Bobby had meant it when he'd said she wouldn't have to cook anything. To think a short time ago she'd thought he was useless.

'Aren't you having spicy food either?' George asked Grandma who ate very little nowadays. In fact whenever Verity visited her at the home, she was often to be found with a biscuit in her hand, crumbling away without her eating it and a cold cup of tea set in front of her. Today however, Jeremy had cooked them both plain chicken wraps with salad and she did seem to be eating tiny forkfuls of chicken, watching George all the time.

'I don't eat spicy food,' she said, sipping at her lemonade with a touch of sherry. She didn't appear to be having any problems drinking her drink today.

'Really?' George said, leaning closer to Grandma. 'Me neither.'

'I don't like garlic either,' she announced, which made Verity smile.

'Same here,' George said. 'Jeremy doesn't put garlic in the Georgian Pie.'

'He's off,' Jeremy winked at her and whispered, 'Dad will talk for hours about his stomach. It's always an ordeal for him eating out. He often says he'd rather just take a pill and be done with it.'

'Well, I wouldn't,' she whispered back. 'This is absolutely delicious. He doesn't know what he's missing.' She was tucking into the main course now. 'What is this?'

'Barbequed Mixed Shawarma,' he said. 'I'll show you how to make it sometime.' Grandma had taught her the basics, but this was all on another level.

'Oh sorry, George, your glass is empty,' she noticed, feeling guilty she wasn't being much of a hostess. 'Would you like a beer next?'

'No thanks, I don't drink a lot of beer either,' George said.

'His mates call him Half Pint Harry,' Jeremy said. We were sitting slightly apart from the others on the end of the table now, as Bobby had moved to the other end to join in the ailments conversation. She was feeling slightly fuzzy and mellow and surprised to find she was enjoying the evening. Of course it must be the wine.

'You certainly don't take after him,' she remarked, looking at Jeremy's full glass.

'Oh, he's not my real father,' Jeremy said. 'He's my stepfather.'

'Oh,' she was taken aback. 'Sorry I didn't know.'

'Don't worry, its fine.' Jeremy moved his chair closer, so that his thigh was pressed close to hers. 'You see, I've always thought of him as my real father. In fact I've never known anything else. I was adopted at birth and had a very happy childhood. I always thought of George and Cassie as my real mum and dad.' Jeremy paused to pour some more wine.

She felt surprised and just a tad emotional. 'I think I just assumed…'

'Don't worry, everyone does. It's been difficult for him since Mum died and that's when I came back from my travels. Then Dad retired and we decided to have a change of scene and move to the North East.' Jeremy took a gulp of his beer. 'I know you must think it strange living with your dad when you're thirty nine. I did leave home once. But my career as a writer is what you might precarious and Dad has always supported me. So you see, I'm very grateful to Bobby and yourself, for giving me a job.'

'Not at all,' she glanced over at Grandma Anna. 'I understand the importance of family.'

Grandma Anna's voice reached across the table and Verity heard her ask George, 'Everyone has a name story. What's your name again?'

'George,' he said.

'Don't you have a surname?' she said, her faded, light eyebrows raised.

Yes, it's Soderland.'

'Soderland?' Grandma Anna put her head on one side. 'That's unusual. 'Never heard of any Soderlands around here. Where do the Soderlands hail from?'

'From the Isle of Wight in Hampshire,' George answered.

'Don't know of any Soderlands,' Grandma Anna repeated, looking a bit nonplussed. 'Now Verity's dad, our Adele's husband was a Raffin. And touch of the Irish he did have in him.'

Grandma Anna turned her gaze on Jeremy. 'Such a nice looking young man. Are you a friend of hers?' She pointed at Verity.

'Yes, I hope I am,' he smiled.

'And I hope you're a better friend than that Ellen was.' Verity couldn't believe she was actually remembering Ellen now. Although Ellen used to live next door, Grandma hadn't seen her for years. 'Proper little madam that one. I used to say to our Verity, if Ellen jumped off a bridge, would you jump off as well?'

Jeremy laughed and went to sit closer to Grandma. 'Tell me more about Verity and her friends.'

Grandma played with her empty glass.

'Would you like some more of that nice lemonade Mam?' Bobby asked.

'Ooh yes please, with some more of that lovely sherry in it,' she said, then turned to Jeremy. 'Do you know what I used to say as well? If you lie down with dogs, you'll get up with fleas. True in that Ellen's case. Such a gobby lass, she was.'

Jeremy began to laugh and soon they were having an animated conversation.

'What's your name again, young man?' she said.

'I'm Jeremy,' he said, turning on his full dazzling smile.

'Ah, Jeremy. Jeremy Soderland? That's right.' Grandma nodded her silvery head. 'Did you know our Adele died when Verity was just a baby?'

Oh no, she thought, why is she coming out with this stuff now? Maybe it was the touch of nice sherry with the lemonade.

'No, I didn't know that.' Jeremy was listening intently.

Grandma Anna shook her head. 'Yes, she never really knew her because she was only six months old when our Adele died.'

'Really?' Jeremy had moved back to sit next to Verity. 'So…' He reached for her hands and held them both under his own. 'I'm so sorry to hear that Verity, I really am. Is that why you were living with Grandma Anna when we first met?'

Grandma Anna nodded and went on talking as if she wasn't there. 'Oh yes. She used to say that her life didn't really begin until she moved in with me.'

'Go on,' Jeremy said, as he began stroking her wrist gently. She pulled her hand away, feeling embarrassed and wondering what Grandma Anna was going to come out with next.

'Uncle Bobby found her when she was fifteen and working as a waitress. He took her to meet me and I showed her some photos of our Adele, her mother. At the first meeting she asked her if she could live with me. *She said to me, I won't be any trouble grandma, I promise.*' Grandma was staring off into space now, smiling and remembering.

Verity picked up the story then, taking up her wine glass to take another sip. Her throat felt dry. 'I wanted so much to live with Grandma and find out more about my mother. It was heaven after sharing beds and rooms with other people's kids all my life.'

'Where was your father in all this?' Jeremy asked.

She shrugged. 'After some other woman. And then another one. My mum was twenty when she left home and married him. Micky Raffin was the local bad boy. Grandma never knew why she ran off with him. Maybe she was on the rebound.' She replaced her glass on the edge of the table and he took hold of both her hands again, resting them on his denim covered knees which was strangely comforting.

'Rebound from what?' Jeremy looked puzzled.

She took a deep breath. 'She was engaged apparently. Her fiancé went on a day trip to London and was run over. Killed outright. She was devastated. Anyway it caused an enormous family rift. Grandma Anna and Grandad only found out she'd eloped because the village taxi driver called in and couldn't wait to tell them.'

'Phew,' Jeremy shook his head as Verity paused.

'They moved in with his family who lived in two council houses knocked together, overflowing with kids.' Then,' she paused again, looking into Jeremy's blue eyes which had misted over as he listened, 'she developed Hodgkin's disease and died in hospital when I was six months old.' She spoke quickly, trying to get the words out over and done with. Jeremy gripped my hands tighter.

'What a sad story.'

'You know, in this day and age they may have been able to save her. But she didn't stand a chance. Poor Grandma Anna spent most of her days travelling backwards and forwards to the hospital on the bus whilst my father was…she looked down. 'He was with some other woman whilst my mother was dying in hospital.'

Grandma Anna focused on the conversation again. 'Then he took the huff with me and refused me any contact with the bairn, whilst she was passed from pillar to post until she was fifteen.'

Jeremy was shaking his head, as if assimilating all this information.

'Bastard,' Grandma Anna said loudly. 'He was one of them, that's what he was. He was a …'

Verity stood up. 'Right, that's enough chat about me. 'Would anyone like another drink?' She had to try to change the mood of the conversation.

Grandma Anna raised her glass. 'Have you got any of those snowballs?' she said. 'Like we used to have at Christmas?'

She took her glass, shaking her head. 'Sorry, I haven't Grandma Anna, but what about another lemonade?'

'I'll have a touch of brandy in it this time I think,' she said, holding out her glass. 'That one was a bit weak.'

'Wow, that's quite a story,' Jeremy breathed.

'I'll get the drinks. Another beer?' Uncle Bobby handed Jeremy another can, and as he moved away for a few seconds, she immediately missed the warmth of his thigh pressed close to hers.

'Go on,' he said, returning and cracking open the can.

'I'm so sorry to spoil this evening,' Verity said. 'This is supposed to be a happy occasion, your Dad's birthday and I've said far too much.' She gulped at her wine. 'I don't normally talk about any of it.'

'No you haven't. Not at all,' Jeremy said. 'And I'm glad you did. It's good that you feel you can talk to me. It puts it all into perspective. And it's not good to bury feelings deep.'

There was a pause and then he whispered, 'By the way, did I tell you that you look beautiful tonight?'

'Yes, you did actually,' she basked in his admiring gaze, feeling a heat right down to her toes. Then she shook herself and tore her gaze away to look down the garden. A bubble of happiness rose up in my chest. Did he really mean that? The warmth in his eyes left her in little doubt.

'Come on, let's go and get some air.' Jeremy rose and grabbed her hand and abandoning their drinks, they went off into the garden, leaving the others deep in conversation and laughter.

It was a warm, muggy evening now and the kids next door were shrieking as they played on a makeshift waterslide with toy super soakers. 'Well I suppose they couldn't get much wetter,' she peeked over the fence.

A lovely sweet scent of summer flowers drifted as they strolled to the bottom of the garden where there was an old, sheltered garden seat and Jeremy pulled her down close next to him. She smelt the same aftershave she'd noticed on George earlier. She could imagine Jeremy wandering into his dad's room and picking up his bottle of aftershave to use because he'd run out of his own.

'So, Verity,' Jeremy said. 'Why aren't you married?'

'What makes you ask that?'

'I'm curious that's all. About your situation.' He stretched out his muscled, tanned legs. 'I just can't believe that you're not spoken for.'

She noticed one purple and white, black edged passionflower eyeballing them from the hedge. 'Well, why aren't you married?' she capitulated.

'Because I've been there and done that.'

'Well, same here.'

'So you have been married?'

'Yes, very briefly. It is the one area of my life I most definitely don't talk about. It was the biggest mistake I ever made.' She shivered slightly and Jeremy moved closer and put an arm along the back of the bench, his hand resting lightly on her shoulder.

'I presume you don't have any kids?'

'You presume right. How about you?'

'No, I don't have any children, although I wouldn't have minded some.' He sounded wistful.

'What's Pedro got there?' she noticed Pedro sniffing about in the hedge at something brown and orange coloured. 'Oh, look it's a tiny caterpillar.'

Jeremy laughed, calling for Pedro to leave it alone. 'Did you know that on the Isle of Wight, when I was a kid, we used to call them mallyshags?'

'No way. I've never heard that one before. You don't half come out with some strange things. In fact I think you're a bit crazy.'

He laughed again. 'Oh, I'm definitely crazy. But only about you.'

Verity moved a fraction along the bench. 'Tell me about your marriage.'

Jeremy sighed. 'I was married to Yasmin for two years. She was the girl from the Café Yummy. I met her when I was working at the Jazz Rooms in Dalyan, Turkey. It was love at first sight across the kebab counter.'

She couldn't help laughing, although the mirth was quickly followed by a sharp pang of what felt like jealousy. 'So what happened?'

'Oh, it didn't work out,' he said. 'We got divorced.' He squeezed my hand. 'Sorry, I didn't mean to upset you before with all my questions. I can totally understand now why you fell for Callum. Knowing what I now know about you, it's the whole idea of being in love that you liked. The image of him. It's safer that way for you. It was probably older man syndrome.'

'He's not that old.' She must be the only one who thought so. Who was she trying to kid? Why was she defending him anyway?

'Think about it. With your upbringing, you didn't want to be hurt again so you picked someone who was already spoken for. There you go.' He made a hand gesture with open palms. 'Reverse psychology.'

'You've got a nerve.' She wondered if it was a mistake by telling him so much about the past.

'You're far too good for him anyway.'

'Why are we talking about him?' she squirmed a little.

Jeremy shrugged his shoulders. 'I just needed to check he was definitely out of the picture before I asked you go out with me instead.'

'Now why would I want to do that?' she leaned closer, enjoying the sense of power she imagined she held over him, enjoying the flirtation and the expression in his eyes.

'We'd be good together. You've got a bit of feistiness about you and I'm a complete idiot most of the time.'

'And you talk a load of rubbish.'

'You know I've always liked you. A lot. All those years ago.' He stroked her hand where it laid on the bench and she didn't flinch. 'And I like you even more now.'

She felt shivers of electricity down her spine. Goodness, how much wine had she drank?

'Tonight, I really wanted to impress you.'

'You've certainly proved you can cook. What else can you do?'

'My other talent is writing, as you know, it's my profession most of the time. I'm passionate about it. It's an itch I just have to scratch.'

'What are you working on at the moment?' she was genuinely curious.

His eyes lit up and he moved closer again. 'I have a new play in the pipeline. That's a writer's life you see. It's a bit like being an actor.'

'Do you have an agent?'

'I do but she's gone very quiet at the moment. That's what happens. Sometimes there's no outlet for my work for months. The opportunities dry up and that's when it's hard to pay the bills. So you see, I've had to turn my hand to other things.' He gestured with his hand. 'Tour guide, holiday entertainer, typist, gardener, chef. You name it, I've tried it. But I can't stop my desire to write.' His eyes sparkled. 'It's just what I do.'

'Have you a special place to write at home?' she asked, stalling for time, wanting to savour the deliciousness of the moment, keeping him talking in case he was planning to make a move, yet secretly hoping he might.

He gazed at her thoughtfully. 'In Hampshire, I had an attic conversion with loads of space. Here in the North East, I've made an office of the back bedroom. But I can write anywhere. A lot of writers can't write 'out' but I'm not one of them. I take my tablet with me most places so I can make notes if something inspires me.'

And then without warning he threw both arms around her, pulling her close and hugging her so tightly against his denim clad chest that her ribs almost hurt. She could feel his heart beating as the clean smell of him enveloped her.

'Thank you for letting me cook here in your fabulous kitchen and for the use of your barbeque.' He whispered in her ear. 'George is having a lovely time.'

'And you?' she whispered, trying to disentangle herself but not too much and laughing. 'Are you having a lovely time?'

'Oh I'm having a wonderful time,' he said. 'Aren't you?' He held on to her tightly and for a moment, strong arms wrapped around her, she just wanted to stay like that. How could this be that she wasn't adverse to him, like she should be? The next thing she knew they were locked in a passionate embrace and she didn't pull away. She could taste beer on his lips. Soft rain began to fall around them but all she could feel was the heat of his chest pressed close to hers. It felt like their bones were fusing together. In the background, she was vaguely aware of the riffling breeze in the apple tree. He pulled her even closer as the kiss became more passionate.

'So can I take you out tomorrow night for dinner?' he asked, as the kiss finally ended.

She sighed and sat back against the bench, pushing back a strand of hair. What was she thinking about, getting carried away like this? This wasn't part of the plan.

'Look, I thought I told you I needed some time.'

'I've waited ages.' Jeremy spread his hands. 'Well, at least a week.'

She laughed and lifted up her hot face to the sky, feeling the coolness of the intermittent raindrops.

'Glad I can make you laugh. Sorry, I know patience isn't one of my virtues,' Jeremy continued.

'I'd never have guessed,' and they laughed together.

'Sorry, sarcasm isn't one of my virtues either.' They laughed again.

'We should go inside out of the rain.' Verity knew she liked him a lot. There was no doubt about it but she was still raw after Callum.

'I'm still waiting for an answer.'

'Look, I'm sorry but you're just going to have to ask me again after the Big Event.'

'What?' Jeremy sat back. 'I couldn't possibly wait that long.'

'If I'm worth waiting for then you can wait for a bit longer.'

'You are, you really are but the Big Event is ages away.'

He looked so crestfallen she wondered if she was being a bit harsh. 'I just can't focus on anything else at the moment but this event, I'm sorry.'

'Could we at least see each other just to go for a walk or something? Away from work?'

She was just about to answer with, 'Maybe,' when a horrendous noise ripped through the air. Yapping. So frenzied it was almost anguished howling.

'Pedro?' Jeremy jumped up and Uncle Bobby came out into the garden to see what was going on. Closely followed by Grandma Anna carrying her cardigan over one arm and a glass in the other, exclaiming, 'Oh my stars and garters!'

'What the…?' Jeremy said.

'Tom,' Verity realized. 'Oh no, Tom this is not a good time.' He was strolling gracefully along the top of the back fence, looking down upon Pedro with disdain, his tail held high. Pedro continued to bark furiously.

'Such a silent dog,' she said. 'My neighbours will be complaining at the noise.'

The animals eventually placated, they moved back inside out of the rain and settled around the table again. She avoided his eyes but there was no doubt about it, something had shifted inside and her heart felt lighter. Why hadn't she pushed him away? Because she hadn't wanted to. It had been so enjoyable to feel solid arms around her. It had been such a long time since…she shook herself mentally.

She felt her cheeks burn and lowered her head slightly. Had anyone seen? Did she care? What was she thinking? Had she really forgiven him for breaking her heart all those years ago? Well, they were both very different people then.

'Oh, I nearly forgot about dessert,' Jeremy said, getting up.

'I don't think I could eat anything else.' Verity tried to calm the thoughts crowding into her brain.

'It's very light, don't worry,' and he disappeared back into the kitchen.

'Here we are - Baklava.' He said, setting out a large tray on the table. 'Help yourselves.'

'What's this?' Grandma Anna asked.

'Filo pastry with chopped nuts and sugar and stuck together with syrup and honey.' Jeremy said. 'A little goes a long way. It's lovely with a tiny cup of strong coffee.'

'I don't know,' George looked dubious. 'Just a little bit maybe?'

'Have you got any vanilla ice-cream?' Grandma Anna asked. 'Do you like ice-cream George?'

George said he did and the two of them carried on with their lively conversation. She'd never known Grandma Anna have so much to say for such a long time. George was certainly bringing out the best in her. She didn't think he was just being kind either; he looked as if he was really enjoying her company.

She was glad of an excuse to escape into the far end of the kitchen and open the fridge, grateful of the coolness on her burning cheeks. Her heart was still fluttering and her head was spinning a little. She'd never felt like this with Callum.

Pedro skittered back in and sat and looked up at her with those beseeching eyes.

'He wants you to…' Jeremy said.

'Yes, I know. Pick him up.' She picked up Pedro and was glad of his solid warmth on her lap, even if he did smell of wet dog. Jeremy reached over to stroke Pedro's ears, only Pedro moved slightly and he stroked her arm instead. She felt shivers down her back again at his touch. They both laughed. Pedro licked his hand and then settled into her lap. It was a good job that Tom had skulked off along the street or else there may have been another showdown.

She remembered another summer barbeque, many years ago. How strange that she should be sitting opposite the very person who had broken her heart at seventeen. And feeling not too different from the way she had then. Maybe it was time to take him at face value and forget the past? They looked shyly across at each other, eyes locked in understanding and she saw the smile slowly forming on his face. Soon they were both beaming at each other as if they'd won the lottery together. She felt happier than she had felt in ever such a long while.

Chapter Twenty Two

Later that evening when everyone had left, Verity started thinking about the first time she went to see her mother's grave. Maybe it was the emotional throwback of Grandma Anna talking about her that brought back such memories?

Every second Sunday Grandma would cut some of the best roses from her square front garden, wrap them up carefully and place them in a shopping bag with some other items. At first she didn't want Verity to come in case she got upset but she was determined to go.

Verity remembered standing on a thin strip of road with beautifully manicured hedges to left and right, with wood pigeons cooing in the background. Directly in front was a gatehouse with rounded windows which stretched across the road, forming a triangular shaped archway to walk under. Two turrets with spires and weathercocks reaching for the blueness above, loomed on either side, whilst a black and white clock nestled directly in the triangle overhead. Through the gap was a tall fountain, which filled her view. Then the road stretched on behind as if going on for ever and ever.

'Aw, look at the rabbits Grandma,' she said, pointing to two fat bunnies frolicking in a patch of dappled sunshine on the emerald lawn.

Grandma Anna tutted. 'Pesky things, they nibble the flowers I leave on the grave. Now, help me with this water, please, would you Verity?' She produced a flask from her big shopping bag which she handed over to be filled with water from an outdoor tap at a little gate house. Verity carried it as they walked.

Presently Grandma Anna stopped and Verity watched as she carefully placed items from her bag on the grass. 'Put the water down for now,' she instructed, as she carefully laid out secateurs, a trowel, the flowers and a pair of scissors next to each other.

Then she went down on her knees and Verity watched as Grandma Anna expertly snipped and dug out a few stray dandelions, bits of grass and weeds, then began deftly arranging the different coloured roses in the vase, placing it at end of the slightly raised mound that was Our Adele's grave. Her daughter and Verity's mother. She was good at this. It looked very neat, and tidy, although bare. Verity felt a bit awkward, this was obviously a ritual and she didn't want to intrude by helping. She hunkered down beside her. Something was bothering her.

'Why hasn't she got a headstone?' she implored. 'Or a plaque? Or anything with…with her name on it?'

Grandma Anna sighed and there was a long pause before she spoke. 'Well, our Adele was estranged from the family when she got married. Then when she died, the plot belonged to her husband Micky, your father and he couldn't afford a headstone.'

Verity's legs ached so she sat back on her heels. 'Then why didn't you buy her one?'

Grandma turned her head away to the side, so her face couldn't be seen.

'He…he wouldn't let me. Not that I could have afforded it either but even so… he owned the plot you see. He was her next of kin. Not me, her mother and her flesh and blood family.'

Verity was stunned into silence. This was way beyond her understanding. She was learning stuff here about her own father which flung her into bewilderment and shame. He wouldn't let Grandma Anna buy a headstone for her own daughter's grave. His wife. Her own father… Silent tears sprung from her hot eyeballs and raced down her cheeks. What sort of person would do that? She dashed them away, not wanting Grandma Anna to see.

It just seemed the worst thing ever in the world to her at this moment, in this beautifully manicured graveyard with its rows and rows of black shiny monolithic headstones and gold lettering, that her own mother's grave was merely a raised mound of earth with nothing to mark her existence. No headstone. Plenty of flowers though, Grandma Anna was doing the best she could. But it wasn't enough. It didn't seem right. She felt ashamed of him.

At that moment, she never wanted to go back to that graveyard again.

Chapter Twenty Three

Verity didn't quite know how it happened as she couldn't remember inviting them, but Jeremy and George dropped by the following Friday evening with Pedro and a bottle of wine.

'We thought maybe we can go for a walk along the river bank?' Jeremy asked. 'It's such a lovely warm night.' She wondered if he knew Bobby usually called in on a Friday evening anyway.

Soon we were all walking along the quayside path with Pedro trotting patiently alongside. Jeremy had promised him a proper run around her garden later. There was a relaxed Friday evening sort of thrill in the air with several people out walking their dogs, joggers enjoying a leisurely run whilst others heading for the Staiths Café for a well-deserved drink.

'What's the story behind the Staiths?' George asked Bobby, as they walked alongside the stunning backdrop of the partly blue painted structure which loomed up on protected mud flats and bird habitat. Like an old fashioned roller coaster, Verity could just imagine the chutes filled with coal trundling up the incline. Across the mud banks and river, tall flats and the spire of a church rose way above the greenery, reaching for the blue sky and white, swathing clouds.

'Bobby said. 'Have you heard the saying, 'Bringing coals to Newcastle?'

'Yes, I have,' George said, 'but I wasn't sure what it meant.'

'Well, this is where it originates from,' Bobby said. And he was off, explaining the history behind the Staiths. Then they began talking about their hobbies and Bobby was explaining to him that when he was off work ill he had taken up wood carving in his shed. Making owls, animals, and a cat for Verity. He loved it and George said he was interested in wood carving as well.

Back home, she said, 'I'll make a pot of tea for us all.' They were all congregated on stools around her kitchen island whilst Pedro skittered about, making for the back door and sitting looking hopefully back at them.

She jumped off her stool and opened the door for Pedro, letting in the late evening breeze and a waft of scented flowers.

'You're a strange mixture V,' Jeremy said looking at her admiringly. 'I'll open the wine I brought as well shall I?'

'How am I strange because I'm making tea?' she said, filling up the kettle and switching it on.

'So in tune with modern life and yet so old fashioned in some ways,' Jeremy continued, jumping off his stool to open the wine and search for glasses.

Bobby smiled. 'Ah, well that's because she's spent a lot of her life with old tea wives,' he said, but with a glint in his eyes.

Jeremy raised an eyebrow.

'He means,' Verity indicated to Jeremy the cupboard where the wine glasses were kept as he seemed to have forgotten, 'that when I first moved in with Grandma Anna, I did spend a lot of time with her and her sister Auntie Dora, going on bus trips to Hexham and Morpeth and drinking tea and eating cakes in quaint old teashops.'

'Nothing wrong with that,' Jeremy said, setting out the four glasses and a bottle of *ruby* red wine on the bench.

'I remember once when we were all in a teashop in Seahouses,' Uncle Bobby said, 'when that young lad came over and asked Verity if she wanted to sit with him. "Poor thing he said, being a teenager and having to go out with your Grandma for the day." '

Verity squashed down the annoyance of Uncle Bobby talking about her so much. She did remember that day though, and thinking that she didn't see it like that at all. How happy she'd felt just to be with people who genuinely wanted her to be there. She knew that this affinity to be happy to spend time with one's family members and appreciate their company didn't usually kick in until many years later for most people but then her childhood hadn't exactly been the norm. Her Grandma Anna often said Verity had an old soul.

'You see,' she explained, 'I was so grateful to her for taking me in that if she asked me to go out for the day with them, I went. Until I got a job of course and made friends with the girl next door.'

Jeremy's eyes darkened at the mention of Ellen but he continued, 'A lot of people call me old fashioned because I like cooking.'

George and Bobby wandered off outside to have a look at the flowers and Jeremy opened the wine he'd brought and put the opened bottle down on the bench.

Jeremy said. 'You know, you're right when you say that sometimes you'd never even guess that Grandma Anna has dementia. I bet she was a driving force at one time. How long ago was she diagnosed?'

Verity shook her head. 'It was about a year and a half ago now. It was so sad the way that it happened. I knew something was wrong at Christmas time when she got all flustered making the dinner. She kept taking the Yorkshire Puddings out of the oven over and over again and of course they sunk and then she got upset.' She hesitated and sighed. 'She'd never ever had sunken Yorkshire Puddings before. She was devastated.'

'Go on,' Jeremy said, taking a sip of wine.

'Then she became more and more agitated when the men were late back from the club down the bank after their pre-Christmas Dinner drink.' Verity ran her finger around the rim of her mug. 'She seemed confused and…and a bit panicky as she mashed the potatoes, adding far too much salt and putting their place settings away, when they hadn't even had their dinner.'

Jeremy squeezed her hand across the table.

'In the end I had to take over, which was unheard of in Grandma's kitchen.' She swallowed another mouthful of hot tea. 'Then one day soon after that I came to visit her as arranged and found the back door wide open and Grandma Anna nowhere to be seen. A neighbour in the back street told me she'd seen her walking very fast down to the town of Fell Ridge. I got straight back into my car and found her striding down the country lane at a brisk pace whilst carrying a large shopping bag. She just smiled when she saw me and climbed straight into the car.'

'I was just taking some stuff down to my mother's house,' she explained, indicating the contents of her bag.

Verity continued, 'I had a look and in it there were two dinner plates, two knives and forks, slices of cooked ham wrapped up in kitchen roll and a slab of butter.'

'Oh dear,' Jeremy said, squeezing her hand again.

'It was all downhill after that. We arranged for carers to visit every morning and night but often the same would happen and Grandma Anna wouldn't be in. We had yellow Post It notes stuck up everywhere saying - DON'T GO OUT, WAIT FOR BOBBY - but it was a waste of time. She was always a determined woman and strong physically as well. She could walk for miles carrying heavy shopping. In the end it just wasn't safe for her to live on her own.'

'I can understand that,' Jeremy nodded. 'You did the right thing for her.'

She gave a little shiver. 'Let's change the subject. I think I'll have a little glass of wine now.' Jeremy was quick to pick up the bottle of wine and pour the rosy liquid into her glass. She watched as it tumbled, focusing on the tinkling sound.

'Can I ask you something?' he said, his eyes soft.

'You've never bothered to ask me if you can speak before,' she said, taking a sip and savouring the taste. 'Oh that's really nice.'

He squirmed a little on his stool and then took a breath. 'Why didn't you ever reply?'

'Reply to what?' she asked.

'My letter.' He looked down at his hands. 'You can't tell me you don't remember.'

'I can because I don't remember.'

'I sent you a long letter declaring my undying love.' Jeremy shifted about on the stool then looked into her eyes.

'I never received any letter.'

'I gave it to Ellen at the last minute to give to you and she promised she would. I didn't have your address. She promised me.'

'Why didn't you give it to me yourself?' she reached for her mug of tea again and took a drink.

'I wanted to but Ellen said you didn't want to speak to me. She said you would never be interested in a good looking nowt like me.'

'She said what?' she picked up her wine glass so she had wine in one hand and tea in the other. 'She had no right. I can…could speak for myself.'

'I often wondered if she'd given it to you.' Jeremy shook his head slightly, shaggy curls bouncing.

'Well she didn't.' She walked into the conservatory and sat down on the comfy sofa pretending to look out at the dogs in the garden as she set her mug of tea and glass of wine on the coasters in front of her.

'Huh. Some friend she was.' Jeremy continued, following behind me.

'She was my best friend.' Verity cradled her mug of steaming tea.

'She was so jealous of you V.' Jeremy bounced into the seat next to her, draping his arm along the backrest.

'Rubbish. Not true. It was the other way around.'

It was always you I fancied.'

'You broke my seventeen year old heart.' She buried her nose in her mug.

'You broke mine.'

'Yeah, right.' She sat up straighter and her voice rose. 'Look, we've been through all of this already.'

'Are you two going to argue all night?' Bobby said, laughing as he and George prepared to leave. We're off now,' and before she knew it Jeremy and herself were left alone. He filled up their glasses with the last of the wine.

'Do you know what I think?' His lips twitched.

'That they're trying to set us up?'

'No, not that, well maybe.' Jeremy placed his glass on the coffee table and turned to me. 'I think that you've been hiding behind your affair with a married man so you don't have to face up to the fact that you've fallen for me.'

'Sorry, Jeremy, I can't joke about it yet.'

'Who's joking?' his eyes twinkled. 'Seriously, I think because of your past, you're scared of having a proper relationship.'

The audacity of the man. She shook her head.

'Isn't it time that you learned to let go?' he said as Pedro wandered back in and sat by her side. She shrugged and drained my wine. There was a sharp silence.

'I love food and cooking.' Jeremy said, getting up. 'Do you mind if I have a look in your cupboards?'

'I'd never have noticed,' she answered, watching him go back into the kitchen. He did eat an awful lot and she had noted he had the beginnings of a little paunch, just showing over the top of his jeans. Hardly surprising, the amount of scran he ate.

Jeremy opened the fridge.

'My Grandma Anna taught me traditional cookery,' she joined him back in the kitchen and perched on a stool, 'she used to make her own bread. She looked after me so well - roast beef on a Sunday, mince and dumplings on a Monday and my favourite – corned beef and potato pie on Fridays.'

'Sounds amazing,' Jeremy said.

'It was. I think I was the happiest I've ever been living with Grandma Anna. I can still taste the bacon sandwiches she used to make me for supper, made with her own bread buns.'

He bounded round the kitchen, prompting her to ask, 'Why are you peering in my freezer?'

'Looking for chicken. Aha, here we are. I guessed you'd have some.' He fished out a pack of frozen chicken pieces. How do you fancy a Shish Chicken Wrap? You start defrosting the chicken, I'll be back in a second.'

Out he went to the car and returned with a carrier bag full of goodies including fresh red and green chillies, a jar of garlic sauce, various jars of spices and some Lebanese bread. Then he produced an enormous bottle of sparkling water out of the bag which, he placed on the table. 'Seeing as I'm driving. Got any ice?' She looked at his broad back as he rummaged in her freezer.

'Unless,' he turned around, 'you let me stay the night? On your sofa of course? Pedro can sleep on the rug in your bedroom and keep you company.'

Pedro gave a little bark.

'No. Definitely not.'

'Oh well, worth a try,' his blue eyes twinkled.

'Well, you certainly came prepared.' She feasted her eyes on all the goodies he'd brought.

'Sorry for being presumptuous.' His eyes widened.

'Anyway, haven't you had any tea?'

'Oh yes, ages ago. This is supper. I'm a man who enjoys his scran.'

'I'd never have guessed.' She began preparing the chicken for the microwave, thinking to herself, how weird is this, so soon after being dumped by Callum, here she was now cooking for another man, or rather cooking with another man, (incidentally she remembered she'd always done the cooking whilst Callum sat and watched or read the newspaper). And she was enjoying herself. All the while Pedro sat in the middle of the floor watching the proceedings, tail battering the floor.

'I know you like puffy bread because we had it at the barbeque,' Jeremy said.

She watched him expertly chop onions and peppers, prepare a quick marinade for the chicken, and then rummage in the bag for tomatoes. 'Got any lettuce?'

She produced some iceberg lettuce and began to wash in it the island sink. Then she began to follow him around, picking up utensils once he'd put them down and washing them up in the island sink as she went.

'Why are you tidying up after me?' Jeremy looked up from chopping the chicken into cubes. 'Do it later. I always do.'

'No way', she replaced the utensils on the draining board.

'It's just like being at work,' Jeremy began throwing onions into the bubbling fat. 'You're always tidying your desk up but I like mine like a tip. I can still find everything easily enough.'

'I can't stand having my space in a mess.'

'Part of the fun of cooking is having the whole place upside down,' Jeremy said, grinning and tossing the lettuce with vigour and stirring the pan with his other hand. 'It's my way of unwinding and clearing my mind before I get stuck into some writing. And I can talk at the same time as make a mess. Ask me any question?'

She had been wondering about his past but what I did say was, 'What makes you think I want to know anything about you?'

He pretended to look hurt. 'You must want to know something. Go on.'

'Okay - why are you so down on your luck that you need a job working for me?'

'Very direct V.' Jeremy chopped some green chillies and added them to the mix. 'The truth is and I may have told you this already. Being a professional writer is a bit like being an actor and being in between jobs. I'm busy writing a series of plays which my agent is looking at marketing at the moment.'

'I see.'

'I worry about you V,' he opened a jar of jalapenos. 'I'm sure you don't always eat properly.'

'I do eat properly,' she indicated her stacked kitchen cupboards. 'I love cooking too.' She set two places on the island table and vigorously splashed more sparkling water over ice into their glasses.

'Well then, next week you can cook me a traditional meal,' Jeremy said. 'I tell you what I really fancy – Shepherd's Pie with Dauphinoise potatoes?'

'Tea and supper in one? With homemade apple pie and custard for sweet?'

'Sounds fantastic.' He reached over and kissed her cheek. 'You're on. Can't wait.' As if it had all been her idea in the first place?

'Good night,' he gathered up his carrier bag and Pedro and off they went.

This set the pattern for the next few weeks.

She knew he liked her, but had the feeling he was holding back. But then she had told him to wait until after the *Big Event*. When she heard him on his mobile arranging to meet someone, she began to wonder if he did like her after all or maybe he just liked having a walking companion for Pedro? She was surprised at the stab of jealously which pierced her heart. And someone to cook and enjoy eating food with? Or maybe she only liked the idea of someone being interested in her? Uncle Bobby always said she thought too much. Why couldn't she just enjoy things as they were for now? Because, surprisingly enough, she was enjoying things. A lot.

On reflection, she knew that Jeremy, since she'd met him again, had done everything to try to help and please her. Is he really the bad person she thought he was for all these years? Surely he had been nothing but kind and helpful?

'For such a professional person, Verity and for all the professional façade you present to the world,' she spoke out loud, 'and at your age, why are you so naïve when it comes to men?'

Chapter Twenty Three

It was the last week of August, late afternoon and conference preparations were in full swing. The conference was now constantly referred to by the team as the *Big Event* and it was all they thought about. Delegate bookings were still coming in thick and fast and the phone rang constantly.

Verity noticed Jeremy had taken a few calls from his agent and he said he'd been working until very late on a project most evenings. It wasn't affecting his work though and she had to admit he was proving to be a grafter. The team were having a well-earned tea break when Jeremy nipped outside to take a call on his mobile.

He was beaming. "Do you mind if I get away early tonight please boss?'

'Well, yes, I suppose so if you need to.'

He was hovering. 'Go on, ask me why.'

'Why?' Sophie obliged, as she stacked shiny conference programmes high on her desk.

'I've got to go to a rehearsal tonight,' Jeremy answered. 'A script in hand performance.'

'What does that mean?' Sophie asked.

'It's a read through of my play. Last one before opening night.'

'Yes, you go. There's nothing much else we can do today,' Verity told him. She had to admit he had worked extra hard lately. All three of them had.

'Would you both like to come along on Friday night to see the proper performance?' Jeremy looked over the piles of delegate packs on his desk. 'Oh come on please, we all need a break and it is on at the weekend?'

'I don't know, we've got a week and a few days to go before the *Big Event*,' Verity said.

'George and Bobby will be there too. Oh and I think George is hoping to bring Grandma Anna along?' He ran a hand through his unruly curls. 'Oh go on please. I need as much support as I can get. I'm sure you'd enjoy it. Please?'

'Mmm, maybe.' She was hesitant but excited by his enthusiasm.

Jeremy stood up. 'I can't wait, I'm taking the play on tour, performing in some of the local bars in the area.'

'Where's the venue on Saturday?' she asked.

'Congburn Cricket Club.' He was practically hopping from foot to foot. 'Have a guess what the play's about?'

'I have no idea.'

'Cricket?' asked Sophie.

'Of course. Cricket.' Verity paused. 'What do you know about cricket?'

'What do I know about cricket?' Jeremy said with a flourish. He began to mimic a bowling action, his hair flopping. 'I used to play for the First Team in Alton. Wicket keeper no less. Part of my childhood and growing up. So it seemed natural to draw on my happy memories to write a comedy about it which has now been commissioned by a company who have a project on the go called *Beer and Bites*.'

'That sounds interesting.' Verity sipped from her mug. Was there anything he couldn't turn his hand to?

'So you'll come? What about you Soph?' Jeremy asked.

'Ooh, defo, yes if there's food.' Sophie said. 'I get so excited for food.'

'Yes, the concept is you watch the play as you drink the venue's beer and tapas. Or whatever nibbles which they provide.'

Jeremy leapt to one side to catch an imaginary ball. 'The play itself is quite short, only thirty minutes in length and it's performed twice on each evening so that more people can come in and eat and drink and then move on.'

'Like second sittings in a restaurant.' Verity thought it sounded like a good concept.

'Exactly.' He leapt to the other side, his fringe flopping over his eyes. 'More money for the venue. And the brewery. And me. I'm so happy I've won the contract. It's good money as well.'

'So you may have to move on?' she asked, surprised at how her heart plummeted at the thought. Office life would be so boring without him, now she'd kind of got used to him being around.

'Don't sound so hopeful. I'm sure you'd miss me loads.' He brushed his hair away from his forehead impatiently. 'I don't know, it all depends on whether it takes off or not. There is talk of a tour further afield next year.'

He jumped in the air to mimic taking a catch. 'Howzat!'

'So you'll come then?' as he sat down again heavily on his chair. 'Please?' he whipped out his phone. 'I'll book you the best seats in the house. I'll text Chezza and Jacko now.'

'Who are they?' Sophie wanted to know.

'Landlord and landlady,' he began texting. 'Translated as Cheryl and Jack.'

'Make it tickets for the second performance of the night,' Verity insisted, 'so you've had time to get it right.'

'Glad you've got such faith in me,' Jeremy said, grinning.

Sophie looked and sounded sulky. 'A play about cricket? I hope it's not too rubbish.'

'As if?' Jeremy said. 'Two tickets it is then.' He leapt in the air to catch another imaginary ball.

'Yes!' she heard him whisper as he came back down to earth.

Chapter Twenty Four

'This must be the place,' Verity clung onto the seat as Sophie drove them along the bumpy drive to the carpark, navigating several ruts and potholes on the way. Congburn Cricket Club said the sign on the arched doorway of the clubhouse with its red dormer windows and russet coloured roof.

'It looks like we've parked behind the cricket pavilion.' Sophie got out first. She'd offered to drive this Friday evening as she'd not long since passed her driving test and was happy to show off her new skills.

'You look stunning,' Verity told her, looking at the younger girl who was all dressed up in a short sleeveless black dress and skyscraper stiletto heels complete with a little silver clutch bag and false eyelashes.

'My false tan's still developing,' Sophie said, surveying her bare legs. 'Ooh, look, there's still a match going on.'

Verity looked around her and drank in the scene. They were in the middle of a quintessentially English country cricket ground, with white figures on the pitch in front of them, all set against a backdrop of greenery and layered hills. It was a fine summer's evening with just a tang of rain in the air, intensifying the intoxicating smell of freshly cut grass. Sheep baa-ed in the distance and pigeons cooed overhead.

'Howzat,' came the cry from in front of them, followed by clapping and a few shouts of 'Well done lads.'

'Looks like the cricketers are just coming off,' Sophie said excitedly. 'Hey, this evening might not be as bad as I thought. They look pretty fit.'

'Come on,' Verity hurried her on. 'We're here to see the show.'

''Ouch!' Sophie tripped over a stone and grabbed onto Verity for support as she inspected her right shoe, hopping to keep her balance.

'Hey, watch out,' Verity steadied her.

'Wait a minute, I've got an idea,' Sophie announced, opening her car boot and producing a flat pair of Uggs from a carrier bag. 'I don't want to wreck my fake Jimmy Choos, so I'm going to walk along in these.'

Verity waited patiently as she pulled on her Uggs and put the revered designer heels in the carrier bag. Honestly, that was the kind of thing Grandma Anna would have done but Sophie wasn't your typical teenager in many ways.

On entering the clubhouse, Verity found herself in a narrow hallway with painted brick walls which had huge noticeboards and posters plastered everywhere, one of which was an advertisement for tonight's play. She perused this while Sophie went into the ladies loos to change back into her cripplingly high shoes.

NOT QUITE CRICKET

Performed by

'Beer and Bites Theatre Company'

Writer - Jeremy Soderland was the wording underneath and there was a tiny photograph of Jeremy underneath, all gelled blonde hair and big smile. Verity felt as if her heart was turning over. She longed to see him again. It must be all of a few hours since she'd last seen him, she chided herself inwardly.

Through the first door, they were immediately engulfed in a wave of heat and cricketers still in their whites, amid loud chattering voices. For a moment they were the centre of attention as all eyes swivelled in their direction. Sophie struck a pose and smoothed her hair, flaunting her curvy tanned legs. She was obviously enjoying herself already.

Verity hoped that her own outfit of her favourite dreamy ocean coloured silky dress with matching greenish gold earrings would see her through. She had felt so comfortable in it at home.

She looked anxiously around the sea of people standing at the bar or watching the huge television screen or crowding around the one armed bandit. This couldn't be the right place.

She spotted another door marked *Hall*. 'Come on Sophie, we're in here.'

The first thing she noticed was the sea of grey and silver heads. Sophie was going to absolutely freak out. She was by far the youngest in the room and Verity wasn't far behind her. Some of them looked like they'd been bussed in from the nearest old folks home. 'What? You've got to be joking me.' Sophie hissed in her ear.

Where was he? Verity felt a delicious thrill of anticipation as she stood on the edge. Voices filled her head as she scanned another crowded room. What was up with her? She couldn't help the feeling of expectation which kept rising, as if she was on the brink of something very important. This was daft. Why was she was looking forward to seeing him again when she'd been working alongside him only a few hours ago?

Then there he was, at the far end of the crowded room, talking animatedly and waving one arm about with a pint glass in the other. His face broke into a broad smile and he bounded over and enfolded her in a bear hug which made her heart beat faster.

His fresh, clean, woody aftershave caught at her throat. He looked incredibly smart in a pair of dark blue jeans and casual white jacket, with a blue shirt underneath which mirrored the blueness of his eyes. 'You came,' he beamed. 'I've been looking out for you.'

He pumped Sophie's hand. 'You both look amazing, Verity that colour really suits you. Come on, come and see. I made sure Chezza kept you a good table. George, Bobby and Grandma Anna are already here.'

The room was long and narrow with faded blue velveteen seating along the walls and lined with tables parallel all the way down, leaving a long space in the middle. Although there was a tiny raised area at the far end of the room, it looked as if Jeremy's play would be performed right there in the centre.

'Looks like a good turn out,' he remarked. 'If rather a more mature age group, dare I say it? Apparently the Old Soldiers meet in the hall on Saturday nights with their wives and they all forgot that there was a do on this week. So they've just joined in. And the same has happened with the bell ringers. Still, the more the merrier, hey.'

He led them to the top table nearest the door, his arm under her elbow and they sat down with cool air streaming in from the windows behind which looked onto the pitch. Soon Verity felt warm air rising up from under the seats.

'This was good material once,' Grandma Anna remarked, running her hand along the seats.

Sophie did the same but pulled a face as she encountered a rip in the fabric. She fanned herself theatrically with a beer mat, a perpetual look of dismay on her face as she looked around at the audience. 'It smells like old beer mats in here,' she grimaced.

'Can't do anything about the heating I'm afraid,' Jeremy whispered. 'It's stuck on a winter setting but I secretly think Chezza keeps it like that to make the punters drink more.'

Verity soon felt her cheeks growing hotter and hotter, aware of Jeremy's gaze. Sophie looked marginally more comfortable in her sleeveless dress. She was certainly subject to some admiring glances from several old fellas as she swept off to the bar to help Jeremy carry the drinks.

'Well, this is rather exciting,' Verity settled herself deeper into the comfy velvet, and picked up one of the leaflets strewn about on the table. 'What time does the play begin?'

'Now, I hope,' Sophie grumbled as she re-joined them.

Jeremy checked his watch. 'Not quite yet, sorry, after the bingo.'

'Bingo?' Sophie said, her face lightening up. 'My nana used to take me to bingo every week. I'm class at it.'

'Then once everyone's settled with their pies and peas the show will begin.' Jeremy said.

'How delicious dear, pies and peas,' Grandma Anna sipped at her sherry.

'Chezza's famous for her pies and mushy peas,' Jeremy said. 'I must leave you now because the cast are getting ready in the billiard room over there and I need to check on them. Although I'm only the humble writer and I tend to get in the way, I like to know what's going on. See you later.'

'It's all right for you. You're sorted.' Sophie whinged, in the interminable age before anything happened. 'Apart from us and the cast, I think you have to have silver hair to be allowed in this room.'

'Shh, don't talk sh… rubbish.' Verity sipped at her cooling drink.

'I'm not,' said Sophie. 'He's not bad looking for someone older than my dad I suppose. I think you'd make a proper class couple. By the way, do you like my eyelashes?' and opening her eyes wide.

'They're beautiful,' Verity said, admiring the length.

Then there was a bit of a kerfuffle when a silver fox lost his mobile and thought it was in the pocket of his jacket which was lost somewhere on the overburdened coat stand near the doorway.

'He began burrowing deeper as the coat stand began to groan and creak. A few people began shuffling round the coat stand, trying to help, and snippets of conversations rang out:

It's like walking round a lighthouse.'

'We might meet in the middle.'

'Is this it?'

Then someone shouted, 'It's here Dad. Down the back of the seat.'

A hush in the room indicated that something was about to start. Chezza was ready with the bingo balls. She raised her voice, 'If everyone at the back of the room has quite finished dancing around the maypole you might like to know that I am about to announce the raffle numbers.'

A few wolf whistles abounded from the floor, then Chezza then began barking out raffle numbers and Grandma Anna won. Off she trotted down the long room on Bobby's arm to claim her prize amidst claps and cheers from the audience. She re-appeared with a huge bottle of golden sherry, beaming all over her face.

Sophie scrumpled up her raffle tickets in disgust, throwing them on the table, but brightened up visibly again as this time, the tall dark haired guy in full cricket regalia appeared from the billiard room, followed by a second guy, equally tall and hunky. He was pulling on a green cricket cap over his fair locks as he took his place.

A quick game of bingo followed then Chezza announced then that the food was ready so everyone had to go and queue up through another doorway which led to a tiny kitchen. Verity picked up a paper plate with an ample, round delicious looking pie on it and when she reached the front of the queue Chezza ladled mushy peas onto her plate, before she was directed to help herself to gravy from a huge urn. Sophie asked if she had any brown sauce and was handed a squirty bottle.

'This is lovely,' Grandma Anna said, whilst Sophie squeezed brown sauce onto her pie.

'Not quite what I imagined,' Sophie looked under her eyelashes at the dark haired guy in cricket gear chatting to Jeremy.

Verity couldn't stop watching Jeremy, he seemed totally at home, maybe even a little bit pleased with himself. Was it false bravado? She looked up from her pie and peas and he caught her eye across the room as he turned around. He winked and smiled that heart-breaking smile and she smiled back and felt her cheeks grow even warmer.

'Who's that?' Sophie asked, watching as Jeremy began explaining something to him, then illustrating his point by bowling an imaginary ball. 'The room just got hotter.'

'Certainly did', Verity muttered, fanning herself with a beer mat as the hot air rose and rose. 'Must be one of the actors.' The room was certainly filling up still further. She didn't quite know what to expect. Was Jeremy a good writer? She didn't know. Should she be nervous for him? There was definitely was a buzz in the air and she had that feeling again, it refused to go away. She felt excited and happy all at once, she couldn't remember having felt like this since she was a teenager.

Someone dimmed the lights and she saw Jeremy fade into the background as the cast of two took their places, the first guy tapping an imaginary bat on the wooden floor and the other one pretending to polish the make believe cricket ball on his trousers. A cheer went up as they assumed these starting positions at separate ends of the 'wicket', also known as the bar. Verity's palms felt damp.

'Ladies and Gentlemen,' Chezza, now the compere, began to screech into a microphone. 'The moment we've all been waiting for. (She began reading from a sheet of paper). *Beer and Bites,* a renowned and exciting contemporary theatre company are pleased to present for you, for the second time this evening at Congburn Cricket Club - a rev – a reva- a revo - a revolutionary new play, to watch as you eat, a play without props. A play which is on the cusp (on the what?) of success. Let's hear it for the cast of – Not Quite Cricket!'

Cheers and roars went off. Some people banged the tables and stamped on the floor. Verity held onto her plate of pie and peas firmly as the tables bounced. There were obviously a lot of followers and support for the company and cast in the room.

Verity had read the programme quickly and the idea was, that a play was written for performance in a bar or a pub or a club, whilst the audience consumed 'bites'. In this case, 'the bites' were fairly hefty.

The idea was to keep everything as minimalistic as possible with the least number of actors possible in the cast and no props. However, as this was a cricket club, the two 'cricketers/actors' were asked if they wanted to dress up in proper cricket whites and to keep the Committee and Chezza happy, they'd agreed. Apparently that was what Jeremy was talking to the dark guy about earlier on.

The mood in the room was jovial but she was sure if the play was rubbish they wouldn't hesitate to complain and heckle. Older people could be very hard to please.

Verity was soon enthralled. After the first laugh of the evening, the audience just seemed to relax and chortle at everything. The dialogue was natural and skilful and Jeremy had created a story whereby the club had been burgled and the robbers had stolen all the beer and were holding the stash to ransom. It was funny as well, as were the comments muttered from the audience.

'Imagine, a club without any beer,' someone whispered.

'What would we do?' came the reply.

The action was played out by the two cricketers hitting the ball and running the length of the wicket (namely the length of the bar) and relating the story through their dialogue with each other. They did have a rest when it was 'tea-time' and a glamorous tea lady trotted out with an imaginary tea trolley, tea urn, china cups, and sandwiches which brought the house down. She flirted and fluttered her eyelashes at the two lads much to Sophie's disgust, and related a bit more gossip which drove the story forward.

It was revealed that the Cricket Club Steward had not been paid so he'd got his own back by staging a burglary and pinching all the beer under the very noses of the Committee. Only, the audience had been misled into thinking that this was the case but it was revealed at the very end with a twist to the story that it was actually one of the young cricketers who had masterminded the event because he was broke.

There was a brief pause in the action, halting the proceedings when Chezza's voice reverberated out from the kitchen:

'There are a couple of spare pies if anyone wants more?'

Verity couldn't have eaten any more but Sophie was off like a shot, returning with another plate bursting with succulent meat pie, standard Cricket Club gravy and mushy peas dotted with brown sauce. It could have been that she had to pass the hunky actors on the way to the kitchen and did it seem a possibility that the dark haired one's gaze as she went past, was one of admiration.

In fact, Verity had struggled to clear her first plateful. It so was hot and she kept peeping over to where Jeremy was standing in the shadows, apart from the rest of the crowd, watching everything anxiously. For some reason, she remembered that lovely kiss at the barbeque and shivered a little with anticipation. Maybe it was the wine but she just wanted nothing more than to go over there and give him a hug. Oh, just get a grip and watch the play, Verity.

The action resumed just as Jack reached his century of 100 runs by hitting a six but he had hit the ball so far that it hit the church roof next door and broke a window.

'It's a six! The lad's hit a six!' the audience hissed and they began to stand up and clap.

'This is as good as a proper match,' someone else on the next table commented.   'Better because they're actually winning,' muttered another voice and chuckles abounded.

The vicar then appeared – the tea lady doubling up in the role with a piece of cardboard around her neck – to rage at the cricketers for smashing the church windows.

No way, it couldn't be over already. The banging on tables and stamping on the floor resumed with greater force as the cast took their bows amid a standing ovation. The audience absolutely loved it, as did Verity. She'd thoroughly enjoyed every second and her hands were sore with clapping. She realised then at that very moment that there was more to Jeremy than met the eye. He was actually a very talented playwright and she was seeing him through very different eyes tonight. What the hell was he doing working for her? She saw him heading in her direction and butterflies danced in her stomach. Goodness Verity, how old are you?

'You have so got to get me an introduction to that Jack,' Sophie hissed. 'Go on, please.'

She ignored Sophie, all she could see were Jeremy's sparkling eyes and his smile and when he reached her, he put his arms around her and they hugged the life out of each other.

'Well done,' she whispered against his cheek, feeling the heat of his body through the thin blue shirt he wore, the jacket hadn't lasted long. The hug went on for so long that she forgot all about Sophie whom she later discovered had stomped off and took matters into her own hands by introducing herself to Jack, who was following in Jeremy's wake on the way to the bar perhaps or to introduce himself to her, Verity wasn't sure.

When she disentangled herself, she felt her hair was sticking to her forehead. She could feel the sweat trickling slowly from her armpits. She noticed Grandma Anna shooting approving looks at them so, she pulled Jeremy over in her direction. Jeremy shook her hand.

'Well done dear,' Grandma Anna patted his hand. 'I enjoyed that.'

'I was so itching to perform in it but they wouldn't let me,' Jeremy's voice was wistful and his eyes were misty.

'Why didn't you take part?' Verity wanted to know. He would have been great as Jack, in fact, he wouldn't have had to act very hard.

'It doesn't work that way, the writer can't write and perform, he needs to stand back and be in a separate place, not part of it.' Jeremy explained. 'Or so my producer tells me.'

Then Sophie reappeared, rattling her car keys. 'I'm off, you coming?' she asked. But Jeremy was saying, 'I'll see Verity gets home.' He then turned to her. 'You look hot. Shall we get out of here?'

The hubbub in the room seemed to quieten for a moment and all she could hear was the blood singing in her ears. She was both nervous and excited at once. It was as if everything was falling beautifully into place.

'But what about all of this?' she gestured at the throng of people crowding around the cast, talking excitedly. 'Your entourage. How can you just leave?'

He took her hand. 'I'm only the writer, no-one's bothered about me.' It was like there were only the two of them in the room. 'No-one will miss me.' His eyes flickered around the room and then locked onto hers. No-one's eyes should be that blue. 'Can we go to yours?'

She held his smouldering gaze and knew she couldn't hesitate for one second longer. So much longing was swelling inside. She took a deep breath.

'I'll just get my bag.' she turned away to hide her delirious confusion. What was she doing, what was she thinking? Holding onto her hand, he led the way through the crowds of people in the hall and soon they were standing on the cricket pitch under the stars.

Chapter Twenty Five

At least Verity knew she didn't have to worry about her place being untidy because it never was. She felt butterflies swooping in her stomach, nervous but excited too. She glanced at him as he drove and badly wanted to place her hand on his denim clad knee but didn't want to appear forward. They drove in silence but he kept stealing little glances at hr and grinning that wide grin as if he couldn't quite believe his luck. Well, to be truthful, she couldn't believe hers either.

She fished in her bag for my key and opened the door with shaking fingers. Jeremy nearly fell over Tom who appeared, eyes gleaming blue in the dark.

They stumbled into the kitchen and she felt Jeremy's strong arms around her, and without speaking, led the way to her vintage country bedroom. She couldn't trust herself to speak, her voice wouldn't have worked and she didn't want to squeak a reply. What if he thought she was being too pushy? The curtains were open, bringing in the starlit sky and a cooling breeze.

Then she turned to face him and for one moment time seemed to stop as they gazed at each other. Somehow, her seaweed floaty outfit just fell away.

It felt like their bones might fuse together and their bodies would always be as one.

She didn't think they'd slept at all that night, but they must have done because she woke up and found that they were lying on top of the bed, bodies still entwined. The curtains were open onto the fairy lit garden and starlit sky. She felt very content as the sweet smell of summer wafted in on the night time breeze. As she cuddled into his broad chest, her nostrils full of the wonderful manly that was just Jeremy, she could hear contented purring and looked up to see Tom lying on the bedside rug, fast asleep. She felt wide awake.

Jeremy leaned on one elbow on his pillow. 'I knew after you'd worked with me for a while you'd realise.'

'Realise what?' she rubbed the sleep out of her eyes.

'That I'm the only one for you.'

'But I absolutely can't stand you most of the time.' She smiled and turned her head so that they were looking straight at each other.

'You don't mean that,' he stroked the side of her face. 'I absolutely adore you. You know that. You must know it.'

'Do I?' her heart felt like it was bursting.

'I always have. Ever since we first met all those years ago at Chawton, I knew you were the one for me.'

'You can't expect me to believe that.' He had been her first love all those years ago and she'd never forgotten him, yet surely he couldn't feel the same? Could she really be that lucky? No, something was bound to go wrong.

'No-one else ever came close.' It was a long time before they finally drifted off to sleep, arms still around each other.

Chapter Twenty Six

Verity's first thought on waking the next morning was how happy she was. Then she realised Jeremy wasn't next to her, the duvet had been thrown back at his side and noises told he was moving about in the kitchen below. As she sleepily watched the first prisms of sunlight begin their daily creep across the ceiling, a mug of tea miraculously appeared on her bedside table and he jumped back into bed next to her. How deliciously relaxed and warm and cosy she felt inside.

'Good Morning,' he leaned over to kiss her slowly and hand her a plate. 'I've warmed up some croissants as well. I don't care about the crumbs if you don't.'

'I don't care either,' she took a bite and tasted a burst of apricot and honey. 'Scrumptious. I wonder if Sophie got together with that actor.'

'Shame that actor's gay.' Jeremy chuckled.

'Oh no, poor Sophie.' Verity picked up her mug, feeling the steam curling voluptuously onto her face. He could make a decent morning brew as well.

'I wouldn't feel too sorry for her. I gave Jacko, the chef, her phone number'.

'Jacko? But what about Chezza?'

Jeremy gave her a quirky grin. 'What about her? They're brother and sister. Younger brother. Now that Chezza – service with a scowl.'

'I wouldn't like to argue with her.' Verity finished off her croissant, propped up her pillow and leaned back contentedly, mug cradled in her hands.

Jeremy brushed crumbs onto the floor. 'Jacko was going to ring her. He said he had some spare pies with him which were going to waste.'

'What a chat up line,' she giggled and snuggled closer to him. 'Funny how things turn out.'

Jeremy stayed all weekend and all too soon it was Monday morning.

'Should we bunk off work?' he said, wearily trying to open his eyes. They'd been awake until very late. Jeremy seemed to think they had to make up for lost time.

'No! No, we can't,' she scrabbled on her bedside table for her phone to check the time.

'Why not? You're the boss.'

'Oh no, it's nine thirty. There's too much to do. Come on, I'm the boss and I say up you get.'

'So, is this it then?' he said as he lay and watched her get ready.

'Is this what?' she replied, frantically pulling her hair back off her face.

'We are officially together?' Jeremy ran his hands through his untidy curls. 'We can tell George? And other people?'

'Maybe,' she said over her shoulder as she picked up her handbag, 'but if you want a lift you'd better hurry up.' What did it matter who knew now? It felt like the time was right.

'Only if I can come back tonight?' he sat up with the pillow behind his head. 'I promise I'll cook.'

She picked up her pillow which had fallen on the floor and threw it at him.

Sophie was dying to regale her tale of the night before when we arrived at work. She eyed them with wide eyed suspicion when they walked in together much later, but Verity didn't care. She was way too happy and the watercoolers were already buzzing. Let them buzz. How wonderful it was not to have to hide and pretend anymore like when she was with Callum.

'You'll never guess what happened last night?' Sophie said. 'Should I tell you? Or maybe you've both got something to tell me?'

Was it that obvious? 'No, you go ahead,' Verity sat down at the conference table. 'Then we really must all get on with some work.'

'Well,' Sophie began, 'You'll never believe it. I changed my shoes again to walk along to the car but when I opened my carrier bag at home, there was only one shoe inside.'

'No? Only one fake Jimmy Choo?' said Jeremy. 'You're joking.'

'No, I'm not, but then I got a phone call. From Jacko at the Club.' Sophie looked round at them both slowly. 'I have no idea where he got my number but I didn't care. Guess what he said?'

'Let me think - is that Cinderella?' Jeremy said.

'Words to that effect,' Sophie said. 'First of all, he said, how on earth did you manage to get home with only one shoe? Then, he said he had a present for me.'

'Your missing shoe?'

'Yes. As well as putting aside two meat pies and a carton of mushy peas. So I'm seeing him tonight.' Sophie rose from where she was perched on the edge of Verity's desk.

'Ah, romance is not dead then,' Jeremy said as he made off to make coffee in the kitchen.

Then, after Jeremy had left the room, she was back again. 'So, what was he like then? I bet he was class even though he's so old? Sorry, sorry. Way, too much information. Forget I said that. OMG, I feel like I'm talking to my mam.' And she flounced off on the pretext of fetching some water from the most popular water cooler.

She rocked straight back in to tell Verity something else. 'Oh, by the way, Jeremy left his posh white jacket on *that* coat stand.

Chapter Twenty Seven

A few weeks passed by and the *Big Event* loomed closer. Verity couldn't believe how good life was and how blissfully happy she felt. She had a wonderful sensual relationship with Jeremy and they discovered they also enjoyed each other's company, wanting to spend every spare moment together. They tried very hard to be professional at work, although when Uncle Bobby popped in she knew he found it hard not to smile knowingly. She kept looking over at Jeremy when he wasn't watching, thinking how lucky she was.

They spent most evenings together. At weekends, they stayed awake for hours at night just talking, sitting up in bed and watching the stars and the clouds move across the night sky. Or she would look at work stuff, whilst he wrote his plays on his laptop which was set up next to hers on the kitchen island. He was oblivious to anything that went on around him whilst he was writing, and she was surprised at how he switched off into his own world. She could hoover around him or have the television on full blast and he was so absorbed, it didn't bother him.

He was the sunniest natured person ever first thing in the mornings, whereas she was often grumpy and liked to be left alone and take her time to get ready. He could be ready and buzzing to start the day in ten minutes. His flippancy which had so annoyed her in the beginning, she now realised now was a cover up when he was nervous about something.

Sometimes they went for long walks past the Staiths and along the banks of the River Tyne with Pedro. She wanted time to stand still and to feel like this for ever.

He loved to cook and experiment with recipes, taking over the whole kitchen and she was quite happy to let him. His presence was very apparent with jars of homemade hot sauce fermenting on the benches, whilst freshly picked red chillies from the thriving plants standing sentinel on the window sill, provided a pop of colour. Although he was very untidy and she was just the opposite, she discovered she could put up with it as long as he didn't mind her tidying up around him. It helped that he was an excellent cook and it made a refreshing change from her cooking for Callum all the time.

They were both avid music lovers and discovered they had differing tastes, although we were both willing to listen to the other's favourites and spent many evenings curled up on the sofa, watching concerts on YouTube. He leaned more towards Pink Floyd and The Stone Roses, whilst she loved the Eagles. They both enjoyed a bit of country rock such as The Shires. He liked to listen to electronic pop through his headphones as well because he could hop about to it whilst cooking and ambient chill-out tunes when he was writing, kept him in his seat.

The fact that Tom liked him was a good sign. Her Persian pet had taken an instant dislike to Callum and the feeling had been mutual, Callum often referring to Tom as *that haughty animal.* Tom would either ignore Callum or stay away altogether whilst he was there, re-appearing as soon as the sleek black car had disappeared down the drive.

Jeremy always made a fuss of Tom and she remembered Grandma Anna always said if a man was kind to animals he had to have a good heart.

'You don't have to cook all the time you know,' Verity said, early one warm and breezy evening, when she was sitting in front of her laptop, checking the programme for the *Big Event.*

'I don't mind at all. I love it.' Jeremy began to water the plants whilst Tom strolled in and curled up near him on one of the kitchen stools, raising his head as Jeremy approached, to be stroked. Soon he was purring loudly.

Jeremy rubbed behind Tom's ears. 'I really enjoy cooking for you V, you know that.' Was this man too good to be true?

'Yes, but it looks so lovely and sunny out there,' she closed the document and shut the laptop lid. 'Let's walk into town and have a meal at the *Garden of Herbs*. It'll give us both a break.'

Jeremy surveyed the biggest plant for any signs of aphids. 'You've hardly stopped lately. Don't we have to book?'

'No, it's a walk in off the street kind of place.' She jumped off her stool, reached for her handbag and touched up her lip gloss. 'They make the most gorgeous pizzas they call artisan and they've got their own organic herb garden.'

So, they strolled hand in hand along the river bank in the lazy sunshine, passing the blue monolith of the Staiths, a cool September breeze floating off the river. They talked about his writing as they walked, a subject which fascinated Verity who had always been an avid reader.

'What did you study at University?' she asked.

'I did Drama and Economics.' Jeremy admired a piece of multi-coloured graffiti on the wall. 'Afterwards, I tried acting for a while, mainly in stage plays but I soon discovered my heart lay behind the scenes.'

'What made you take that route?' she asked, curious, as it was obvious to her he would have made a fine actor.

'My stepmother, Cassie, wrote and produced plays for amateur dramatic societies and she helped me an awful lot with the craft of writing.' Jeremy slowed down to look at two birds fighting on the mud banks. 'George and Cassie weren't my biological parents, but I certainly had a wonderful upbringing.'

'So you were an only child?' How she used to long for her own space when she was growing up sharing bedrooms with several other noisy and messy kids.

'They couldn't have any children of their own, so they adopted me. Then they fostered short term from time to time.' Jeremy's squeezed my hand. 'I was never lonely. I used to make them all perform in my little plays I scribbled down in my school exercise books.'

By now they had reached the High Level Bridge and were on the narrow pedestrian walkway. Cast iron arches stretched out above and in front of them, whilst trains rumbled overhead and traffic passed by on ground level.

'What are all these?' he asked as they approached a metal grate on the right hand side, between the footpath and the river below. 'What are they for?'

'They're love locks,' Verity informed him, laughing at his delighted expression.

'Love locks?' he exclaimed with delight as she showed him the little padlocks, some brightly coloured, red, purple, yellow, some plain, but each with its own inscription.

'It's a new romantic craze,' she explained. 'They all hold a message of devotion, then the couple throw the key into the river.'

There were dozens of them, heavily clustered, obscuring the view of bright blue sky through the gaps in the metal squares. They lingered for ages reading the messages and looking at the other bridges of the city through the grid. Down below Verity could see the sweeping red and white curve of the Swing Bridge which the

High Level towered over, and the higher, majestic blue arc of the Tyne Bridge.

'Wow, these are fantastic,' Jeremy whipped out his phone to take photos. He was snapping selfies of them both as well, the sun glinting off the silver snail like building that was the Sage, crisscrossed behind the little squares of the grid. Kittiwakes shrieked all around.

'Think of all the love stories behind each one,' he was clearly fascinated. 'Look at this one. *We Got Us. And this one – We Made It.* And this one – *You are forever my serendipity moment.* I absolutely love this idea.'

Maybe this would crop up in one his plays someday. 'It's very popular in Paris,' she remarked. 'I read once that in some cities like Paris, bridges have buckled under the weight of them all. I like to think of Newcastle being the Paris of the North.'

'We'll have to come back with our own padlock,' Jeremy said excitedly. 'What could we have on the inscription?' He twirled around to look at the view of the Staiths from the other side of the bridge. Then he came bounding back. 'Got it – Jeremy loves Verity forever.'

'You're such an old romantic,' she laughed as he grabbed her and took another selfie before pressing her gently against the gridlocked wall of padlocks, for a lingering kiss. This was a wonderfully magic moment. She knew she'd never felt so happy before in her entire life before and just wanted to stay like that for ever, safe in his arms, way up high above the swirling river. So oblivious until she realised they were blocking the walkway.

They resumed the walk along the bridge, arms wrapped around each other.

'Good job one of us is,' he said. 'Look, I've been thinking. I'll get right to the point.' He grabbed both of my hands. 'Why don't I move in to yours?'

'You practically have already. All your stuff is in my kitchen.' Goodness he meant it. Had she sounded too dismissive? Oh my god. This gorgeous, hunky, kind and thoughtful man wanted to move in with her. Was this really happening at last? Her heart began to pound and her head swam and it was nothing to do with the height of the bridge or the dizzying vista below.

He hugged her and swung her round. 'I could go and get more of my stuff right now,' he said hopefully.

She pulled apart and sighed. 'Seriously, would you mind very much if we waited until after the *Big Event*?' Now, why on earth had she said that when it wasn't what she wanted at all? What she wanted more than anything was for them to be together. It seemed like the years of conditioning herself and preparing herself for disappointments which always happened, had come straight to the fore. 'Sorry, sorry I know that's…'

'The wrong answer.' She saw his face crumple and it was his turn to sigh. 'Yes, yes of course, if that's what you want. I know how important it is to you.'

'It is so very important and I need to be able to concentrate on it'. Well it was true, she'd worked very hard to turn things around. She felt like everything was rushing in on her, like the river breeze and brilliant though it was, she liked to be in control at all times.

He continued to look so crestfallen she felt terrible for spoiling the moment.

'It's just that we've been so very lucky to find each other again and I don't want to lose you again.' He reached for her hand again and they linked the ends of their fingers together, bodies not touching.

She felt choked up and unable to speak for a moment, then she said, 'that's not going to happen.'

He peered at her sideways, his blue eyes mischievous and gave her another of his quirky grins. 'Still, you're not saying no, though are you?' he perked up again, linking her arm through his and beginning to walk faster as the wind was now whipping up.

They'd reached a good vantage point now on the bridge where there was a panoramic view of all the bridges below, unhindered by a metal grate and Jeremy took another photograph whilst the breeze grew stronger and birds screeched around them.

'I will ask you again after the *Big Event*,' he said, 'and I'll keep asking until I get the right answer.'

Oh yes please do. And please let her the strength and confidence to say yes. You see, she was wary of her happiness and in spite of all his assurances of the way he felt about her, she was subconsciously waiting for the big fall.

Chapter Twenty Eight

The day of the *Big Event* finally dawned and it was a beautiful, golden morning in mid-September. All the lawns which wrapped around the old building looked lush and green. Verity passed a tiny robin perched on the Reception sign, trilling his heart out, and receiving calls in reply from other birds across the carpark. She was filled with a mixture of trepidation and excitement, she'd worked so hard to make today a success.

She hadn't realised that the Secret Room also had a lift and staircase at the other side of the building so the delegates didn't have to traipse all the way along the walkway. The lift and walkway were flooded with attendees, all dressed up for the occasion, looking forward to a rare half day off. Snippets of different conversations filtered through -

'Do you think, there'll be a decent lunch?'

'Hopefully. It's so good to have a change from a normal school inset day.'

'This is exciting isn't it, right on the top floor?'

Lively background music, rang out as they entered, signed in and were handed their name badges. She noticed of couple of them pretending to dance along, the music was obviously giving them itchy feet.

The team carried out their usual Meet and Greet, signposting people to where they need to be - 'Coffee and tea to the right, loos to the left and here's your Conference Pack. Do please have a seat,' and so forth.

Then everyone was gathered together in the Secret Room. Greyson had had the train set removed and they had laid out 100 plus chairs, horseshoe style on the gleaming floor, with a podium and low level stage rigged up with promotional banners at either side, so that a good view could be had of the speakers. The room looked perfect, even with the blinds all closed. There was an expectant hum of conversation as everyone chatted. The noise dipped as the Chair took to the microphone and Jeremy darkened the lights. Verity felt her stomach swoop with excitement. This was it. There was no going back now, if something hadn't been done it was too late…

The Chair of course was Greyson, who had been delighted to be asked, totally oblivious of the team's need to raise funds. If only he didn't totally ruin the event by talking too much and guffawing as he told silly jokes. He had been warned not to go on too much. Give him his due, he gave a brief, professional introduction as well as the necessary housekeeping information and she thought he might have been about to launch into one of his funny monologues when he announced,

'Ladies and gentleman, I believe I'm being advised that my time is up and I know who the real boss is here,' he turned his head as Verity gave the cut sign from the side of the podium. Those who knew him looked at her on the side-lines and chuckled.

She breathed a sigh of relief as the Chair then declared the event open and introduced the Main Speaker, Martyn Kingston who launched into the most inspirational speech about the need to administer medication for ADHD properly in schools. His talk was also shown on two huge conference screens to the right and left of the podium, so everyone in the room could see. The room was crammed full. She'd heard he was good but had never actually seen him address an audience before. He was better than good. He was passionate and had the audience gripped and listening to every word, nodding to each other here and there.

'He would have made a class actor,' Sophie leaned over and whispered in her ear.

Sophie and Verity were ready at the end of the speech, poised at each end of the windows. They were dressed in their conference uniform which was a smart navy trouser suit, set off with a pink and lemon silky blouse and scarf, replicating the website colours. Jeremy was wearing a dark blue suit with a tie and pocket handkerchief in the same hues, his blond curls tamed to smooth waves. The chairs were all arranged so it was easy to turn and face the windows. At the end of his speech, Martyn had something to add.

'Ladies and gentlemen, if you'd all please keep your seats for a moment. There is one final thing to show you before we begin our Delegate Workshops.' He nodded to Sophie and Verity and then jumped down from his podium, moving to one side.

'Cue ladies,' he gestured. 'Conferenceque in fact.' A few giggles rippled through the room.

Excitement raced inside Verity as she looked at Sophie and mouthed. 'Are you ready?'

Sophie nodded in readiness, her face full of smiles which was an unusual sight.

They opened the blinds simultaneously, peeling them back slowly across the glass of the wide expanse of windows until the view was unveiled. Bright sunlight and warmth poured into the room. There was a moment's silence then a series of gasps and exclamations abounded. 'Wow.'

She heard Sophie gulp and murmur, 'Epic.' Yes, there couldn't have been a better word for it.

The sun glinted and bounced off the four streams and the sky was a beautiful azure blue, the greenery and countryside colours vibrant. She had so hoped for it not to rain and like a miracle, everyone was seeing the view at its very best.

Everyone began to rise to their feet for a better look and then they all started to clap. Was it for Martyn or the view? Maybe both. It took a while before everyone settled down again and they opened the doors out onto the balcony. The energy in the room was crackling. Verity's eyes were filling up with water which threatened to spill over, so she quickly dabbed at the corners with a tissue and tried to blink the moisture away.

She couldn't stop herself looking over to where Jeremy stood and their eyes locked. He grinned and she felt her heart gallop, swelling up with emotion so strong that she felt it was about to burst with happiness. She must be the luckiest person in the room at this moment with the beautiful sight of the four streams spread out below, bathed in September sunshine, and the man she loved smiling across the room at me in pure adoration. Suddenly she couldn't wait for this stressful day to be over, and to be with him, just the two of them. Wait a minute. Loved? Yes, I had actually admitted to herself that she loved him. It was a magic moment. For once, she allowed herself to be happy and enjoy, well, just being.

People were allowed out on the roof balcony a few at a time to gawp at the view, glasses of orange juice or cups of coffee in hand. Birds tweeted. She listened in to conversations.

'Wow, isn't this amazing, I wasn't expecting this.'

'What a fabulous event this is.'

At lunch time the delegates were wowed once again when the table covers were removed from the oblong tables lined against one wall. There was a tiny picnic table loaded with goodies for each guest.

She'd had the idea for these from Uncle Bobby who had always been good at joinery and had a shed full of wood. Whilst he'd been off on the sick he'd taken to dabbling with carving bits of wood, owls, birds, cats and she had persuaded him to make one hundred small picnic tables with soft wood. She was worried that he wouldn't have enough time to make them all because he was busy at work as well but Jeremy had asked his dad George to help and between them they'd done a cracking job.

She'd offered to pay, of course, for the wood and his time with her own funds but he wouldn't hear of it.

'No way, you're definitely not using your own money, I want to help,' he'd said.

'Thank you so much, it's such an important event,' she'd enthused, 'and there's a lot at stake for me riding on its success. We can always re-use them in the future.'

Bobby had replied, 'I think it's a marvellous idea, and it shows that you're going the extra mile.'

So Bobby had painstakingly crafted these with George's help, churning them out one after another in his garden shed. They said they'd really enjoyed making them and were glad to be able to contribute towards the event. In fact, George said it gave him a huge sense of purpose and made him feel useful.

The little picnic tables looked wonderful. Jeremy had made the canapes/sandwiches/patties and she'd baked the miniature chocolate eclairs and vanilla slices, storing them in the fridge of the adjoining kitchen. They were definitely a legacy of Grandma Anna's teaching. The guests were very impressed and loved the idea. Lunch was a huge triumph.

All too soon the last workshop was over and it was time for them to sign them up. The queues at the desks were long and Jeremy was in charge of keeping them in order.

'Will you be doing the training?' one lady asked Jeremy.

'Me? Oh no.' Jeremy said. 'I'm not a trainer.' She looked disappointed. Another lady said, 'That's such a shame.' She looked so crestfallen Verity was scared she was about to change her mind, so she broke in to say, 'It's highly likely that he will be there on the day, doing the administration.'

'I certainly hope so.' Jeremy said, dazzling them with his smile. 'If I'm around, I will definitely be here to help.'

Verity felt a slight shadow darken her day at the thought of him not being around. She shrugged it away.

'You know I'd do anything for you Verity,' he leaned over and whispered in her ear. He'd obviously forgotten all she'd impressed upon him about being professional and business like whilst at work, but at his words she buzzed with sheer happiness. She'd never felt so content in her whole life.

The lady signed up and soon there was a line of people eager to register for the Medication Management training courses. It looked like Conferenceque would have to lay on more than they'd planned for. The event had been a great success.

Verity felt a tap on her shoulder and turned around to find Jan, the Office Manager from the school visit smiling up at her, another two ladies in tow. Verity nearly didn't recognise her, she looked so much better, wearing a lovely summer floral dress and coloured sandals.

'Hello Verity, thanks for a wonderful event,' Jan greeted her with warmth.

'How lovely to see you,' Verity smiled back. 'You look well. I'm glad you enjoyed today.'

'We really found Martyn's speech inspiring,' Jan went on. 'He really knows his stuff doesn't he? And we've all learnt a lot.'

'Yes, we're just going to join the queue to sign up for the longer course,' another of the ladies piped up. 'We're all going to work together to put the policy in place in school.'

'Oh, I'm so glad,' Verity said. 'Martyn was really worried about you last time we saw you, Jan.'

'Oh, no need, we've all pulled together,' Jan said, 'and the new Business Manager is really supportive by the way.'

'I'm glad to hear it,' Verity said.

Jan laughed and turned back from the queue. 'Why don't you come and visit us again in a few months' time? See how we're doing?'

'I'd love to,' Verity said, catching Jeremy's eye and smiling as he winked at her. 'I might bring my colleague along as well.'

She breathed a sigh of relief as they toasted each other much later with a glass of sparkling water before the clearing up. She felt so hot, sweaty and tired, but very happy.

'Well boss, looks like you pulled it off,' Jeremy said when almost everyone had gone, apart from the usual one or two loiterers who lingered behind to talk to the speakers.

'We pulled it off, you mean,' she answered. 'I couldn't have done it without you or Sophie.'

Greyson had to have the last word when he patted her on the back and said,

'Good stuff Verity, good man, you really did have all your ducks in a row.'

Chapter Twenty Nine

'Our Johnny!' Verity cried in delight as a figure turned to her from where he had been standing gazing out of the windows, his round face beaming and displaying deep dimples. Stocky in build, with pale hair spiked up at the front and shaved at the sides, he was wearing a red checked short sleeved shirt which showed off tanned forearms complete with tattoos. He flung his ample arms around Verity and they hugged.

'It's so wonderful to see you.' Verity brushed away a tiny tear.

'What an absolutely dazzling view,' he gushed. 'I couldn't believe it. Did you recognise it?'

'Of course. It's the Four Streams.'

'And the event wasn't bad either. I caught the afternoon sessions.'

Verity beckoned for Jeremy to join them.

'Jeremy, I'd like you to meet someone,' she said, still holding on to the newcomer's arm.

Jeremy smiled, one eyebrow raised.

'This, is our Johnny,' Verity said proudly. 'Johnny, meet Jeremy Soderland.'

'Really? *The* Our Johnny?' Jeremy asked, grinning as he shook his hand with great enthusiasm. 'Your nephew?'

'The very same,' Johnny said. 'Hi, so pleased to meet you Jeremy. How are you?'

'I'm good. I've heard such a lot about you, mate,' Jeremy said. 'Great to meet you.'

'So happy I could make it.' Our Johnny grabbed his bottle of water from the front cabaret table, 'I'm on a tight flight schedule but managed to wangle a stopover in Newcastle.'

'A stop over?' Jeremy said. 'What do you do for a living?'

'I'm an Air Steward,' Johnny said with pride. 'I work for British Airways.'

Verity squeezed his hand. She was so proud of him and remembered when she'd been on a flight to Italy and watched him in action. He was born to do this. Sparked by his love of all things geographical and all the different countries he'd read about, after leaving school he'd applied to be an Air Steward, was accepted and went through the training. He was a natural. Verity remembered how, to promote some giveaways from the In Flight Magazine, he'd produced some very expensive face cream which was reduced in price.

'I use this,' he told the passengers, holding it up for them to see, 'and I'll tell you a secret.' He looked behind him and lowered his voice to a whisper. 'I'm really sixty years old.'

People laughed, liking his youthful, cheerful face and began ringing their buzzers to buy the cream.

'Yes, I'm an Air Steward,' he said. 'I love it. Even at my age! And my husband's a pilot, who works erratic shifts as well, so we work around it. We live in London now.'

'It's marvellous to see you,' Verity breathed, hugging him again. 'What did you think of the event?'

Johnny's eyes clouded over slightly. 'It was superb. Verity, you're doing a really worthwhile thing here. I can't tell you how much I wish I'd had more help with ADHD as a kid.'

Jeremy asked, 'Did you know you had the condition?'

Johnny shook his head. 'No, I didn't. No-one did. There was no-one to dole out my medication – in fact I didn't have any medication. They just thought I was incredibly naughty when I kicked off.' He laughed to himself. 'I can still hear that knock on the back door which meant I was in trouble again with the neighbours.'

He struck a pose, folding his arms, frowning and pretending to be Grandma Anna.

'Oh my lordy stars and garters, what's he done this time?'

He struck another pose. 'Fighting with my son that's what. And rolling about in my hedge. Or knocking on my door and running away up onto the fells.' His voice grew louder and soon they were all laughing together.

He shook his head, wincing a little. 'Poor Auntie Bertha and Grandma Anna. They were always fed up with me. And they were always being called into school about something or other I'd done. Verity was the only one with any time for me.'

'We had some lovely times up on the fells,' she said, linking his arm with hers. 'I just remember those good times.' Now, he had a way of making people laugh and drawing them to him.

'I still have my moments mind,' he went on, lowering his voice, 'and I've had spells of depression over the years which I manage to control with medication.' He looked from her to Jeremy.

'For every school to have a Medication Policy and a plan for each pupil is an amazing achievement. You must be very proud of yourselves. What you're doing here is going to help pupils – and teachers - all over the North East.'

Verity nodded. 'I certainly hope so,' she said, jumping up to retrieve a delegate badge and feedback form from someone who was oblivious to everything but walking out in deep conversation with one of the speakers.

'Talking about Grandma Anna, how is she?' Johnny asked. 'Next time, I might be able to call in to see her.'

'She's doing extremely well,' Verity said. 'Far better than we'd hoped. Better check first though because she's more out of the home than in it at the moment. She goes out to a few concerts and recitals now.'

'That's so good to hear,' Johnny said, chuckling to himself. 'She always was a character.'

'To be honest,' Verity went on, 'she looks younger now than she did when I lived with her.'

'Really?' Johnny swigged from his water bottle.

'I'm not joking. She has her hair done regularly and her nails. She's very well looked after.'

'I'm pleased to hear that,' Johnny looked wistful. 'I had some of my best childhood moments over at her house. Look, I'm really thirsty, if I give you guys a hand with the clearing up would you both fancy a quick drink in the River Bar?'

Jeremy's ears had pricked up. 'Mine's a pint,' he grinned.

Chapter Thirty - Callum

Callum had been to a meeting with the director of one of his charities, which just happened to be housed in the business park near to the building he used to work in with Verity. Walking down the hill, he bumped into one of his old cronies which led to coffee in the restaurant, where he felt a bit uneasy and kept looking over his shoulder. One should never go back, maybe. He was glad to be on his way out of the building and was moving through the foyer when a brightly coloured poster caught his eye. His heart began to beat a little faster as he stopped to look.

The *Reach the Stars* organised by Conferenceque, headed up by Verity Raffin, Business Manager. He felt slightly disconcerted at the sight of her name and wished he hadn't stopped to look.

Loosening his tie, he ran a hand over his sticky forehead and mused that the coffee hadn't really hit the spot. He could do with a proper drink. He was lost without his car as well, which was in for service today, the only advantage being that he could pop in across the road for a cheeky gin and tonic before he caught his train home, if he wanted. He didn't do much walking, maybe he should take more exercise. A steady stream of people were heading out of the building towards the River Bar and so he followed them, his hand sweating on the handle of his briefcase.

The pub was already crammed full of people, most of them looking as if they had just come from the conference. They were spilling out onto the terrace to sit and look over the river in the late afternoon sunshine, vying for a good spot to view the forthcoming sunset. Some were carrying their drinks further down a set of steps which led to the lower balcony. Others perched on the wall, clutching their glasses and chattering excitedly.

Several people were still wearing their badges and were clutching crumpled conference packs. Callum moved through the bar to the far end and found himself a vantage point on a high stool, where he managed to position himself strategically with his paper and his tall glass of iced gin and tonic. It was fairly dark inside compared to the bright afternoon sunlight. People were clustered all around him, constantly shifting around to talk to others, chattering and drinking, and although he was pretending to read the Financial Times, he kept glancing up through the gaps of the constantly dispersing and rebranding groups.

The hub of chattering voices seemed to grow louder. 'Was it a good event?' he had to raise his voice to be heard, as he spoke to a young woman fluttering on the edge of a group, pointing at the brochure she was clasping under her arm.

'Oh, definitely the best,' she said, nodding frenetically. 'Quite the most amazing event I've ever been to.'

'Most excellent,' he nodded. 'What was it about?'

'Managing Medicine in Schools,' she answered, showing him the folder. 'I've learnt loads.'

'Most excellent,' he said, smiling politely. He finished his drink and ordered another.

Then he saw her come in. He caught his breath at the sight of her, glad to know she was oblivious to his presence. He slouched down slightly behind his paper and watched as she threaded her way outside straightaway, followed by a plump young man. By goodness, she looked positively breath-taking, her dark hair shining bright enough to match her smile. And she was wearing the conference uniform in the colours which matched his website. Well, the one he'd designed for them. And they had a new name, which wasn't at all bad. She walked elegantly with confidence, the suit jacket folded neatly over her tanned arm, a pink and lemon scarf crisply bestowed around her neck.

She had a kind of glow about her and he felt a strange feeling in his gut. He knew she couldn't see him from where he sat so he craned his neck until it ached, in order to observe her more fully.

She looked so happy. It couldn't possibly be down to the plump young man who was with her? No, couldn't be him, he looked a lot younger. It must be conference fever. It had obviously been a successful event. He was glad for her. Then why did he feel ever so slightly chagrined? He knew she would have worked hard and made a go of it. She deserved the acclaim. He'd left her to get on with it and that was what she'd done. He would have expected nothing less. He felt a stab of admiration. Was it because he secretly wished he'd been a part of her success? Was he that shallow? And selfish? His wife thought so.

He watched as the two of them perched on the edge of a wooden table overlooking the river, Verity sitting with her back to him. They were right within his line of vision. Shortly they were joined by a shaggy haired blond chap, who navigated his way through the crowds with ease whilst deftly balancing a tray with a bottle of wine, three glasses and a pint of beer on it. It looked like he was wearing a smart suit, but his shirt sleeves were rolled up and the jacket was slung over his shoulder.

Callum watched with growing unease as the scruffy guy put down the tray and caught hold of Verity's outstretched hand as he moved around the table to sit down next to her, throwing his other arm around her. Then they squashed up as close together as they possibly could whilst the other guy poured the wine. The three of them clinked their glasses high across the table, Verity's hair swinging and falling back perfectly into place.

Callum felt jealously stabbing at his heart, like knives. What was he doing here anyway? He'd only come in for a cooling drink and now he couldn't drag himself away.

He'd been thinking about her a lot lately, feeling guilty about finishing with her the way he had. And he'd missed her like hell, like he'd never expected to. His circumstances had changed slightly and he'd had more time to think.

He picked up a discarded Conference Pack. On the back page there were small headshots of the speakers and organisers. His eyes sped to the bottom of the page. Conference Organisers - Verity

Raffin and Jeremy Soderland. That was him. Unusual name. His stomach twisted unpleasantly. What was she doing with that…that messy young whippersnapper anyhow? It hadn't taken her very long to move on. The bloke probably wasn't that young if the truth be told but that lion's mane of hair made him look younger than he was. Callum bet he had a lived in face under all that hair.

She couldn't possibly be happy with him. Could she? She certainly looked it and he imagined her laughter tinkling out, on a separate level to all the chatter and noise around him. It could just be successful conference euphoria. No, they were hugging each other now and he was leaning in for a kiss as the other man left the table, and was swallowed up in the crowds. The pair of them seemed unaware of anyone else around them.

Callum caught his breath, stiffening as the plump young man moved towards him, probably to go to the gents. This was ridiculous, it wasn't as if he even knew who he was. He caught a faint tang of his perspiration as the crowds pressed him nearer as he passed.

'Most irrational,' he muttered to himself. He felt as if the skin on his face was shrivelling up with cold despite the warmth of his surroundings. Time to leave. He drained the liquid in his glass, then folded the conference pack over and placed it in his jacket pocket as he got up to go, keeping his head down and leaving the paper behind. He couldn't resist one final look.

Chapter Thirty One

It was Saturday afternoon and Verity had been into work for a special conference debrief with Greyson. She didn't usually work on Saturdays but this was the only time Greyson had available as he was away on business next week, so she'd agreed just this once. They met in the Secret Room which looked very different, stripped of all the posters, banners and people, the blinds tightly shut against the glorious view.

After all the excitement of the last few weeks, tiredness was now kicking in and all she wanted was a long soak in the bath and a nap in front of the television, or the gogglebox as Jeremy always called it. I remembered Jeremy was out all day at rehearsals so the house should be quiet.

With a damp tang of the river in the air as she walked up the path, she turned the key in the lock and stepped straight into the hallway. Well, she tried to step into the hallway but it was a bit difficult because of all the flowers. They were everywhere. 'What the…?' At first she thought she'd been burgled, but what burglar would leave all these flowers? And the heat in here. It was overpowering. As was the smell.

'What is going on?' she said out loud. She could hardly see the floor for strategically arranged vases, pots, and terracotta planters. The clear glass pots showed woody, knobbly green stems, arranged with pink tissue paper from which billowing bouquets of glorious blooms abounded. The perfume was intense, the air too heavy with the fragrance of lilies.

There was a narrow walkway through the middle of the stunning arrangements which included waxy red roses in vintage teapots.

Oh no. The only people who had a key were herself, Jeremy now of course - and *him.*

Her heart was beating like a drum as she navigated a way to the sitting room as if in a dream. Callum was sitting on the sofa, his jacket and tie off, strewn over the armrest, his hair immaculate. As if he'd never been away. She could see the back of his head in the mirror. How astonishing. The grey at his temples had spread and he had a spreading bald patch.

'What are you doing here, in my house?' she whispered, her voice not working properly. Probably in shock.

'Hello Verity.' He rose and came towards her, his eyes were soft and appealing and he was holding out both hands. 'Most excellent to see you. You look absolutely splendid. I parked just round the corner in a layby so it would be a complete surprise for you.'

It was a surprise all right. She put out one arm and stopped him mid approach. 'Don't touch me.'

'Verity, I've been so longing for this moment,' he went on. 'I've missed you so much.'

She backed off into the hall. 'What? You should have thought of that when you dumped me.'

'I've thought of nothing else since,' he followed steadily. 'I made a big mistake and I'm sorry.'

She shook her head. 'It's all a bit too late,' she said softly, as she took tiny steps backwards into the foliage.

'I turned the heating up I hope you don't mind.' He followed her, eyes beseeching.

These blooms like a bit more warmth.'

He did what? He turned the heating up. It's still summer for God's sake. No wonder it was hot in here. Her limbs felt like there were leaden weights attached to them.

'How did you get in here?'

'I kept the key you gave me.'

Oh no. That stupid key. How she regretted not demanding it back that last time she'd seen him but she'd just wanted rid of him. Like she did now.

He continued to advance and she to retreat, moving through the greenery. Mind in a whirl, she wanted to match his cool assurance but couldn't find the words. She found herself uttering, 'It's like the Gateshead Garden Festival in here.' But she was more than irate. She was bewildered and remembering that deep hurt he'd caused her.

'I know how much you love flowers.'

She glared up into his pale eyes and saw apprehension, reticence, even a touch of hope? He took a step towards her. 'Verity, I swear I was only thinking of you the whole time.'

'Even when your wife was ill?'

'Yes, well you know what I mean. You were always in my thoughts.' He loomed closer.

'What about the budget?' she fiddled with the scarf at her neck. 'You spent it all. And left me to pick up the pieces.'

'What? No, I was only thinking of you. I bought you the Stuff NGo Machine to save you time and effort. I did so hate to think of you sitting and stuffing all those envelopes.'

'And the website?'

'Well, we needed a decent website to showcase to the world.'

'But ten grand? Honestly Callum.'

'Verity,' he shook his head. 'I only wanted the best for you. You know what I'm like with figures. I don't do detail.'

'No, you left that all to me.' Thoughts were crowding into her head, tumbling over and over themselves. 'You spent it all. And left me to sort it all out.'

'I honestly had your best interests at heart.' He moved closer still. 'You were always on my mind. Anyhow, I'm back now. Surely we can, you know, pick up where we left off? No-one need know what happened.' He put one hand on the wall next to her head.

'I know all about the Secret Room and your, your assignations in there.' she snapped out the words.

His throat worked. 'How did you know..?'

'It wasn't hard to figure out. A dirty cereal bowl and a floaty scarf was all it took.'

'That was a mistake,' he removed his hand and scratched his head. 'It didn't mean anything, honestly. You don't need to worry about that.'

No way. 'I'm not so foolish to think you would ever change. Who was it anyhow?' She remembered how hurt she'd felt at the time that he'd been in the penthouse with some bitch.

His eyes flickered. He obviously thought if it mattered to her who it was he might be in with a chance.

'Oh, no-one, honestly. She was just someone from the Food Bank. It wasn't important.'

'You know what? It doesn't matter now anyway. Now I'd like you to take your flowers and go please. Right now.'

Her head and heart were pounding. Could this be happening? Rage was building inside and all she could think about was getting him out of the house.

'Think of all the happy times we spent together,' Callum's voice was nearly a whisper. 'Do you really want to throw it all away?' He moved closer, despite the foliage.

'It's already gone. You're a stranger to me Callum.' She tried to press her spine into the wall. She could smell his cool aftershave or cologne or whatever it was and combined with the sickly aroma of the lilies, it made her stomach churn. She felt his breath hot on her cheek and willed him to go away.

'I've come back because I've got an idea which will save err... Conferenceque isn't it? Most snappy name' His other hand was reaching for hers now. 'You didn't really think I'd leave you to flounder?'

'I don't need your idea,' she knocked his hand away. 'I've gone ahead and organised an event for all schools which was a huge success. 'I've got delegates for the Medication courses coming out of our ears.'

'Ah, so you discovered my plan. Most excellent.'

'Your plan? You were the one that left us in debt.' Her thoughts raced. How could she ever have convinced herself that she was in love with this man?

'But I always planned on coming back to rescue you.' He grabbed at her hand again.

'I don't need rescuing and least of all from you, you… idiot,' she shook him off as if his touch burnt her skin. 'I've managed to break even.'

'Ah, but you couldn't make it work without Martyn Kingston. Ex-Army man. He's the one with all the knowledge. Surely, you won't have got him on board?'

'Martyn's a total pussy cat,' she could hardly keep the smirk out of her voice.

'What? How did you manage that?' He ran a hand over his head. 'Well, I must say I'm impressed. He's one tough guy. I obviously hadn't given you enough credit.'

'Obviously not. Now please leave.'

'Verity I think I've underestimated you. However, I must confess to something.'

'I'm not interested in anything you have to say.'

'But…I must tell you and you've got to believe me. I left the medication information in my drawer where I knew you'd find it. I planned it because I wanted you to succeed.'

Now she knew what the expression - blood boiling meant. 'Really? Is that a fact?'

'Yes. You see, I did help you after all, you see? Now can we forget all this nonsense and get back to the way we were?' He looked at her sideways, smiling that smile she'd always thought of an enigmatic and now she just thought he looked stupid.

He was looming closer now and his large frame was blocking out the light from the front door. He placed his hands tentatively on her arms and moved them gently up to her shoulders. She could see the relief settling in his light eyes as she hesitated for one second. She was only hesitating however as she planned her escape route.

A noise made her jump back. It sounded a bit like the letterbox being dropped shut in haste but when she turned to look back quickly there was no-one there. Must be the evening breeze. This gave her the opportunity to push him away forcefully which he wasn't expecting, and twirl around so he was now standing against the wall. He shifted his position to face her.

She pointed her finger at him. 'Don't you dare touch me again.' She saw a flash of annoyance and faint disbelief in his eyes now.

They stood facing each other surrounded by all the flora and every time he moved towards her she moved backwards slightly, each step taking her further towards the front door. She had a plan.

'Can't we go and sit down and talk further?' he said. 'I still love you and can't wait to get back to the way we were. Darling, I've missed you ever so much. You're not making this easy for me.'

Was he even listening? 'No thanks, you're leaving.' she said. 'I can't stand this whining any longer.'

'Whining? Verity when did you become so hard?' he said. 'Is it because you're Conference Manager now?'

'Business Manager,' she corrected him, stalling for time until she reached the front door.

'I know. It was I that engineered that for you. Your promotion I mean. I talked Greyson into it.'

What? Was this man for real?

Then, she brushed against a pot of lilies which dispersed some waxy orange powder all over her silky blouse. She muttered an expletive and brushed it off.

'Well, none of it makes any difference now. You're going.'

'But I do know you are the one I really want.'

'Tough. You are way too late.' With one last step she'd reached the front door. With a flourish she flung it open, letting in the cool afternoon air.

'Get out.' She gestured to the path.

'Verity, you don't mean that.' His vice was softer, more wheedling.

Oh but she did. 'I repeat - get out of my house.' She hissed out the words, feeling the anger rise and rise in her chest.

'Come on now, Verity, we can sort this out. Listen to me – please?' He put his head on one side.

'Take them all away.' She flung her arms out to the Floral Gardens collection.

'Verity, I know we can move on from this.'

'All of them. I want them gone. And you.'

'Why? I've explained everything. I didn't know you could be so cruel.'

'Me? Cruel? Ha!' Her temper was really roused now and she couldn't stop, knowing what people meant when they said they could see the red mist descend. Her tiredness evaporated. All the anger and betrayal spilt over as she picked up a bunch of blooms from the Rose and Oriental Lily Pot and with the stems dripping all over the floor, held it poised at shoulder height whilst she shot him a filthy look. She then flung it on the front lawn and didn't stop there.

She ripped bunch after bunch of the flowers out of the pots, complete with sopping wet knobbly stalks and threw them out of the door onto the front lawn, grunting and groaning with the effort. It felt like her arms were being pulled out of their sockets, she was putting so much effort into it. How childish she was being but she didn't care anymore.

Afterwards she couldn't believe she'd acted like this. It must have been an accumulation of years of pent up feelings and stress, of always being the one to keep the peace and avoid any unpleasantness. She had simply let go. And it had felt…liberating.

He followed her outside, panicking, his arms flailing. She noticed with relish the look of horror on his face. He hated scenes of any kind.

'Verity, hey steady on!' he ducked as she ran back in for more. 'I'll come back and talk to you when you've calmed down.'

'Don't bother. And give me back my key. Now. Throw it to me. Now.'

'Verity, you don't mean it. Please?' He was walking slowly backwards now, arms outstretched. Pathetic. Maybe she was too.

She threw another bouquet. Then she turned around to find something else and spotted a big terracotta pot which she picked up with both hands and struggled to lift it up high enough to throw.

With a look of horror on his face, he threw her the key which fell on the ground a few feet away.

'At last!' she screeched, bending down to pick it up. 'Hallelujah! Now go away and don't come back.'

'Verity! Hey. Give him a break, won't you?' the next door neighbour stopped mid spray with his pressure hose of his car down and stopped to watch. 'He must have spent a fortune.'

The new young window cleaner stopped halfway up her ladder to watch the drama unfolding on Verity's front lawn. Some blinds twitched on the other side of the street.

A few of the neighbours were still outside chatting in their gardens and several kids were playing football in the field just over the fence. A strong smell of freshly clipped late summer grass pervaded the air.

'Yes, he must have spent the earth,' she said nodding.

'Thank you. Verity, listen to them,' Callum pleaded. 'Listen to me. I'm really sorry I upset you so much. Just give me another chance.' They faced each other on the grass, her hands were clenched and she was surrounded by flowers.

'Aw, go on love,' said the neighbour. 'Give him a chance.' His wife came out of the house and joined him, I think she'd been peeping out of the upstairs window.

'Is it a wake?' she asked in bewilderment.

It might be yet. 'Give me a chance? Give him a break? I'll break both his legs!' Verity's voice rose until she was almost screaming.

'Why, what's he done?' the young window cleaner said, poised mid height, squeegee in hand.

She turned around full circle, hair flying and arms full of squashed hot house blooms. Her lovely silky blouse which had been so spotless this morning was now hanging out of her skirt and was stained with green. It felt uncomfortably sodden and was sticking to her skin. She turned the other way to see who else was watching. A little huddle of kids had assembled at the edge of the path, mouths open, fingers pointing. A couple of them assembled on the kerb.

The kids playing football were now leaning over the fence to watch, giggling to each other. A teenager in a hoody was passing on a bike. He dismounted and joined the kids on the pavement.

A dog walker walked past very slowly, looking back over her shoulder, little grey terrier trotting alongside. She'd never seen so many people in her street in one go. Normally she never saw anyone.

'Where do you want me to start? How's about cheated, lied, led a double life and had assignations with some bitch in the penthouse!' she yelled.

The kids roared with laughter and pretended to cover their ears. The dog walker stopped, the terrier straining on the lead.

The window cleaner whistled. 'No way.' Then she turned her head to the neighbour who had stopped washing his car mid hose. She nodded, nearly dislodging the ladder as the neighbour pointedly turned his hose towards Callum.

'He looks like a ghostbuster.' said the teenager, producing a mobile phone. 'I've taken a video.'

The window cleaner, chortled with laughter as she hurried down the ladder, scrabbling in her jeans pocket for her mobile phone. 'Please send it to me. My hubby will never believe me.'

'Don't worry, we'll have this on U-Tube in no time,' Verity shrieked. The little crowd cheered.

'Please no, I'm going,' Callum backed off quickly to avoid the spray of water and deluge of pelting flowers.

'You can come back for these,' she continued to shout. 'And these!' She went inside and carried out put more containers.

'On second thoughts, forget it. Don't ever come back.' Oh why did he have to go so far over the top? All these flowers were wasted.

He didn't move for a second, wavering on the spot.

'Well go on then,' someone said.

For a second the whole scene seemed to freeze. Then she remembered he'd left his jacket inside. She didn't want anything of his left behind so she broke the spell by running inside, slipping and tripping on the wooden floor which was strewn with water and discarded flowers. Quickly, she slipped out of her heels and discarded them on the way back.

She caught sight of herself in the hall mirror and groaned. What a sight. Her normally sleek hair was all over the place and she looked like a mad woman, eyes glittering with fury and cheeks streaked with black where her mascara had melted and her face looked so white. All her clothes were all sopping wet now and flower stained. She grabbed his jacket and threw it on the grass at his feet.

'There! You can go now. For good.' She didn't watch him go but slammed her front door on the shocked street. Then she opened the door again roughly two seconds later to see the back of his sleek car disappearing around the corner. They were still all standing there in the same position, jaws dropping. There was a paper boy there now as well, being filled in on the action by the teenager with the video on his mobile phone.

When they saw her again, she was mortified when they all began clapping. She didn't know whether to laugh or cry.

'Well done, pet. You certainly told him good and proper,' said the neighbour. 'Got what he deserved.'

'Don't worry Verity, if he comes back we'll get rid of him for you,' the window cleaner said, wringing out her sponge viciously.

'I don't think he'll be back in a hurry', the neighbour shook his head. 'You haven't half got a temper on you haven't you?' he chuckled and patted her shoulder.

'Anyone like some flowers?' She indicated the mess littering the front path and lawn.

'Can I have some of the rose petals to make perfume?' a little girl asked shyly.

'Take your pick.'

'Have you got a vase or something to put them in?' the little girl said, delightedly gathering handfuls of petals to her chest. Had she? There were masses of them. 'Take as many as you want,' she told her.

'Would you like a nice cup of tea pet?' the neighbour's wife said, gingerly putting an arm around her shoulders. 'Then we'll all help you clean up.'

'Where is the Penthouse anyway?' the window cleaner asked.

It was at this point that she burst into tears.

Chapter Thirty Two

A few minutes later, an exhausted Verity was sitting in her next door neighbour's conservatory, with a weak cup of tea in a dainty china cup balanced on her knees, when she was presented with a bunch of slightly flattened, velvety red roses.

'Where have these come from?' she asked. Not more flipping flowers. She never wanted to see another bunch of flowers ever.

'These are for you as well,' kind neighbour said. 'Don't look too bad do they, considering I rescued them from the bin?'

'I don't want any more flowers,' Verity said. 'You have them. Please.'

'Oh, they're not from *him*. Another chap called for you. You're very popular aren't you?'

'What? When?' she sat up straight, holding onto the tea cup. 'How long ago was this?'

'Before you came out. I saw him from my kitchen window.'

'What did he look like?'

'Very, very nice,' she went on. 'Younger. Bit like a movie star but messier. Tall with blond hair. Had an adorable little dog with him.'

'Oh no,' Verity thought, warning bells were beginning to ring. She put her cup down on the coffee table and rested her forehead on her hands. Kind, nosey, neighbour kept on talking.

'He looked so upset, poor chap. In fact he looked distraught. He was looking through your letter box. Even the little dog was up on his hind legs.' She pressed the roses onto Verity's lap. 'Then he opened my bin lid on his way past and dropped these in. Can you imagine that? Then, he sprinted off up the street.'

'I'm sorry,' she got up quickly, scattering the roses everywhere. 'You've been so very kind and I don't mean to be rude but I must go now.' She reached down and gathered up all the roses to her chest feverishly.

'No worries pet, as long as you're all right,' the concerned voice continued behind her as she dashed off. 'Please come and let me know what happens next?'

'Oh no, no, no.' Verity said to herself, turning the key in the lock with shaking fingers and trying to hold on to the roses. Red roses! A sign of his undying devotion and what did he see? Callum's sleek black Mercedes parked in the layby on her street. Her and Callum through the letter box. He knew the registration was CYDL. He must have got totally the wrong impression. How hurt he must be feeling right now.

She rang Jeremy's mobile number frantically but got the answerphone. She thought she'd go round to his house but then she caught sight of the ticket pinned on the notice board in the kitchen which reminded her that *Not Quite Cricket* was being performed in a pub over the other side of town. She was supposed to be going to watch. She'd nearly forgotten, what with everything that had gone on this afternoon.

He'd be there now for the pre-show rehearsal which would explain why his phone was switched off. The show had to go on after all. Like the *Big Event*. She had to go and find him now and explain. Oh goodness, she couldn't go out looking like this, she must get changed first.

Her thoughts were all jumbled as she agitatedly tried to make herself look presentable, splashing cold water on her eyes and flinging off her sodden, flower stained white blouse and work skirt and pulling on the first things that came to hand, which happened to be the floaty sea-green dress she'd worn to the barbeque. No matter how much she hurried, she knew she wasn't going to make it much before the interval. She was going to take the car but as she felt a bit shaky, changed her mind at the last minute and decided to ring for a taxi to take her over to the other side of town. She was nearly falling over her feet in the high heels which were the nearest pair she could find.

'Come on, hurry up hurry up,' she said out loud, as she waited for the taxi which was a few minutes late. Goodness poor Jeremy, what he must be feeling now? If he felt half as bad as she did right now, he would be feeling so awful. She just wanted to see him, feel his strong arms around her and tell him how sorry she was for the misunderstanding and how much she loved him.

Chapter Thirty Three

The taxi stopped on the rain swept cobbled street and in her haste to get out, she snagged her tights and nearly went over on her ankle.

The venue for Jeremy's next performance was in an old converted warehouse in an up and coming area. The place was called Ernestine's, a bar well known for its local music and performance artists. He'd done very well to secure a booking there.

Impatiently waiting for them to spill out for the interval, she went upstairs to the ladies room and noticed that there was part of an old stone arch, painted over with white paint, in the end cubicle. She reapplied lip gloss with trembling fingers, looking at her flushed face in the mirror. She felt feverish. The sound of clapping resounded from below which indicated that it was now interval time.

Pictures of forthcoming events adorned the brick walls and there was a buzz in the air as people trickled out from the function room and milled about. It was noisy and warm and Verity felt her head begin to ache. She craned her neck to look up the stairs, her eyes darting everywhere for a glimpse of the man himself, feeling nervous with a swoop of butterflies in her stomach. She couldn't wait to put things right. Her heart seemed to be galloping away at a tremendous rate. Then she saw him. And her.

They were at the top of the stairs. She could see immediately that this woman was an exotic creature, a natural beauty with classically sculptured features even with her hair scraped back from her face. Yasmin was small, petite with a long dark ponytail falling nearly to her slender waist and as Verity watched her move a few steps away from Jeremy and back to him, it was easy to notice she moved with a dancer's grace. She was obviously the touchy feely type because she was draping herself all over him, one arm around his waist and the other on his shoulder, and as he looked down at her, they were both was gazing at each other in what appeared to be adoration.

Verity felt like she'd been punched in the stomach. He didn't look bereft or upset at all. In fact he looked just the opposite. How was this happening? Had he forgotten all about her already? And the last few hours?

Then another betrayal. As she watched, Yasmin bent down and picked up a shaggy bundle and hugged him closely, Pedro attempting to lick her all over her face in his excitement. Pedro, the silent dog who was very selective with people, was all over her. Verity stood watching the little tableau that was the three of them, it was as if there no room for the outside world, and felt growing dismay inside which threatened to rise up and choke her.

'Who's that?' she asked George who had just appeared at her side, although she knew the answer. 'It's her isn't it? The girl from Café Yummy.' Her voice sounded strange and wobbly, even to herself.

'That's Yasmin', George said. 'Jeremy's ex-wife.'

Wow. They made such a stunning couple – was that what they were? He looked to be very protective of her.

Then Kat arrived at her side, kissing her on the cheek. They were on very good terms now that she had attended the Big Event and established herself as one half of Conferenceque's lead trainer team. She'd come along with a few friends to support Jeremy.

'Verity,' she said, 'Good to see you.'

Her heart felt as if it were thudding out of her chest and her mind jumped around searching for an exit facility.

'Have you seen Yasmin?' So even Kat knew about her.

'Yes, I have.' She replied calmly, not knowing how she found her voice. Her throat was so constricted with trying not to cry.

'She's exquisite isn't she?' Kat said, then she whispered half to herself, 'so that was what he meant by the love of his life,' shaking her head wistfully.

'Yes,' she knew when she was beaten. She felt so very, very tired.

'Two beautiful people together,' Kat's eyes were misty.

'Come on, I'll introduce you.' George took Verity's arm went to lead the way but she stopped him.

She was finding it hard to breathe, her head throbbed and all the laughing, happy people seemed to be closing in all around.

'Are you alright Verity? You've gone very pale.' George put a protective hand on her back.

'It's just the heat in here and I feel rather ill, it's been coming on all day.' Liar. 'Please apologise for me George, sorry, but I've really got to go.'

'But, wait, I'll get Bobby to go with you.'

'No, don't bother him, I'm fine honestly.'

'Then let me walk with you to the door.' She heard George's voice from behind but she knew she had to get out of there for some air before she passed out.

She fought her way through the bar, hearing people's voices as if from a long way off and stumbled out of the side entrance onto an uneven pavement in the middle of a block of refurbished warehouses. Her shoes pinched her toes as she struggled to walk on the gleaming cobblestones. Cool evening rain was falling and the night air grabbed at her throat as she took great gulps of it, her chest heaving. She heard fading laughter and noise behind her, as if in mocking.

Chapter Thirty Four

Verity didn't go into work the next day as she did genuinely feel ill and had hardly slept, being disturbed by vivid dreams of Jeremy and Callum. She kept waking up feeling like her tongue was too big for her mouth and her throat was sore and her headache thumped. Maybe she was slightly delirious? She was refusing to let herself think about what had happened yesterday. It was just unbearable. She felt numb inside and as if the last few weeks with Jeremy hadn't taken place. Her mind didn't seem to be processing anything, all she could think about was how wretched she felt. Tom meowed softly from his position at her feet, he knew something was up.

She was shaky on her feet when she got up to ring in sick. Having never been off ill before, she wasn't sure who to ring, so she left a message with Sophie, then was so exhausted by the effort of getting out of bed that she gratefully flopped back into it. Half way through the morning, she was woken from an uneasy sleep by the beep of her phone on the bedside table. It was Uncle Bobby texting to say he was outside so she had to haul herself up again to answer the door, still clutching her hot water bottle which was now lukewarm. He followed her inside, 'Sorry to disturb you, I'll quickly shut the door, it's cold and windy out there.'

'You look terrible,' he fussed. 'I knew it must be bad because you're never off. Have you rung the doctors for an appointment?'

She shook her head. 'It's just a touch of flu. All I need is some rest.' Her throat hurt with the effort of using her voice. She sank down onto the settee and he sat opposite, on the edge of the seat. Tom joined her, pushing his head into her side.

'Can I get you anything?' he said, 'some hot lemon maybe?' He kept fidgeting with something in his inside jacket pocket.

'No thanks. I've had paracetamol. What's up?' she said, leaning her aching head back against the soft cushions.

'I've got something for you but I don't know if I should bother you with it, the state you're in,' he said. His brown eyes were full of compassion as he pulled out two oblong envelopes. She felt even more chilled and pulled her dressing gown closer. She felt as if her cheeks were shrivelling up with heat although her body was cold.

'I'd rather know. What is it?' she asked faintly, looking at the envelopes. The one addressed to Bobby looked as if it had been opened.

'I'm so sorry Verity,' he said. 'This one addressed to me is from Jeremy.' He patted her hand which rested limply on the chair arm. 'It's his resignation.'

His what? His resignation? Immediate hot tears flooded her eyes. Her head throbbed although her mind still felt frozen, and refused to register. 'But it can't be.'

'I'm afraid so, it came to me as I was the one who hired him in the first place.' Uncle Bobby took a deep breath.

'And this one is for you.' He tentatively handed it over.

She took it from him slowly and just stared at her name on the front – To: Verity. She recognised his scrawled handwriting and turned it over and over before putting it down.

'I'll read it later.'

Uncle Bobby produced a large handkerchief and she wiped her eyes. Futile because more tears just kept coming. She couldn't remember the last time she'd cried like this and in front of someone else. She hadn't even opened the envelope yet. Poor Uncle Bobby.

He hadn't a clue what was going on except that he knew she was devastated.

'I don't understand. I thought that you two were so happy,' he said, shaking his head.

So did she. Until yesterday when her world fell in on itself.

She remained silent, too choked up inside to try to speak.

'Look,' he said, getting up and pacing up and down the length of the settee. 'I don't know what's happened between you, but would you like to talk about it?'

'No thanks,' Verity mumbled, continuing to stare at the envelope on the settee next to her. 'Definitely not.'

'Aren't you going to open it?' he said, as she picked it up again. 'Look, I'll go and warm up that hot water bottle.' He took it from her and Tom shifted his position to cuddle in even more closely. At least he still loved her.

'You go back to work,' she said, laying down full length on the settee. 'I don't know why you left work anyway to see me. I'll be fine.'

'Not a chance, I'm not leaving you like this. No arguments, I'm going to ring the doctors in a minute.'

She was shivering so Uncle Bobby hurried upstairs where she guessed he was dragging the quilt off her bed. He draped it over her clumsily and made for the kitchen where she heard the kettle begin to boil and him rattling about in the medicine cupboard.

Tom pushed his head into her elbow as if to remind her he was still there, then he snuggled closer. 'Tom, thank goodness you're always here for me,' she thought as she closed her eyes which felt like they'd been rubbed with sandpaper, and fell asleep, her fingers still curled around the letter.

Chapter Thirty Five

It was much later that day when she actually plucked up the courage and found the energy to sit up and open the envelope with trembling fingers. Her heart pounding, she began to read.

To my dearest Verity,

By the time you read this I'll be gone. I'll be on the train and well on my way to Margate. Not so very exotic I know but it's a job. My agent has managed to secure me a tour of the South Coast with a longer version of *Not Quite Cricket* and it's just too good a chance to miss.

As you know, the nature of my job is that you've got to take the breaks when they crop up, because when you get to my age they sometimes don't come as often. And the offer came at just the right time. Besides without you, there's nothing for me here.

I hope you're happy in the path you've chosen. It's not what I wanted for you. For us. I only wish things could have been different but I know you've got a mind of your own and nothing I say will make any difference. So I'm not going to try to make an idiot of myself (this must be a first I know you're thinking). You're a very determined character V and you've been through enough.

You deserve to be happy in life. There'll never be anyone else like you and my life is far, far enriched from having known you. More than you'll ever know.

This was where Verity stopped reading.

Chapter Thirty Six - Jeremy

Last Saturday afternoon, Jeremy, with Pedro in tow, parked the car in town and called in at the florists for a bunch of twelve red roses. He knew how much Verity loved flowers. He parked the car round the corner from her house as he felt like he needed a walk and some fresh air to give him courage, not that he really thought he needed it. It was a warm afternoon and the sunlight danced off the water and reflected off the silver of the high rise buildings across the Tyne.

He was taking a break from the dress rehearsal, well he was only the writer, no-one of great importance. They were managing fine without him and anyway, he'd be back this evening for the performance. They wouldn't miss him for a little while.

As he walked along with Pedro trotting jauntily beside him, clutching the roses and drinking in their heady perfume, he felt like skipping to one side. It seemed to be taking forever to reach her house. He couldn't wait to see her again, even though it was just a few hours since he'd last been in her bed. The girl of his dreams and at last she would be his. He felt like he'd come full circle. After all these years. At last the jetties and chutes of the Staithes loomed into view, birds basking and roosting in the heat on its timbers. Now he'd left the river behind and was walking through the houses.

He noticed how the flower heads of purple Michaelmas daisies and the stars of passion flowers precision edged with black, nodded over garden walls. There was a tang of wood smoke in the crisp air and pigeons cooed rhythmically overhead. He didn't normally notice flowers or see everything so vividly, unless it was for something he was writing and he wondered if it was love that made him see everything differently?

Pedro was happy too. 'We're going to see her soon, mate,' Jeremy said out loud. 'She said to ask her again about moving in after the *Big Event*. Surely she'll say yes this time? I'm sure she loves me. I can't bear to be apart from her you see.'

Pedro gave a little bark and pawed at his ankles excitedly, gazing up at him with his tongue hanging out.

Then, Jeremy stopped abruptly when he saw the sleek black Mercedes parked a couple of houses away. And the registration CDYL. Surely that was his car? Dr Callum Doyle himself. Oh this can't be happening, he thought. What's he doing here? He immediately felt sick to his stomach. Jeremy was a fairly laid back type of guy, but something unexpected like blinding rage was building up inside him at the thought of him trying to worm him way back into her life. Wait, though, maybe it's not what it seems? Could he have just called by to pick something up?

'No chance mate,' Jeremy muttered to himself.

He hesitated, but still hoped there might be a simple explanation so they walked tentatively up the drive and Jeremy made to go round the back because he had a back door key. Something made him stop at the front door. Why was he feeling this way when for Christ's sake, he'd been practically living here for weeks? He had his own key hadn't he? Jeremy stood back for a second then he stooped down and pushed open the letter box. Pedro was on his hind legs beside him, his tail wagging like crazy.

Jeremy gasped as all he could see in his line of vision were flowers. Pots and pots of them. What the f… was going on? Then a man's broad back came into view, blocking out the flowers. He heard voices. He felt his heart dropping like a leaden weight in his chest as he saw him putting his arms around Verity and, she wasn't pushing him away. What? Had she taken him back? No, she couldn't have, she wouldn't. Would she? Every inch of Jeremy rebelled against what he was seeing. Should he confront her? Them?

No, he couldn't do it. He couldn't face the look of guilty pity and rejection on her face and the gloating look that was bound to be on his. He would smash his face in. Or try to.

Jeremy dropped the letterbox lid in a hurry, feeling sickened and sad. He turned away and walked down the path, then he leant heavily against the next door neighbour's bin catching his breath. He knew when he was beaten and couldn't compete. After all, what the hell did he have to offer a woman like Verity? He didn't even have a regular job. How had he ever thought he'd be enough for her? A struggling writer working as an agency temp in her office?

He didn't stand a chance. He moved away from the bin, wrenched the lid open and threw the roses inside where they fell with a soft thud. He let the lid close with a bang. He felt shaken up.

Pedro looked up at him and uttered a soft whine as if he understood.

'Come on Pedro, she doesn't want us here,' he said. 'Not today. Not ever.' And clasping Pedro's leader tight in his hand, they began walking quickly back along the road to the Staiths, Pedro's tail facing downwards.

Chapter Thirty Seven

One morning a couple of weeks later, Verity woke up with what she called crying eyes and no amount of wet, used teabags (Grandma Anna's remedy) would put them right. Her touch of flu had turned into a nasty chest infection and on seeing the doctor, he'd said she was suffering from anxiety as well and offered to prescribe her some tablets. Anxiety? Load of rubbish. She'd refused and so he'd prescribed some sleeping tablets instead. These were helping a little as the nightmares had lessened and she was now managing to sleep right through.

He wanted her to take some more time off work but she'd declined. Two weeks off were more than enough. She'd never missed a day of work before. She did promise to come back to see him straightaway if she felt any worse. She'd thought she was doing okay but last night she'd read Jeremy's letter again and cried again. She'd never wept so much as she had lately and the strange thing was, it didn't make her feel any better afterwards. She wanted to scream, no, no, you've got it all wrong. Callum was not her chosen path. And why, if Jeremy had come to ask her again to move in and declare his love, why did he go off so quickly with his ex, once described as the love of his life? She didn't think he was so fickle.

We're *taking it on the road. There's talk of **us** taking the play further afield.*

He was with Yasmin. Hadn't she meant anything to him at all? Had she imagined the last few months? Okay, they'd only had a few short months together, no time at all really, but she'd believed in him. If this was for the best, why did she feel so bruised and bereft? Somehow, without realising it, he'd got right under her skin and she'd fallen deeply in love with him. Again. And for what purpose?

Too late, she'd realised he was everything she wanted in a man. Yes, he was dishevelled at times and untidy, and disorganised but he was also kind, caring, helpful, gentle and loyal. Loyal? Well obviously not that. The things that had so irritated her in the beginning like his trailing laces, his odd socks, his messy man bun, his never ending smile – now she'd give anything to see them again. Jeremy was the whole package and the pseudo heartbreak she'd felt over Callum was nothing compared to this crippling sense of real loss.

Jeremy had been totally right. She'd been trying to hide behind the idea of being in love with Callum, because deep down she knew she'd never have to commit to him fully. Maybe there was something wrong with her? She'd loved and lost two men in such a short space of time, less than a year.

On the plus side however, if there was one, she was still Business Manager, having succeeded in her quest to raise funds for Conferenceque. The team were solvent again thanks to the *Big Event* and the first tranche of courses were already oversubscribed. Greyson would never know of the plight Callum had left them in and was delighted that they had secured solid bookings for well into the coming year. More staff were needed to help out at events. For the moment it was just Sophie and Verity and they were working flat out which was a bonus for her. She determined to throw herself into the job and not dwell on what might have been.

'I'll see if I can find another Jeremy for you,' Greyson said, raising his eyebrows as she shrugged her shoulders, the familiar pang of loss stabbing at her chest. That he would never be able to do. Almost everyone that rang up to make a booking asked if he would be there on the day of the course and were very disappointed when told he'd left to tour his play.

Continuing on the count your blessings theme, as well as her job, she had her own house, Uncle Bobby, Grandma Anna and of course, Tom. Uncle Bobby had recommended a Lakeland cottage this weekend for a few days break and she was looking on this as the start of a new episode in her life. She was desperate to have a change of scene. Then, when she returned, she would be stronger and ready to work even harder for Conferenceque.

She knew the memory of Jeremy's skin and the perfect way their bones had seemed to melt together would haunt her for the rest of her life, but she was going to try to focus on her job. No more men. Ever. It was too painful to dwell on, so it would all have to go. Out of her mind for ever. She was good at that. She would cope. Somehow. The doctor said she was stronger than she imagined. Who knew what else she could achieve? One thing was for sure, she vowed to herself that today would be the last day she woke up with crying eyes.

Chapter Thirty Eight

Jeremy

Everyone was talking about the new statue which was on loan to Ilfracombe and had just been delivered a few weeks ago. Opinion was divided, and Jeremy could see why the locals loved to hate it. The enormous bronze and stainless steel figure stood proud and tall, lording it over the harbour at Ilfracombe Pier with a sword held valiantly in her left hand, scales in the other, feet placed on two greyish green law books. Jeremy had read with interest that it was believed the books were added in order to elevate the statue 10 inches higher than the *Angel of the North* back in Gateshead. He'd passed that particular landmark many times on his way up and down the A1 on route to Verity's house and had grown very fond of it. This sculpture however, was very different.

She was 67 foot tall and depicted a pregnant woman with layers of skin and flesh removed from one side, exposing a fœtus developing inside her womb, muscle layers and a skull underneath. A structural cross-section and the other side was normal. Grotesque really, but intriguing. No wonder everyone was talking about it. That's modern art for you, he supposed.

The brilliant blue skies and sunshine of his arrival had given way to grey storm clouds, with raging waves lashing at the harbour walls and gusting over craggy rocks. He'd hurried down to the Quay Head, passing fishermen untangling their ropes and hardly noticing the boats painted blue, red, and white, bobbing on the choppy waters, tall masts jangling and clanging in the wind. He'd been dying to have a look at the statue in the flesh so to speak, since he'd heard about it on the news a few weeks ago. Now here he was on the wind ravaged pier, walking through the middle of a few fairground attractions not doing much business, as the few people there were about only wanted to look at the statue. A statue named Verity.

Verity. How could this be? Was he never to have any respite? He grimaced inwardly, thrusting his hands deep into his denim jacket pockets. That wind was nithering. Hadn't she'd told him he'd have to buy a warmer coat for the winter? And he'd said, did he have to, because he loved this old faded blue one. It seemed ironic to him that he wasn't being allowed to forget about her in one way or another. As soon as he left one Verity behind, another one showed up. He couldn't quite believe that he now stood looking up at a statue of the same name.

A few other people joined him on the quay, some standing eating fish and chips from white cardboard boxes with little wooden forks. A strong smell of vinegar wafted over, making his stomach rumble. He stood there for a long time, taking photographs and thinking.

He'd been warned by his agent that he may have to drop everything and shoot off on his tour of the South Coast but he hadn't realized it would happen quite as quickly. His whistle stop tour had started off in Margate, taking in Brighton, Southampton, Bournemouth, and ending up in Ilfracombe last week in October. Ilfracombe was the climax and the highlight of the tour because his agent had managed to book them in at the iconic Landmark Theatre. Then, maybe he'd take himself off to Turkey for a quick holiday before the rains started over there.

He just felt, well rootless. Suspended in time. He'd left the South behind, worked abroad for a few years, back to the South again and then he'd grown to love the North East in a way he hadn't anticipated. He'd been in a good routine with his writing as well there. When he was at home with George he'd get up early and write for an hour with a view of the Greek temple from his window and the same most evenings. When he'd stayed at Verity's, he'd simply set up camp in the middle of her kitchen and switched off to anything going on around him. He had the bones of a new screenplay which he was becoming excited about. He'd enjoyed the research and the preliminary brain storming. But now, how could he go back to the North East and his dad after this and not be with her? Knowing that she was only a few miles away?

He'd barely had time to visit the Hampshire village he'd grown up in or the Isle of Wight where he'd lived when he was a kid. Half a day in Alton to catch up for a quick pint at the pub near Jane Austen's house museum, with a couple of his old mates and that was it. In normal circumstances, he'd have loved every second of the tour and the performances.

He'd taken on an acting part as well as someone had dropped out at the last moment. So he was twice as busy as he might have been, yet being erratically busy suited him and he tried even harder to put on a good show, so to speak. He hadn't had time to think about her and what had happened, which was a good thing. He had to get through each day. He kept telling himself that it was for the best but he hadn't realised just how hard it was going to be, going on without her. It felt like a kind of grief, subdued each day as he had to work. Without working, he couldn't have coped.

Jeremy looked down at the leaflet he'd picked up earlier. Verity - An allegory for truth and justice. That described the Verity he knew implicitly. Verity is a statue measuring 20.25 metres high tall and weighing 25 tonnes. Truth? That got him thinking. What if – and this thought had been niggling at him since that fateful day he'd seen *his* car parked on her street. What if he'd got it wrong and she wasn't back with Dr. Doyle after all? By some miracle she was missing him as much as he missed her? His heart raced with hope which he quashed down straightaway. Fat chance. He'd seen her with him. With his own eyes.

He looked at his watch. He knew they had sounds checks and a dress rehearsal in half an hour at the Landmark Theatre which was a landmark in itself. It was of a double conical design, often likened to Madonna's bra, set on the promenade with green grass and rocky cliffs sharply falling away down to the sea. It was what he called a proper theatre instead of performing in pubs and inns and he was very lucky to be finishing up the tour there.

He looked back at the statue, at the sword held aloft. It actually looked better when viewed from the back. One side of her was normal and the other outlandish. Truth. A true principle of truth, especially one of fundamental importance according to the leaflet. What if this was a sign? Jeremy wasn't one who believed in fate, thinking you had to make your own luck, which he'd done on many occasions. But something still niggled at him.

A particularly strong gust of wind struck the quay and he had to admit he was finding the weather strangely exhilarating with sea birds shrieking and squalling overhead and the white spray tumbling against the cliffs. Then, making a decision, he reached into his jeans pocket for his mobile phone. He scrolled down and rang a number, his heart beating a little faster than usual. Drops of spray obscured the glass surface, and he wiped it dry with his denim sleeve, turning away to shelter as the number began to ring out. Tasting salt on his lips, he turned up his collar, hugged his denim jacket more tightly around him and leaned back against the cold stone of the harbour wall, phone clamped against his right ear. It seemed to him that in a place like this, anything was possible.

A voice answered. 'Hello?' Then, 'Hello, Jeremy, is that you?'

Chapter Thirty Nine - Jeremy

'Hi. Yes it's me, Jeremy. 'How are you, Bobby?'

'I'm fine, thank you.' His voice sounded guarded. 'What do you want?'

'Just to talk to you, I'm ringing from Ilfracombe,' Jeremy's words rushed out.

'Oh. How nice for you. You're not after a job are you because…'

'No, no, nothing like that.'

'Good, because there's nothing going at the moment.' Jeremy could practically hear the relief in Bobby's voice. 'Then I suppose, if it's not a job you're after, then that means…'

'I was kind of hoping I could talk to you.' Jeremy jumped in. He realized he was clenching and unclenching his free hand. 'About Verity.'

'Hmmm. Yes, well, I'm not sure I should be talking to you.'

'Please. Look, I'm so, so sorry for everything. But it's not like you think. Not at all.'

'O - kay.' Bobby's voice was measured.

Jeremy ploughed on. 'The thing is, I've checked my schedule and I'm going to be back in the North East next week for a couple of days to visit my dad. (He had quickly changed his plan of going to Turkey). 'Could we meet for a drink? I'd like to be able to explain properly and well, ask your advice I suppose. Please?'

Jeremy could hear Bobby sighing. 'I don't know if…'

'Please?' Jeremy could hear the urgency in his own voice and hoped Bobby wouldn't think him too needy. Or desperate. What the hell, he was both. 'I promise I won't take up too much of your time. I know how busy you are.'

Still silence. 'Look, Bobby have I ever let you down before?' he pleaded.

'No, not until now. Well, I can't say I'm not curious. I suppose there's no harm in meeting for half an hour. In confidence of course.'

'Oh yes, yes of course.'

'I'll come to you. Meet me at *The White Horse* next Wednesday evening. Eight p.m. Sharp.'

'Thank you so much.' Jeremy breathed a sigh of relief. 'I'll be there. See you then.'

But Bobby had already ended the call.

ooooooooo

The White Horse was actually Jeremy's local pub, being only a five minute walk from where he and George lived. He often called in with Pedro when he was out walking. Bobby must have thought it would be safer to drive over to Jeremy's village, instead of running the risk of them bumping into Verity in Gateshead. He felt a pang as he remembered that Verity always liked to stay in on a Wednesday night, to catch up on her midweek emails and stuff.

Jeremy, with Pedro in tow, made his way to the heart of the tiny village where tucked in between a church and another inn, was *The White Horse*, it's cream walls washed to a golden glow by three strategically placed lamps above the top storey windows. From the pub garden, a segment of the gothic monument could be seen looming over the rooftops from its elevated position high on the green hill and the temple was lit up like a beacon against the star sprinkled sky.

In front of the pub was a horseshoe of grass with a few picnic tables, empty flower tubs and a sign on top of a pole which read *The White Horse* and displayed a picture of a white horse against a backdrop of green knoll and monument. The sign gleamed pale, swinging and creaking in the evening breeze. As Pedro lifted his hind leg on the pole, Jeremy looked for Bobby's car but couldn't spot it anywhere yet. But then, it wasn't quite eight o'clock. He felt a tad nervous, although excited for news of Verity, any news at all would be welcome. He was glad he was doing something, hopefully which would ease the crippling heartache which never left him.

He could smell the open fire as soon as he opened the door. As he scanned the room for a decent seat, a white neon sign behind the bar caught his eye which said *Wet Wednesday. Reduction in beer prices.*

Jeremy slung his coat onto a table tucked away in a corner near to the red bricked, open fireplace, as far away as possible from the pool table area and the old gogglebox which constantly blared out Sky Sports football. He motioned to Pedro to keep the seats and the little dog obediently trotted over to sit on the floor under the table.

He said 'Good Evening' to the one or two locals who were stood chatting around the bar area and ordered himself a pint of real ale from Meggie, the grumpy faced barmaid.

He often joked with her, knowing she didn't seem to mind because he always took the time to ask how she was. She even ignored the fact that he wasn't a Sunderland supporter. In fact the locals had taken to him as well, even though he was a Southerner, probably because he had nothing but praise for the North East and would spend many an hour putting the world to rights, listening to everyone's point of view. He was a people person and enjoyed engaging others in conversation and watching what made them tick. It also helped for character authenticity in his screenplays, if he was honest. So many different characters came in here…

Back down South it was so different in the pubs, everyone seemed to be in a hurry with no time to talk. Jeremy sat down and Pedro jumped up beside him and curled up comfortably on Jeremy's coat. Jeremy moved to the edge of his seat and began tapping his foot and looking up every time he heard the door open. He didn't have to wait long.

Bobby came in, looking different out of his work clobber, wearing casual jeans, jumper and padded jacket. He spotted Jeremy, who jumped to his feet and came to greet him.

'Thanks so much for coming,' Jeremy said, jumping up and shaking his hand. 'It's good to see you.'

Bobby didn't smile and his hand felt cool. He patted Pedro and sat down opposite Jeremy. After a long pause, he pushed his glasses back onto his nose and said, 'Well, I always thought a lot of you, Jeremy and I'm a pretty good judge of character. You worked very hard for me and were a very loyal employee.'

'Absolutely,' Jeremy agreed with him. 'You were a brilliant boss and I'd like to think we had a good working relationship.'

'Which is why I agreed to meet you, but I can't stay long.'

'Let me get you a drink,' Jeremy jumped up. 'What would you like?'

'Just a half please, I've got to drive home,' Bobby said, peeling off his coat.

'Meggie's bringing it over,' Jeremy said, returning from the bar.

'She looks a bit scary,' Bobby whispered, which broke the ice slightly, after Meggie plonked his half pint glass down in front of him.

'Heart of gold,' Jeremy said, taking a gulp of his real ale. 'Honestly.'

'Now then,' Bobby said. 'What's all this about?' His deep set eyes bored into Jeremy's.

'How is she?' Jeremy asked, unable to stop his voice wavering.

' Bobby picked up his glass and took a sip. 'Well, she's been ill.'

'Ill? Verity was ill? Is she all right?' Jeremy knocked his glass with his arm, nearly spilling his beer. He couldn't bear to think of her being poorly or in pain. 'What's been wrong with her?'

'She's fine now.' Bobby didn't raise his voice, speaking in a monotone.

'What was it?' Jeremy felt physically sick to think he might have contributed to Verity becoming ill.

'It was flu combined with tiredness and a bit of stress, that's all. She was off work for a couple of weeks but she's back now. And coping well.'

Jeremy sat back, feeling the relief flood over him. 'Thank goodness for that.'

'No thanks to you.' Bobby said, shaking his head, both hands clasped around his pint glass. 'How could you leave her high and dry like that? When I think of the state you left her in, I nearly didn't bother to come today.'

'Me? What have I done?' Jeremy pushed away his pint glass. 'It wasn't me that was left high and dry. I didn't want her to get back with him, that…that low life rapscallion. That Rasputin, that b…'

'I've no idea who you're talking about.' Bobby looked perplexed.

'The great and the good Dr Callum Doyle.' Jeremy spat out the words. 'I saw them -together.'

Bobby frowned so hard that his eyebrows nearly met in the middle. 'You couldn't have done. That ended ages ago.'

'I swear I did. I looked through her letterbox and all I could see was flowers like Kew Gardens and him and her…with their arms around each other.'

'Ah,' said Bobby, and Jeremy saw his shoulders relax and his deep set dark brown eyes lighten a tad.

Jeremy went on. 'I was going to ask her if I could move in. Properly I mean. I'd asked her before, several times, but she'd persuaded me to wait until after the *Big Event*. I plucked up the courage, bought her some flowers – hah that was a laugh considering how many he'd already showered her with. Then I looked through the letter box and saw what I saw.' Jeremy shook his fringe out of his eyes.

'I think I know now what might have happened.' Bobby began feeling his pockets and checking his coat pockets for his phone. 'Have you got U-Tube on your phone?'

'Yes, but why?'

'I've forgotten mine. I'm always doing that. I'll show you in a minute. But,' he leaned forward over the table and stared straight into Jeremy's eyes. 'There's still something that doesn't make sense to me. Something I need you to explain.'

'What do you mean?' Jeremy asked. 'Ask me anything. Anything at all.'

'Well,' Bobby said. 'Verity told me that you were back with Yasmin, your ex-wife.'

No way. Whatever made her think that? 'Yasmin?' Jeremy spluttered. 'No, that's simply not true. I'd never go back there. Whatever made her think that?' Pedro jumped up next to Jeremy and snuggled in close to him.

'She saw you together at your gig. At Ernestines. Looking very cosy together, the three of you. With Pedro. I saw you too, come to think of it.'

Jeremy felt like his head was going to burst. He pushed away his pint. 'I can't drink this.' Pedro whined slightly.

He thought back to that night. 'The thing is, Yasmin is always very touchy feely. She's a very passionate woman. But we were rubbish together. Neither of us would dream of getting back together. Anyway, her husband was in the audience. After speaking to me, she went to sit with him and their kids. I was only talking to her for a few minutes.'

'Verity told me you were going on tour with her.'

'Oh what a tangled web we weave,' Jeremy shook his head. 'What a mess. I was on tour with my team. With Mike, my co-writer. I was on standby, you see, with my agent, waiting for her to come back to me with arrangements for my *Not Quite Cricket* tour.'

He leaned forward across the table. 'I didn't expect it to be in the South of the country but to be honest, I believed it was a good thing because she was back with him and I wanted to put some space between us. I was so…so gutted I couldn't wait to get on that train.'

Jeremy saw how thoughtfully Bobby was watching him, eyebrows almost meeting in the middle.

He pushed away his pint. 'Bobby, Verity was the best thing that ever happened to me. I regret so much what happened and I'd do anything, absolutely anything to get her back. I just want to look after her. You've got to believe me. Do you think there's any chance at all of her forgiving me?'

'Right, one thing at a time.' Bobby said. 'Can I borrow your phone a minute?'

With slightly shaking fingers, Jeremy passed it over the table and Bobby located the video of Verity and Callum and the window cleaner. 'I'm surprised you didn't see it. It almost went viral.'

'I've been very busy with my tour,' Jeremy said, then as he watched he felt his eyes growing wider and his heart swell with hope. 'What a woman. Isn't she absolutely magnificent?'

Bobby sat back in his seat and pushed his glasses back on his nose. 'Well, I'm biased of course. She's my niece and my protégé, so to speak. And I don't enjoy seeing her get hurt. I was the one who had to pick up the pieces. She's been through such a lot. All I want is her happiness.'

'Oh, so do I. Honestly, I can't begin to tell you how rotten I feel.' Jeremy couldn't help his eyes filling with tears. He dashed them away quickly with the back of his hand. 'I'm so sorry. I can't believe it, yet once again I have spectacularly managed to ruin things between me and Verity.'

'True.' Bobby leaned forward, resting his elbows on the table, so that his eyes were once again level with Jeremy's. 'I must admit, you have screwed up rather badly.'

Pedro put his head on one side, looking at Jeremy and emitted a low, throaty whine.

'Too right I have,' Jeremy muttered. He looked down at his hands whilst Bobby glanced at his watch and Pedro nudged his arm with his wet nose.

Jeremy felt stricken. This had been a total waste of time, Bobby didn't believe him and now he was going to leave. 'I must go,' Bobby said, draining his glass.

'Oh, must you?'

'The thing is,' Bobby said, standing up and reaching for his coat, 'what are you, sorry, I meant to say, what are *we* - going to do about it?'

Jeremy looked up slowly. Bobby believed him. He was going to help. He felt the beginnings of a smile attempting to lift the corners of his mouth.

Chapter Forty

Before setting off for the Lake District, Verity visited her mother's grave as she did once in a while. The spire of the nearby church in the village rose above the bright autumn colours and skylarks treaded air above her.

As she placed the flowers she'd brought on the mound, looking at the gold lettering on the headstone in front of me, she felt a sense of pride. It was all thanks to Uncle Bobby, who'd talked to her dad and come to an agreement. Uncle Bobby paid for an engraved headstone to be put in place.

She was just about to climb into her car when she heard a voice behind her.

'Verity, is that you? It is isn't it? It's me, Ellen.'

She turned and there she stood. Ellen. She hadn't seen her for years but recognised her straightaway.

'Wow! You haven't changed a bit Verity.' She drew back quickly as Ellen reached over to hug her.

Ellen had. She'd gained a lot of weight and had a double chin, although there was still a glint in her green eyes.

'Hello Ellen,' she said, 'what are you doing here?' Of all the people to bump into, why did it have to be now when she felt so vulnerable?

'I'm visiting my auntie,' she said, 'She's buried just over there.' She pointed over the grass. 'I'm only here for a couple of days, I live in Scotland now with husband Number Three.'

'That's nice,' Verity forced a smile.

'What's your situation? Are you married?' she asked, then as she shook my head, her eyes clouded over and the words came rushing out. 'Oh, I am ashamed for what I did. I think about it often. I was so envious of you Verity.'

'I can't understand why,' she remarked, her heart sinking like a stone. 'You were the pretty one with all the boyfriends.'

'Is that what you thought?' Her eyes were bright with unshed tears. 'It was just everything we did, like…like when we went to the ice-rink, you were always the better skater. I was rubbish next to you.'

'What?' She couldn't believe what I was hearing. 'You were the one that had skating lessons and did all the fancy footwork. I couldn't even skate backwards.'

'Oh that was just showing off stuff.' Ellen's phone beeped and she pulled it out of her bag. 'Then I couldn't believe it, when I won the writing retreat competition and you turned out to be the one that could write, not me, remember?'

'That was just luck.' Verity shifted the position of her bag which was digging into her shoulder.

'Still, it was a terrible thing to do,' Ellen went on, her eyes filling up still further. 'I fancied him like mad and I was so selfish and didn't want you to have him. I was very childish and I am sorry. Can you find it in your heart to forgive me?' This time she did fling her arms around her in a tight hug.

'He was a really nice guy to be truthful,' she went on as Verity pulled away. 'And only ever interested in you. Still, it was a long time ago wasn't it?'

'Please keep in touch on Facebook?' she said, as her phone beeped again.

Not in a million years. Verity turned away.

'Oops, I've got to go, he's waiting for me. Did I mention I've got two step grandchildren?'

Load of emotions were crowding in on Verity, anger, hurt, annoyance. She'd never really had any doubt since meting Jeremy again that he was innocent but why did she have to have it shoved down her throat when it was too late anyway?

'I feel so much better for seeing you,' Ellen said.

Good for you. So pleased about that. Then one of Grandma Anna's favourite sayings came to the forefront of her mind, she often used to come out with this one to warn her about Ellen,   'If you lie down with dogs, you'll get up with fleas.' This thought made her feel marginally better.

Then as Ellen opened the door, she looked back and flung a remark over her shoulder. 'You know what? You're such a lovely person. I'm still jealous.'   And off she went, happily scurrying away to husband Number Three.

Chapter Forty One

Verity arrived at the cottage in the Lake District later in the evening. Uncle Bobby insisted on driving her there picking her up two days later. All she wanted was a couple of days completely on her own, two days of peace and quiet in a cottage she'd been to many times over the years with Uncle Bobby and his family. She loved it here.

It was perfect and she'd kept reiterating she didn't want any company although he and his wife had offered to stay. She'd somehow managed to convince them this was just what she needed for rejuvenating purposes.

He fumbled in the dark for the sneck of the cottage gate and she sniffed at the country air, smelling at once the strong, earthy cattle dung from the farm across the fields. In the tiny back yard, she looked over at the darkened panorama which was the rolling hills of the Pennines in the daytime and at night, the stars were so very bright they reminded her of a planctarium she'd gone to on a school trip many years ago. The air was so cold it caught her breath.

Once settled and Uncle Bobby had left, she found herself in the kitchen, walking past the cupboard which started at this end of the house, roaming underneath the whole space under the stairs until it reached the other end. It had two doors, one in the porch entrance and the other next to the staircase. It was a great space for hide and seek when kids visited, as was the cupboard at the other end of the house which was crammed full of wellies and mousetraps.

She noted the stillness. There was always this lovely peaceful silence in the cottage. There was a faint whiff of paint and she noticed the kitchen with its original sash windows and shutters had been newly painted and everything looked very light and bright. There were some new black tiles around the black leaden cooking range in the kitchen and the place smelt of fresh clean linen which had been flapping in the wind and dried by the sun in a country cottage garden.

There was new white embossed wallpaper up the winding stairs and along the wide landing with its window with view of the back garden. It was too dark to see the view.

She loved her bedroom which was all country style with roses on the wallpaper and a wonderful view of the Pennines from the large window. She unpacked her few clothes and hung them in the tiny wardrobe. There was a white painted fireplace in here with a picture of the cottage above it and to the left was another door. This door was very stiff and after years of coming to the cottage, she finally discovered that if you pushed it really hard it did open and there was a space behind it under the roof with a few hangers, which served as a walk-in wardrobe.

She slept better that night in the cosy bed on the front of the cottage than she had for a long while, waking up to the fluttering of birds up the chimney breast. The bed was so soft, comfortable and warm she didn't want to leave it. She opened one eye and saw the chintzy wallpaper and from a gap in the curtains opposite the bed, the mist was just lifting off the layered hills of the Pennines.

She opened the curtain of the window on the stairs and looked up the length of the back garden with its privet hedges to the apple trees at the top and circular sheep pen beyond. A couple of plump grey rabbits chased each other on the grass.

She looked up to the grey sky and saw a patch of gulls swirling overhead, milling about, crisscrossing, intermingling, back and forth, just managing to miss bumping into each other, as if searching for something elusive up in the air.

'Thermal currents,' she remembered Uncle Bobby telling her. 'The gulls are probably coming off the sea and finding warmth.'

Orange and russet leaves tapped at the tiny porch window, filling it with colour. She was surprised to notice that there were still lots of red, rosy apples on the apple tree at the bottom of the garden as it was now November, although now they were wizened and the ones on the ground had been mauled and pecked by the birds. The sight of the apples were yet another stabbing reminder of how she and Jeremy had sat at the bottom of her garden with the apple tree behind them.

After a calming day walking out in the open air followed by a delicious cream tea at a tea garden in Pooley Bridge, she felt herself unwinding although her heart was still sore and being totally alone afforded thoughts of Jeremy to crowd into her mind. She wished she'd arranged to stay longer but told herself she still had most of tomorrow to look forward to until Uncle Bobby came to collect her.

Chapter Forty Two

They had arrived in a rugged, country valley surrounded by steeply rising peaks, striving to reach the bright blue sky. Uncle Bobby parked the car in a National Trust car park. 'Here we are.' he said, opening the door. 'You'll need your coat.'

Verity tied her bulky walking coat around her waist and followed him up a single track to where a traditional stone built bridge strode over a fast running beck. The hillside in front of them was ablaze in a riot of late autumn colours including shades of green, gold, amber and caramel as the afternoon sunlight moved over it, leaving the lower half in shadow.

'Isn't this an absolutely lovely spot?' Uncle Bobby said, flinging out an arm to the sky. 'Do you remember it?'

'Oh, Uncle Bobby,' she said and gave him a hug in pure delight. 'You've brought me to the Four Streams. This is the spot where the Four Streams meet isn't it?' She was standing at the lowermost point of the glorious tableau viewed from the Secret Room.

He nodded and smiled as she picked out the four little streams, glistening as they tumbled down the rocky hillside behind them, converging into one foamy mass under the bridge. There was a muffled peace about the place. The only sounds were that of sheep bleating occasionally and the tinkle of running water.

'We used to come here for picnics with Grandma Anna and our Johnny.' Verity twirled around in glee. Oh, those golden days. She closed her eyes and listened to the silence, breathing in the country air, fresh with a tang of earthiness.

She remembered vividly how strong the tea tasted from the thermos flask, the fizz on her tongue from the dandelion and burdock pop, the red checked tablecloth Grandma Anna used to spread on the grass. Oh, the joy of peeling a hardboiled egg and dousing it with salt, and eating it out in the fresh air. Nostalgia washed over her like a wave.

When she opened her eyes, Uncle Bobby was back in the car down the hill, tyres screeching slightly as he pulled away. 'I'm going to the pub, I'll pick you up later,' he mouthed.

'What? Hey, wait for me!' she yelled, the magic moment gone. 'What are you doing? How am I supposed to get home?'

'Look over the bridge,' he called out of the open car window as he sped past. 'Go on!'

Perplexed and annoyed, she stood for a couple of seconds just watching the car disappear along the winding road, not understanding what was going on? Why would he do this? Then she looked over the bridge and the shock made her legs feel weak and her heart punch against her ribs.

Jeremy was standing on a rock skimming pebbles into the swiftly flowing water, the fading sunshine illuminating his hair to gold, a sharp contrast against the dark battered leather of his jacket, and outlining his body against the backdrop of layered, sunlit hills and bright sky.

'Oh no,' she said out loud. What was going on here? She was totally unprepared for the wave of suppressed longing which welled up and up and tightened her throat. Whilst, despite herself and everything that had happened, inside all she was shouting, 'Oh, yes, yes, yes.'

Jeremy got up when he saw her. There was such a look of sadness, hope and understanding all at once in his bright blue eyes and his mouth curled in a large smile. She moved closer until they were standing face to face, noticing a few more crinkly lines around his mouth. Well, there was no escaping him here, was there in the middle of the countryside? Might as well be face to face.

'What are you doing here?' she asked, feeling her fingertips begin to throb with the cold. 'I thought you were in Margate.'

'Well, I thought I was going to have a look at Uncle Bobby's allotment,' he thrust his hands deeper into his pockets. 'Then, next thing I knew, George was dumping me here with all this.' He gestured at a large wicker picnic basket and a flask which stood nearby. She hadn't noticed them. She'd only seen him.

She nodded. 'Uncle Bobby said we were going for a walk in the hills on the way home.'

'I think we've been set up, don't you?'

'I believe so.' They were very close now and it killed her inside not to be touching him. How fickle was she.

'Come and sit down.' He gestured the rocky outcrop and they both sat down, stretching out their legs towards the stream. She stole a sideways glance at him and noticed how long his hair was, it had grown really quickly. A pang of stifled longing struck as she remembered how soft it felt brushing against her face.

Her mind was racing, what was going on here? He was back with his ex-wife, the love of his life wasn't he? Then if so, why was he looking at her as if she was everything he needed?

'How have you been Verity? You look thinner. I heard you'd been ill.' There was concern in his voice.

'Oh, it was nothing, just a touch of flu,' she said, now looking at him properly and feasting on his craggy features. 'Anyway, how did you know about that?'

'Aha.' He reached for the flask and unscrewed the lid. 'Uncle Bobby and George called in at your house. You weren't there, so they talked to your window cleaner.' He handed her a cup filled with milky coffee.

'Oh, I see.'

'Then she showed them both a certain You-Tube video.'

She pulled a face, taking the proffered cup with a shaky hand. 'Oh no, I'm afraid I made a total show of myself.'

'You really have got a filthy temper haven't you, my dear?' he grinned.

'Only when provoked.' She took a sip. It was hot and delicious.

'To be honest, I thought you were magnificent.' His face creased in a grin. 'It made a change to view chaos without me in it. Also,' he gulped at his coffee, 'it told me everything I needed to know.'

'Really?' Was that good or bad?

'You see,' Jeremy said. 'Before I saw the video, I thought I'd lost you for good.' He shook his head. 'So when my agent rang with the job offer that was it. I was off.'

What about Yasmin? The girl from Café Yummy.'

'Yasmin?' Jeremy set his cup down. 'What about her?'

'The love of your life.' She hardly dared look at his face in case she saw something she didn't want to see, but he only looked puzzled.

'You've got to be joking,' Jeremy shook his head. 'She's my ex-wife for a reason.'

'But I saw her with you at the venue,' Verity rubbed her cold hands together. 'You were together.'

'There couldn't have been much to see. Yasmin and I are friends that's all. Our marriage was an utter disaster.'

'But you looked so happy,' she remarked, remembering how desolate she'd felt watching them together. 'It was as if you'd forgotten all about me already.'

'I could never, ever do that.' He moved closer. 'I must be a better actor than I thought.'

'Oh no.' She rested my face on her cold hands. 'I even thought Pedro had betrayed me.'

'Pedro was her dog in the first instance. She gave him to me when we split.'

'But what about your letter? You said *we* were going on tour. I thought you meant with her.' She threw the dregs of her coffee away onto the grass and set down her cup.

'We? I meant Mike and Colin and I. My team.'

'Oh. So Yasmin really wasn't the love of your life?'

Jeremy laughed. 'Verity, the love of my life whom I'd never forgotten was you.'

'No way.' She gasped. 'Me? After one meeting all those years ago? You're kidding me.'

Hope was starting to rise up now unchecked and she wasn't going to stifle it any longer. She wasn't that little girl any more being passed around from relative to relative, she was a grown up. Could it be that she was truly wanted now?

'No-one else ever came close.' He moved nearer still on the rock and took her hands in between his broad ones. 'Your hands are absolutely freezing.' He raised her frozen fingertips to his lips and blew gently on them. The warmth of his breath sent a sharp wave coursing through her body. She felt like her heart was going to explode with happiness. There was no mistaking the pure love in his eyes.

'There is one thing I must say, she said seriously. 'It just goes to show how little we really know about each other, for us both to make such absurd assumptions.'

'Well, we've got plenty of time to find out now, haven't we?' Please?

'How are you here?' she asked in confusion. 'I thought you were on tour.'

'I am, but I managed to get a couple of days off to see George.' He took a light breath. 'You see, yesterday was, or would have been Cassie's birthday.'

'Your stepmother.' How thoughtful he was to want to be with George on such a sad day.

'Yes. Oh, but I must tell you about Ilfracombe.' Jeremy covered her hands with his again, resting them on her lap, while he gestured in the air with his as he spoke. 'I did a gig there at The Landmark Theatre, which is an award winning building and incidentally looks like the shape of Madonna's bra but never mind that. When I heard there was a statue in the harbour called after you, I had to go and check her out.'

'There's a statue named after me?'

'Yes, there is actually a statue called Verity. She was standing all proud and tall looking over the Bristol Channel.

'Did she look like me?'

'See what you think.' He let go of her hands to find his mobile phone in his jeans pocket, and began scrolling through photos. 'Here put your hand in my pocket where it's warm,' he said, moving closer still so she could feel the heat of him through his denim clad thigh.

'Can you imagine how I felt when I saw it? Your namesake. It was as if I just wasn't allowed to forget you. I took loads of pictures.'

'Really? Let me see.' She reached for the phone.

'Look.' He showed me the first photo.'

'Like me?' She was horrified to see the statue was an enormous bronze and stainless steel monstrosity type of woman holding a sword aloft in one hand and the scales of justice in the other, overlooking the harbour as if she owned it. The side view of her showed her internal anatomy, including a barely formed embryo.

'But that's hideous,' she gasped at the sight.

'Then look at the next photograph of the other side.' Jeremy showed me.

'That's better,' she felt mollified. The other side was normal, quite beautiful actually.

'The name of the piece refers to Truth. That much is right. You're very truthful.'

'Yes, but I'm not pregnant or…hideous.' She pretended to be annoyed with him and turned away. 'Am I?'

'What do you think?' He pulled her back gently by her shoulders, looked right into her eyes and leaned in for a kiss and she immediately put both her hands on his head and felt his messy, golden hair, soft under her fingers. Their lips touched gently. At last. Then she remembered her appearance.

She pulled back a little, feeling shy. 'Oh, I forgot, I must look such a mess,' and she looked down at her black waterproofs, clumpy walking boots and creased walking coat tied in a lump around her middle. Uncle Bobby might have warned her. Then she saw Jeremy's cornflower soft blue eyes glaze over slightly with desire and she was sure he must have seen the same thing mirrored in hers. Her heart was soaring now.

In one swift movement, Jeremy pulled her onto his knees. 'I don't care what you look like. I love you exactly as you are,' he said, trying to wrap his arms around her bulky waist. 'In fact I love everything about you. Always have.'

'Even au naturel?'

'Especially au naturel. They kissed again with growing passion and she could feel his heart beating against her chest. She could smell the leather of his jacket and taste coffee on his lips.

'By the way, I've got something really important to tell you,' Jeremy said, as they broke apart after a long while. 'I've got a job for a year.'

'Oh that's wonderful news. Where?'

'At the Little Theatre in town.

'When do you start?'

'In a couple of weeks.'

'That's amazing.'

'Thing is, I need somewhere to live,' he went on. 'I was hoping you might let me move in at yours?'

This time she didn't hesitate. 'Yes, that would be perfect,' she said, feeling so happy she might burst.

'Then we need to celebrate,' he leapt up to open the picnic hamper, producing two plastic flute glasses and a bottle of Prosecco. 'How about a nice glass of fizzy…?' he asked. He paused while looking at the bottle. 'I can't believe it's not champagne.' With a weak smile he added, 'Sorry, budget and all that.'

But she didn't care, she had him and where the fizzy wine had been made didn't matter at all. They clinked glasses.

'They've really set us up haven't they?' she said, taking a sip. 'Oh, that's lovely.'

'Yep. Thank goodness they did.' Jeremy drained his glass, set it down on a smooth rock and did the same with hers.

'It'll be turning dark soon, do you think they'll bother to come back for us?' she asked.

'Hopefully not.' He reached for her again.' So do you think we've got time or not?' His lips brushed her neck and his warm breath made her shudder.

'Depends on what you have in mind?' she wound her own arms around his neck and they rolled over onto the smooth rock.

The four streams tinkled away merrily in the background as they kissed, bodies fusing together. How perfect, she thought as she clutched at his body under his leather jacket, how dependable, as well as desirable, he was. She felt so elated and happy never wanted to be prised apart from him. She felt like she'd come home.

Then a few sharp barks disrupted the silence as Pedro appeared from under the bridge, tail wagging furiously and launched himself on top of them, barking excitedly, his silky ears smothering her face, until they had to give in and sit up.

'Where did you get to?' Jeremy said, stroking him.

Then Pedro sat back in front of Verity and put his head on one side, tail beating the ground. The sunlight was moving quickly down the hillside now and it was growing chillier. She heard a car approaching – Uncle Bobby was back. She looked down at Pedro.

'I suppose he wants me to pick him up?'

Chapter Forty Three

Back home the next day, Jeremy had let Pedro out in the back garden. It was chilly now in the evenings and becoming dark earlier, so Verity tugged on a warm fleece to go outside to see what they were up to. Then she noticed Jeremy, pint glass in hand, talking to the lovely neighbour over the fence, the one who'd made her tea the day of the flower festival. She was so happy that they were now back together. Oh, how much at home and happy he looked here in her garden. She'd never felt so safe and content in her entire life.

She heard a loud meow and the usual commotion of barking, scrabbling and jumping up at the fence, began. Tom had arrived and was strolling along the back railings, back arched, looking down upon Pedro.

'Coo, coo coo,' came the repeated, soothing chorus from the pigeons on the roof above. 'Coo, coo, coo.'

Jeremy turned to her, smiling and held out his hand.

'Oh, by the way, I've got something for you. Close your eyes.' Jeremy fished in his pockets and was holding something in his hand.

'What is it?' she asked, curious as he pressed something into the palm of her hand and closed her fingers around it. It felt small and cold and metallic.

'You can open your eyes now,' he said.

She opened her eyes and uncurled her fingers from the object.

'Oh!' she laughed with delight as she realised what it was. 'That's wonderful. You remembered.'

It was a little love lock, with the inscription in bold black lettering:

Jeremy and Verity Forever.

She held it tightly in the palm of her hand.

Jeremy pulled her to his chest with one arm, spilling some of his beer. She drank in the delicious smell of him, his cedar fresh aftershave and his own unique Jeremy smell and once more she melted into the warmth of his body. As they clutched at each other with their free hands, she felt an overwhelming sense of happiness and peace. She knew she belonged in his space and he in hers, be it here in the North East or anywhere else in the world.

Much later he said, 'Come on, let's go and throw our love lock in the river.'

THE END

About the Author

Arlene Pearson lives is Penshaw and is a writer of blogs, plays and prose.

Also by Arlene on Amazon

NORTHBOUND
Take a journey across the North East through the medium of verse. Northbound is a joint poetry anthology with Arlene Smith.

2.4 TEENAGERS
A collection of shorts from the author, looking back at revealing aspects of everyday family life with two teenagers.

INSPIRATIONAL PLACES
A collection of anecdotes about some of the author's favourite places, ranging from leopards and lions in the bedrooms at Biddick Hall in County Durham to triffids in Turkey.

Printed in Great Britain
by Amazon